DARKSIDE OF SUNDAY

By

Geoff Leather

This novel is entirely a work of fiction

The names, characters and incidents portrayed in it are the work of the author's imagination. Any resemblance to actual persons, living or dead, events or localities is entirely coincidental.

A catalogue copy of this book is available from the British Library

ISBN:978-1-9163494-6-9

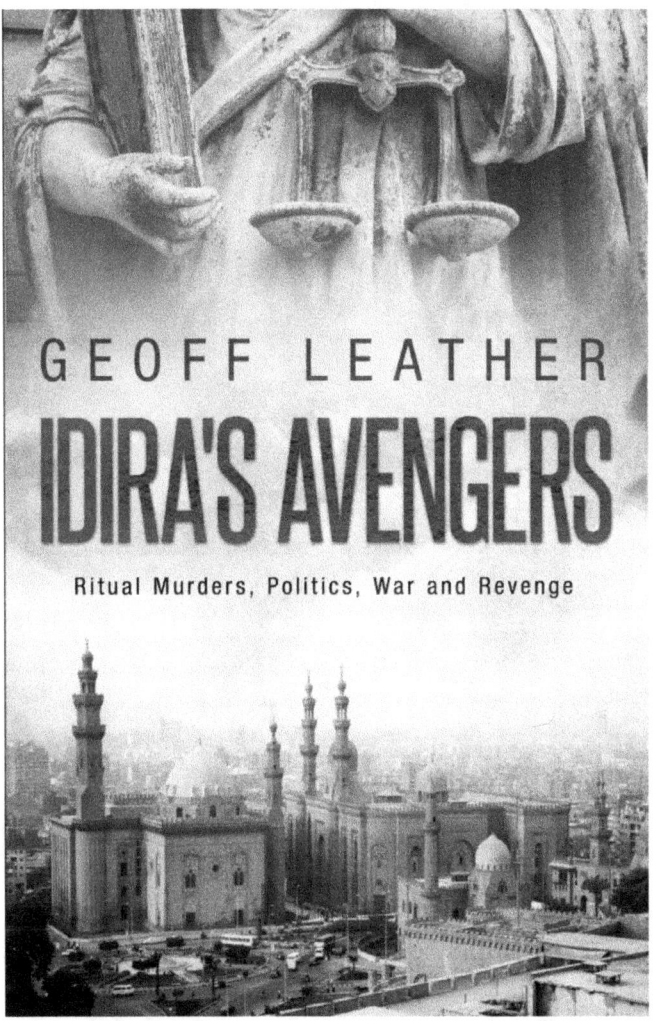

To the memory of Lieutenant-Commander Lionel Kenneth Phillip Crabb, OBE, GM. I hope he would have approved of this fictional story.

JACK SANDERSON

CHAPTER 1

Autumn 1954 Southern England

Crabb had just telephoned. Jack Sanderson looked at his wife sleeping peacefully, kissed her forehead as he crept out of bed. It was 'Buster' Crabb's nature to call unannounced out of the blue.

'I need to see you urgently, son. We have been summoned. I will be arriving about 0700 tomorrow. You need an overnight bag.' With that the receiver clicked, the call was over.

The previous night Jack had told his wife that he had an early morning start and would be back in a couple of days, no need for any worry simple assignment in the U.K. She never pressed him to elaborate. She knew he would not, and in any event, it would be clothed in the Official Secrets Act. He crept into each of the children's rooms stepping carefully over the previous night's array of teenage bedlam on the floor and looked at peaceful sleeping faces. Susan aged 16 going on 24 had the untidiest room ever; he kissed her gently as he pulled the sheet over her shoulders. Nicholas aged 15 was spread-eagled over his bed in the other room. He kissed him gently on the cheek and went downstairs.

'Good morning, young man,' whispered Buster through the letterbox just before 7am so as not to disturb the Sanderson household. Jack opened the door and Buster stuck out his hand in greeting.

'Sorry about the hour!'

Jack had no time to ask questions as Buster had already turned and was walking towards his car. Jack threw his overnight bag into the rear seats and struggled to squeeze his six-foot four frame into the front seat, ducking to avoid clashing with the door frame. As usual the car stank of stale cigarettes and the footwell evidenced several years of stray ash that had failed to find a home in the overflowing ashtray.

Buster wore his favourite raincoat and tweed hat. His gold-headed sword stick sat on the back seat together with battered and scuffed multi-labelled suitcase.

'Well, come on, fill me in?'

'We've a rendezvous tonight at Vernon.'

Buster turned off the A3 trunk road to Portsmouth as they were talking. The little Austin A35 battled against the wind especially up the hills. The threat of rain darkened the sky overhead with morning light struggling to appear.

Buster appeared not to be his usual confident self., thought Jack.

'O.K. What are we up to this time?' broached Jack, sensing Buster was more than a little pre-occupied and trying to find the right way of disguising his concerns.

'We're going to take a look at the bottom of that Russian cruiser, Ordzhonikidze.'

'Ah, Ordzhonikidze. He was one of those Bolshevik leaders in the 1917 Russian uprising, if my memory serves me correctly.'

He started to give Buster a short history lesson but suddenly stopped short as the car lurched to the left clipping the curb before Buster regained concentration and took another drag on his cigarette wafting the blue smoke away with his hand.

'It is nice to know your time wasn't wasted at the Admiralty's expense at the London School of Economics studying the Russian language with history and culture. It has its rewards, my son. Yes, Jack, you're right. He was a revolutionary and wanted to create a modern new world. This ship is also revolutionary and modern, part of the pride of the Russian navy.

'She tied up this morning. Premier Krushchev and Marshall Bulganin doing their bit to ease relations with the West. I think the Labour Government expect to teach the Yanks a thing or two about how to achieve a lasting world peace.'

'I don't suppose the Americans will know or want to know anything about this. We'll be on our own until we are successful,' replied Jack.

'So it seems. That is why I didn't say anything to you earlier so that Mrs Sanderson would not worry.

'It was Matthew Johnson who rang me. Apparently, we are not under orders from the Admiralty this time. They don't want to get involved directly. I am advised that it is a private covert Anglo-American operation.

'You've met Johnson, haven't you?'

Jack was silent, his mind raced back to the American Embassy a year or so ago. Yes, he remembered Matthew Johnson. He had a long conversation with him. He did not like him from the outset. Worse, he felt he couldn't trust him. It was an intuitive reaction. He was an opportunist at best.

CHAPTER 2

Portsmouth England

Crabb's thoughts returned to Pat Rose, his fiancée. He had found it very awkward explaining to her yesterday that he must cancel that night's long-standing dinner appointment and skipping through his lunch at the Grove Tavern without a convincing enough excuse. He should have lied to her. Told her about some experimental equipment to test, but for some reason unknown to himself, he told her the truth. What had she said to him last night? *'Since when have the Admiralty been approaching you through some doubtful American adventurer? You going to do what? That is sheer lunacy.'*

He unknowingly shrugged his shoulders.

'It will be all right,' he said under his breath.

'What did you say?'

'Nothing. Just musing, Jack.'

'Buster, I know we have got to do it, but how the hell do you think we will get away with it? The Russians will be expecting it and the ship will be curtained and guarded day and night,' said Jack clearly concerned for the second time that day.

'Jack, you know we did it with the Sverdlov last year. It was nice and easy.'

'So. You don't think they will have learned anything from that?'

'Why should they unless you told them about our success. They don't even know we were there.'

Jack was silent in reflection.

Crabb lit another cigarette and puffed at it in relief.

'I didn't think Johnson was a US Naval Officer.'

'He isn't. As you know some naval matters are engineered and carried out by civilian intelligence officers and this is especially true where the Americans are concerned. Johnson has his own security firm with links to the Navy, small fry at the moment.'

An hour later, they arrived outside the Sallyport Hotel in Portsmouth where Johnson had agreed to meet Crabb. There was no-one in reception when they entered the hotel. Jack searched for and pressed the bell. Several minutes elapsed before a short grey-haired woman wearing a misshapen cardigan and floral dress came running down the stairs.

'Sorry to have kept you waiting. I've been showing another gentleman to his room. A yank by the sound of him.'

She looked up from the open register. Surprise overtook her face. She stumbled to find some words.

'It's a great honour to meet you, sir. I have read so much about you. If you don't mind me saying so, I think you are wonderful and so are you for looking after him.' She said looking at Jack. A flicker of envy passed over her face.

All three of them stood momentarily in silence.

'I am told you'll be here one or two nights. Is that so?'

She looked at the register and then turned and handed the keys to Jack, lingering slightly before releasing them.

'Breakfast is served between seven and...'

Before she had finished the sentence and both men had started up the stairs, Jack turned and smiled at the elderly lady. The first-floor corridor was lighted by a flickering wall lamp; the carpet runner had seen better days and the walls had not witnessed a paint brush in years. They found the room at the end of the landing and let themselves in. Jack threw his bag onto the floor and slumped onto the nearest bed and closed his eyes.

All arrangements so far had been choreographed by Johnson, thought Jack as his mind fought sleep and concern. Not easy bedfellows.

Crabb unfolded his copy of the official charts of the south west jetty and the tide times on his bed and began to study them closely yawning noisily as he did so. He must have fallen into a light doze because he was startled by a rapping on the door. He rose to open it and there stood Matthew Johnson.

'Welcome to Portsmouth, Commander Crabb.' He stuck out his hand as he half entered the room. Crabb took it and acknowledged his enthusiastic greeting. He stopped suddenly as he saw Jack lying on the other bed, now wide awake. His eyes flickered surprise and worry almost imperceptibly. Jack noticed.

'You remember Jack Sanderson?'

'Yea, we met at the ...'

'The American Embassy, last April'

'Yea.' He turned to Crabb.

'You didn't tell me you'd have company.'

'No. This operation needs two, especially at my age! A dive to thirty feet or more with the equipment we need isn't trivial or simple in these waters.'

'Well. O.K. We'll catch up later.' With that Johnson left the room. He had an urgent telephone call to make.

'Right, no time like the present. Let's be off the Vernon.'

H.M.S. Vernon, the Naval Base in Portsmouth harbour, housed the Navy Diving School. As they set off towards the gated entrance, Jack took hold of Crabb's arm to slow him a little.

'Did you notice anything unusual about Johnson's demeanour when you introduced me and told him we'd be diving together?'

'No. He's a funny bugger, but I trust him. Obviously not used to changes without his say so.'

'I'd say it was more than that. I don't think he's telling us the whole truth.'

The two stopped just before the gatehouse to Vernon. Crabb turned to Jack. There was nervous concern on his jovial face.

'Look, you know you don't have to do this. You've proved yourself countless times and you have too many scars for an old man,' said Jack pushing Crabb forward in jest. Crabb laughed.

The Duty Officer within the base saw them approach and before Crabb could reply, he had taken his hand and was ushering them inside.

'Well, well. What brings you two here. No. Let me guess. It hasn't anything to do with the 'Ordzhonikidze' by any chance.' He had lowered his voice to a whisper and smiled knowingly.

'Not a chance and even if it was, you wouldn't expect me to tell you. No. we are here on a flying visit. You would have heard it from others and been offended if we hadn't come over to say 'hello',' proffered Crabb unconvincingly.

'We have only a few moments.'

Jack, meanwhile, had been eyeing up the shelves of equipment stored beyond the counter. The telephone rang precisely according to plan; the Duty Officer listened intently.

'I'll be back shortly, don't go away.' He disappeared upstairs catching every other step. Within seconds, Jack had located their diving equipment and checked the oxygen cylinders. One was too low and he replaced it and returned to the front of the counter before the Duty Officer returned.

'Strange that. Some American wasting my time on trivia. God knows whose idea that was.'

They took tea together in the Officers' Mess and reminisced. Crabb could talk for England and did so at every opportunity. That is what made him so much more than a colleague to Jack. He had to remind Crabb that they were getting late for their dinner appointment. Outside, there was more activity than usual. Alongside the south west jetty lay the Ordzhonikidze and her accompanying destroyers. The dockside was milling with people who had come to see the warship that had brought Soviet Premier Nikita Krushchev and Marshall Bulganin on their goodwill visit to Britain. They were not on board now but were safely ensconced in Claridges Hotel in London. Jack and Crabb walked casually along with the other sightseers. Their expert eyes taking in all the surrounding details. The usual lookouts at all quarters which they assumed would be around the clock.

'Entry point?' asked Jack.

'Over there.' Crabb nodded his head towards a point he'd selected. Jack followed his eyes. They would be unobserved from the warships and not too far to swim. They both knew these waters like the backs of their hand.

'Come on then, let's tell our American friend.'

Johnson was already sitting in a secluded corner away from the main part of the restaurant and away from prying eyes and ears.

'Under cover of darkness is the obvious and best option but is the most likely time the opposition will expect us. So, we've decided to show the buggers and go early in the morning.'

Johnson looked surprised, he had assumed that night time would be their choice. He tried not to show it. He had made the wrong assumption earlier.

'Wednesday, it is then.'

CHAPTER 3

Portsmouth Harbour Southern England 1954

'O five hundred hours.' Crabb checked his watch. It was just after 10 pm and he turned off the bedside light.

Matthew Johnson lay awake fully clothed on his bed in the adjoining room. He waited patiently until he was convinced that the others were asleep. He turned off the bedroom light and opened the door onto the landing. With his shoes in his hand, he crept along the corridor keeping as close to the wall avoiding the creaking floorboards. He descended the stairs and carefully opened the front door putting on his shoes as he stepped into the rain.

'Damn'. He wasn't prepared for that. Nevertheless, he strode towards the telephone booth, entered and dialled and fed the coins into the machine. Drops of rain trickled down his collar. He shivered a little.

'Amphi one and two. 0.500, 18.' There was a click and the line went dead.

He got back to the hotel and relaxed, shutting his eyes. He could now sleep well. Everything was under control.

Jack opened his eyes to see Crabb hunched over the washbasin rinsing the lather from his face whilst trying to stifle a cigarette induced bout of coughing.

'Couldn't sleep?'

'That's about the truth of it. Feel fine now. Come on young 'un. We have a Russian bottom to inspect.'

They left their bags in the room and walked under a leadened sky towards the drop off point where, the previous day, they had arranged for their diving equipment to be left. The two of them readied themselves in minutes checking each other before stowing their clothes, picking up two small limpet devices that would be attached to the hull of the Ordzhonkidze and slipped quietly into the water and submerged. The limpet would register signals from the underwater detection equipment on board the ship giving the American and British valuable information before eventually detaching itself and disappearing.

They resurfaced momentarily to check if their entry into the water had prompted any tell-tale Russian activity. Reassured that it had not, they swam in tandem for the first two hundred meters. They could see the hull of the vast ship looming up in front of them like some black unmoving leviathan.

Security nets had been lowered by the Soviet crew after docking as standard security procedure.

Crabb and Jack removed their cutters and began to create an opening, their emergency exit. They then swam another fifty meters and created another opening. Crabb swam through and beckoned Jack to follow. Crabb motioned Jack to the bow and held up both hands indicating ten minutes.

Unknown to them but observed by Matthew Johnson from the other side of the water, two Russian divers slipped overboard.

Crabb made his way along the hull towards the stern, unaware of the two Soviet divers hidden from view by the vast rudder complex. He swam slowly along the hull committing to memory the construction details and the sonar equipment bulging from the underside.

Almost imperceptibly in the grey waters behind him one of the divers withdrew from his waistband a coil of rope and loosened it so that one end floated downwards. The other diver moved forward into Crabb's path. They were a meter apart when Crabb removed his knife. The Russian moved back towards the rudder to avoid the swing of Crabb's knife as it cut through the gloom. Crabb followed, adrenalin coursing through his veins. The Russian counter-attacked, swinging low towards Crabb's waist as he moved upwards. They circled each other, each trying to gain the advantage, then Crabb kicked upwards towards the surface.

The Russian lost sight of his quarry. Sensing his confusion, Crabb dived again to his left under the propeller shaft in pursuit. He struck the netting and turned. The Russian was now upon him and cut through Crabb's rubber suit just above the wrist of his left arm. He could feel no pain, just the coldness of the water as it mingled with the blood that oozed from the severed skin. Momentarily, he lost the advantage, so he dived deeper. The Russian followed. Crabb turned violently and thrust upwards at his attacker. Their masks met as the Russian looked into the eyes of a man many years his senior and a hero of his generation. Crabb's knife sank deep into the Russian's right shoulder, whose knife drifted in cartwheels through the water into the darkness below. Crabb sped forward crashing into the Russian whose body hit the netting billowing it outwards under the impact. Crabb grabbed the man's leg as he curled under the force, twisting him downwards. He grabbed a loose piece of rope that secured the netting and pulled it upwards with all the strength he could muster catching his prey within the netting and tying him securely to it. He had no desire to kill, just preserve his own life. He'd be collected later by his comrades.

Crabb moved towards the rudder again watching the wounded man's blood circle around him as he tried to struggle free. The second Russian waited his opportunity.

Crabb came within feet of him and with one swift movement Crabb was pulled backwards by the force of the tightening rope that had been thrown over his head. The tension around his neck became more intense. He tried to loosen the grip with his hands in vain. His left arm was already weakened and as he turned with knife in hand, he struck the ship's hull and the knife fell from his grasp.

The Russian watched Crabb's face through the mask as his colour changed from a reddened hue to purple. The eyes started to bulge. His arms flailed desperately as darkness began to descend over him. He felt himself beginning to rest in the few seconds before consciousness was lost. His struggle was over, his body became limp.

The Russian tightened his grip on the rope and guided Crabb's lifeless body to the surface.

Several of the Russians comrades were already in the water and as the two broke the surface, one of them ripped off the mask from Crabb's face. The blank stare of a dead man looked back. They let go and watched the body slowly tumble into the depths of the harbour.

Almost immediately, the Russian who had killed Crabb, sped down to find his brother in the netting. Now there was only one Englishman and two of them and the element of surprise. As Jack made his way to the pre-arranged rendevous, he could just make out Crabb's form beckoning him. As he got closer and the gloom evaporated his smile turned to horror. He plunged deeper to the second exit. Too late, his leg was caught by the Russian and he tumbled with him downwards. The second Russian grabbed Jack's head with his only good arm. Jack could see the fury that met his eyes as he momentarily twisted his head. Too late, he felt the blow that severed his oxygen supply. The bubbles gurgled upwards at an alarming rate. He only had a few minutes left.

He swung his right leg into one of his attacker's face and his fist into the other's ribs. He wriggled free and kicked upwards. He knew that if he could get into open water, he could outpace most opposition. As he surged forward towards the opening, the dark outline of a third diver confronted him. The underwater light flashed into Jack's eyes. Time was running out and he could not hold his breath much longer. He raced back towards the hull, hoping he could surface under the huge overhang of the hull unseen by those on deck who must now be aware of something untoward going on in the murky waters beneath them. As Jack felt the cold grey steel of the Ordzhonikdzi, he saw the third diver approach. Using his momentum, he grabbed the man and slammed him headfirst into the steel. The impact dislodged the divers mask and oxygen tube. Jack grabbed the tube and took a great lungful of the compressed air.

The rush of bubbles and the shouting from the third Russian as he surfaced brought several other divers into the water to aid their comrades. Jack now realised that he was alone and hopelessly outnumbered.

CHAPTER 4

Ordhonikidze Portsmouth Harbour England

In the pale green light of the guardroom, Jack stared at the senior of his captors. He recognised the Murmansk accent. Jack had spent many years studying Russian language and the Soviet Union.

'Well, Lieutenant Sanderson, welcome on board the Ordhonikidze.

'I could have told you that your mission was doomed from the start, such a futile effort. We know such a lot about you and Commander Crabb. You should be sorry to have caused such much trouble and grief, but I do not expect an apology. Like you, I do my duty as and when commanded.'

With that the officer left to be replaced by the guard who had been hovering outside waiting for his chance.

The guardroom door was closed. Without warning Jack sank to his knees crippled with pain as the guard's right fist struck, quickly followed by the back of the guard's left hand across Jack's face. As he regained some composure, the guard stamped down with force on Jack's left hand, turned his boot ripping the skin from his knuckles.

'Bastard, English. Put these on and come with me.'

The guard threw a set of dark grey flannel trousers and shirt at Jack and waited as he removed all his diving gear, underclothing and his watch, a gift from Crabb years earlier, and redressed.

Jack was bungled into a small cell that was to become his home for some time to come. Just long enough to accommodate a narrow-slatted bed with mattress. It smelt damp and musty with an overlay of oil paint to scent the air. The steel bolt on the outside of the door scrapped into its locked position and all went quiet.

**

On deck, the Russian flagship commander flashed a signal from the Ordzhonikdze.

Matthew Johnson left his observation post immediately and returned to the Sallyport Hotel. The reception was empty. He picked up the register, turned the page and removed all trace of the three guests who had stayed overnight. He took the keys from the board behind the counter and collected the two divers' personal effects and made his way undetected to the carpark. He searched the car for any private property, taking Crabb's gold-headed swordstick and a few other identifiable items and put them with the wallets into a separate holdall.

He drove out of the carpark in Crabb's car and headed west out of Portsmouth. He knew exactly where he was headed and after an hour, turned off the coast road through an open gate towards the disused quarry.

It was isolated enough that no casual observers would distract him. He removed the holdall and placed it on the grass beside the car. The ground was surprisingly dry and there were no noticeable tyre marks leading from the gate down the slope to where he now stood. He rechecked the car and opened all the windows. He removed from the holdall a coil of rope, bolster hammer, a piece of shaped wood and a metal stake. He drove the metal stake into the ground and tied the rope to it. He then tied the other end around his waist and shoulders checking to satisfy himself the coil was free to unfurl when necessary. Johnson then sat in the passenger seat and started the engine, leaving the driver's door open. The ground in front of him stretched on for a few hundred meters or so.

He selected first gear. Punched the accelerator and the little engine responded. He then wedged the shaped wood between the accelerator pedal and the front seat. The engine screamed in protest but did not falter. He needed to keep the car pointing straight ahead to ensure it kept the trajectory that he had calculated would result in it being lost, never to be found again. The only way was to keep control until the last second. He took a deep breath and let out the clutch, the wheels spun then the car lurched forward gathering speed. Johnson lunged through the open door. It caught him, tearing at his leg dragging him towards the edge of the cliff. He struggled ripping his trousers, gashing his leg but freeing himself and crashing to the ground. The rope pulled tight around him forcing the air out of his chest as his momentum slowed. He turned his head to see Crabb's car leaping into space with all four wheels spinning. He could hear the screaming engine until it hit the water a few hundred feet below. He dragged himself to the edge to witness the last death-throws of the little car as the water engulfed it. Slowly the concentric ripples spread outwards dissipating as they did so. It wasn't long before silence spread over this little corner of forgotten England bearing final testament to his betrayal.

He closed his eyes for a moment, then examined his leg. He untied the rope and removed the extra clothing he worn for protection using a couple of strips to cover the superficial cuts. He packed his holdall and walked unsteadily back towards the road. He sat obscured by the hedge next to the gate and waited.

CHAPTER 5

Same day on board the Ordzhonikidze

There was a click of heels outside the cabin. The key turned in the lock and the bolt slid back; the door swung violently open and banged against the metal bed in the wake of the entrance of two men.

'This is Colonel Petrov. I want you to remove your borrowed clothing and hand them to me', snarled Vitaly.

Jack started to protest but was swiftly reminded that he was in no position to argue when the Russian struck him across the face with the back of his black gloved hand. A small trickle of blood oozed from the bridge of Jack's nose.

'You should mind your manners now that you are our guest.'

'That is enough, Vitaly. Just remove the clothes of Lieutenant Sanderson and let us be on our way.'

Jack shrugged off Vitaly's attentions and began to undress, leaving his underwear. The floor was icy under his bare feet, but Jack did not show his discomfort. He knew it was the start of the process of debasement, loss of self-respect. He was ready for it. The training started to kick in. Both men turned and left. The room was plunged in darkness without warning. Jack lay on the bed and curled into the foetal position to keep warm under the meagre blanket. He must have dozed a little because the abrupt illumination of the cell surprised him. He rubbed his eyes and felt the swelling across the top of his nose. He rose unsteadily into a sitting position. Without warning the cell door flew open. Vitaly grabbed him by his bare shoulders and guided him into the corridor.

They bumped their way along until he halted outside the cabin. Vitaly knocked and opened the door. Colonel Petrov sat at his desk. The Colonel stood and asked Jack to sit down. Vitaly obliged him with a double-handed shoulder press that drove Jack into the seat. Jack bent to rub his numb toes.

'I am sorry to tell you that your accomplice, Commander Crabb, is dead. He was intercepted by two of my comrades whilst the two of you were carrying out your spying mission. During the struggle he received injuries that attributed to his death, although we think he died from a heart attack.'

'Where is he? Can I see him?'

'I am sorry that will not be possible. We were unable to find him after the attack.'

Jack fell silent for several seconds. Anger welled up inside him. He rose from the chair and grabbed Petrov by the lapels of his jacket and pulled him over the desk. That was as far as his protest reached. Vitaly was on him in a flash, sending Jack comatose to the floor with a full swing of his pistol butt to the side of Jack's head.

'Remove this man immediately and take him back to his cell,' ordered a frustrated and angered Petrov. 'And remove his blanket. I want a full confession. Get it. Remember he must not die in the process or you'll be spending some time in Siberia instead of him.' On reflection as he sat down in his cabin alone, Petrov thought he'd probably have reacted in the same way if he'd lost a close friend.

From outside Petrov's cabin, Vitaly summoned assistance and the two men dragged Jack's inert body down the corridor and dumped him heavily on the floor of his cell.

'Strip him,' bellowed Vitaly.

The guard fell on Jack like a hungry jackel on a carcass and tore the remaining clothes from him and flung him onto the bed. He was the lone survivor. No Crabb to comfort him. He remembered his friend's thumbs up sign earlier and his smile as they entered the water. Full of hope and confidence. Where was he now? What had they done with the body? There was no propaganda in a dead body. Alive, he would have found much celebrity as a spy in the Soviets'. hands. Jack was no substitute in the international stakes, he was a nobody. He shivered again, this time not out of cold but the realisation that he must now make up his mind to survive, fight or not. Short intervals of sleep were interrupted by pain and aching. No matter where Jack's body made contact with the bed each limb rebelled to keep him on the edge of consciousness.

He was now very hungry, but the empty ache of his stomach had to go ignored and continue to be ignored until he was free again. He would have to keep his memories alive. The visions of his recent past, the last few weeks and months, the colours, the smells and the sounds. What would they tell his wife? What would she tell the children? The older memories would take care of themselves. He fumbled for his watch but then remembered he had been forced to give it put to his captors hours ago. He was now too cold to sleep, too hungry to rest and too confused to be sensible.

Then they came. Roughly they tried to haul him to his feet, but his legs gave way and he fell back again.

It was now Vitaly that sat in the chair behind the bare desk. The traces of daylight were visible behind the curtained porthole at his back. Jack was thrust into the chair. One floor lamp was switched on. Jack immediately closed his eyes as the intensity stabbed into him. The heat of the bulb warmed his face as he shivered a little. Almost immediately the chair was kicked from beneath him as he jack-knifed to the floor. A steel–tipped boot pinned him down as the second guard's boot struck deep into his ribs. The air was expelled violently from his lungs and he gasped in pain. He was dragged back into his chair. Vitaly's lips curled and his nostrils flared as he stared at Jack.

'Who gave the orders? What exactly were your orders? Who else knew about the mission? Were the Americans involved?'

'I have nothing to say.'

The palm of Vitaly's hand crashed against the side of Jack's face. Blood seeped from the cut from Vitaly's ring and ran down Jack's face dripping onto the bare floor. Jack's ear rang out in protest. More questions were bellowed at him but were only faintly heard. He said nothing.

His hands were pinioned behind his back, allowing one of the guard's clenched fists to slam into his stomach. His physical torture continued at intervals, each pause heralding another round of questions. Each time Jack remained resolute and refused to say anything. He was then returned to his cell. He was determined not to betray those who trusted in him. The trouble was he did not know exactly where his orders had come from and the chain of command behind them. Who could he betray by saying what he knew. Crabb was dead or so he was told. He knew the scientific target of their mission. It was obvious to him that the Russians already assumed this was their mission. Johnson was his only known contact. None of this mattered, they would assume he was lying even if he told them everything he knew. If he faltered, they would continue to dig deeper into his mind. What known information would be useful to them. No, he'd have to fight, withstand the physical and psychological pressure because at some stage it would end. It always did.

They returned. Again, the threats, his denials and the beatings. This continued each day throughout the voyage east. The routine never varied. Jack gained additional inner strength from his resistance, knowing and hoping that the punishment would not go beyond a careful tolerance. Jack varied his reactions. First, the denials, then the protestations of innocence and now he started to resent his captors.

He was lying on the bed drifting in and out of consciousness when he heard the lock click open, again. Vitaly stood there alone. To his side but slightly behind him stood another man, the ship's surgeon. Jack tried to stand but slumped back onto the bed. 'Damn it', he thought. 'They won't get the better of me.' He tried to stand again and succeeded. He had survived.

The examination only took a few minutes, checking the swelling and bruising at the back of skull, the bridge of his nose, ribs, back and then finally his heart rhythm. The surgeon nodded.

Vitaly gripped Jack under the elbow, causing him to wince as his injuries confirmed he was alive but not in good shape. The two of them shuffled down the corridor. This time Colonel Petrov was ready and waiting. He dismissed Vitaly whose protest went unheeded.

'I am sorry about your treatment. Vitaly is a loyal man but perhaps a little over-zealous at times. You should be more careful. It was not a good idea to attack me. It could have been your death penalty anywhere else but here. You understand that don't you?'

Jack sat down in silence.

'Let me remind you that you are now on Russian soil and subject to our laws and regulations. Now, would you like to explain to me exactly what you were supposed to achieve in your doomed and futile mission?'

Jack noted the use of the same words again as he drowsily gazed around him, trying to focus on his surroundings. His mind had picked up the words 'doomed and futile'. His eyelids narrowed and opened and shut again. His head drooped and rested on his chest. Petrov came around the desk and leaned into his ear.

'You have no choice, my friend. There is no escape. Co-operation with us is your only future. We will talk again,' he whispered quietly.

The interview was over. Jack grimaced as Vitaly's hands tightened around his shoulders as he was pulled upright and escorted to the bathroom where he was ordered to shower and was given clean grey overalls.

'Sleep well,' sneered Vitaly as he closed the door on Jack's solitude.

The cell light was extinguished before Jack could find the bed. He held his quivering hand in front of him fumbling through the cold air. The ammonia from the bucket caught his nose. His hands found the bed and he collapsed onto it searching for the sheet and pillow. The bastards had removed them both. He curled up tucking his knees into his chest and wrapping his hands around his legs, trapping the little body heat within. He closed his eyes. The images of all those dear to him passed through his consciousness fading into darkness as exhaustion took over. Dry sadness fell from him, no tears. Time passed. The lights flashed on. He expected company but none came. The lights dimmed a little and the vibration of the propellers, shallow to begin with but growing louder and stronger kept his attention. Life in England was now over. What lay ahead was the agony of a Soviet prison.

Jack's physical state deteriorated as the voyage continued. The questioning soon ceased but their determination to break him mentally continued. The light and the dark, the sleep deprivation, meagre food rations, all these had disoriented him. He mumbled to himself to keep his concentration. Must use your mind. Keep thinking of your life, the colours, the smells, the names and places. Sometimes he failed hopelessly, but it was the times he succeeded that gave him hope. He was sorry that the questioning had ceased, these sessions kept him alert and on a high being in different surroundings, he had stimulation, not alone in a cold cell. Perhaps they were waiting until he was too weak to resist.

After what he calculated to be about four days at sea, Vitaly threw open the cell door without warning. He coughed involuntarily and put his hand to his face trying to hide the pungent aroma of stale urine and body odour. Jack cowered into the corner of his bed.

'Change into these,' he barked stepping back a pace into the corridor as he threw a set of clothes at Jack.

Painfully and slowly, Jack put on the black cloth workers overall and slipped into the canvas shoes. He lay down exhausted by the effort. Vitaly grabbed him by the arm and dragged him to his feet, propelling him into the corridor and towards Colonel Petrov's cabin.

'Wait here.'

Jack eased himself into the cabin and remained standing so that he could glimpse the view through the porthole. The cruiser was making preparation to dock. Jack could make out, in the grey damp dawn illuminated by the dockside arc-lamps, ship after ship all bearing the Soviet flag. He wasn't sure but the geography looked familiar. Just as he realised where he was, Colonel Petrov entered.

'I see that you are admiring our Black Sea fleet. Welcome to....'

'Odessa,' interrupted Jack.

'Correct.' Petrov stroked his chin in thought. Knowledge and culture are things no Russian can resist. He drew himself up proudly.

'Our most famous port.'

Jack nodded. His stiff neck reminded him that Colonel Petrov was the enemy but could not resist hearing what this educated Russian had been taught of his own history. Petrov was no thug like Vitaly. There appeared to be an affinity between the two of them. Jack prompted him nervously.

'1905.'

'Indeed. It was the beginning of the end the Romanovs dynasty. We didn't necessarily realise it at the time, but history begins with momentous events and this was one of them although it took until 1917 to finally overcome the Romanov's rule.'

Jack interrupted hoping to see what the Soviet navy propaganda had instilled in Petrov. Despite Jack's physical state, it was his mind that was important today.

'We learn things with a different edge in England. The winners write history, but the losers have their chance to correct it later, even re-write it on some occasions. It is only when time fades for those with power that the truth eventually rises from the ashes.'

Petrov stroked his chin.

'Let me tell you what our history books tell us, Commander Sanderson. You will already know that the crew of the battleship 'Potemkin' had served their Tsar Nicholas II with great courage and duty risking their lives for Mother Russia. Nicholas was an intelligently stubborn man who did not have the foresight or the courage to see what was happening all around him in Europe. He appeared not to give a damn about his people. That may be true. I am not sure.' Petrov lowered his voice as if these words maybe treasonable. 'I believe he was manipulated by those around him, particularly the Tsarina who was under the influence of the mad monk, Rasputin. She believed he had such spiritual powers that he could cure her son's haemophillia. Such influence in the court of St Petersburg was a dangerous thing. Nicholas was too weak to deal with the conflicting advice that he was getting from all sides.'

'Are you saying that the crew of that ship had no alternative but to mutiny?' questioned Jack.

'All I am saying is they had tolerated appalling conditions. Life in the Russian navy of 1905 was very harsh. Do you know what prompted the mutiny, Commander Sanderson? The bloody ship's doctor told the crew that the maggot-infested meat was fit for those heroes to eat. What would you have done?'

Petrov's eyes were sad and regretful. 'The ship's second in command, Giliarovsky, threatened reprisals unless the crew backed down. He mustered all of them on deck. A tarpaulin was laid out on the deck surrounded on one side by armed marines. The crew assumed they were going to be shot and rushed the marines and overpowered them and killed seven of the ship's officers including Giliarovsky and their Captain, Golikov.

'The ship arrived in Odessa where a general strike had been called that day. The Potemkin proved a focus and incentive for the strikers, but the ambitious uprising failed. Six thousand. Six thousand were butchered by the Tsar's Imperial forces. Cut to pieces in the bloodbath.'

'You asked what I would have done. I don't know. Power can corrupt but absolute power corrupts absolutely. This was just one example of the results of that power. The excesses that have taken place since then by those that sought to change the regime have been just as inexcusable.'

Petrov nodded.

'Colonel Petrov, we all know you have lived in fear. In fact, Stalin's behaviour leading up to his gaining power and the subsequent purges after the Second World War were far worse than Hitler's extermination of the Jews. Twenty million innocents have died in state-controlled famines, five million in great purges of the military, the bourgeois, opponents and colleagues, even the husbands of wives he wanted to sleep with. Stalin knew no bounds to his megalomania driven by his paranoia. In the Crimea, his action amounted to genocide. There were no constraints to his delusional persecution of thousands of innocents.'

Jack felt he had clearly said too much as Petrov stood up clasping his hands behind his back imperiously. He looked at Jack. He was unaware that the British had such details that he thought were locked carefully behind the fear and curtain of terror that still existed now as it had only three years earlier when Stalin had died.

'Yes, but to us they are still rumours.'

His face tightened. Colonel Petrov was frightened. The GRV bullies had put the fear of God into everyone. Jack looked away.

'I would have liked to have had time to show you the steps that lead from the harbour into town where the slaughter took place. Where the Cossacks ......'

He stopped abruptly as Vitaly knocked and entered without waiting.

'You have come for the prisoner?'

Vitaly nodded and grasped Jack's hands cuffing them behind his back and marching him out of the cabin up the gangway stairs into the night air. On the quayside stood a black car with the driver standing to attention adjacent to the open rear door. Jack's head was tucked down as he was pushed into the rear seat. Over his shoulder Jack could see Colonel Petrov standing astride the gangplank, his gaze fixed on Jack's. Was that a deferential nod of one officer to another? Jack could not be sure. The car made its way through the quiet, tree-lined streets and rickety wooden houses to the railway station. All seemed starved of a fresh coat of paint. Jack thought it reminded him of an unlikely fusion of Brighton and a sleepy Italian village. Both places had fond memories for him and his wife before the children were born. The only thing missing was the people enjoying themselves; even the railway platform seemed deprived of humanity. A few brave eyes watched from a distance as he was marched onto the train for what was to be a thirty hour journey to Moscow; the last on board was Colonel Petrov in the carriage reserved for high ranking officers.

CHAPTER 6

23rd May 1954 Moscow

Outside Moscow's Kievsky railway station standing at the bottom of the steps was Colonel Petrov flanked by two guards holding open the rear door to an unusually large black car. Now he was dressed uniform. Jack immediately recognized the peaked grey wool felt cap with royal blue piping and band with two brass laurel wreaths attached to the visor, the steel grey tunic and trousers, double breasted, open neck and blue piping and stripes, white shirt and grey silk tie, high ranking KGB. Petrov took Jack hand. It was a vice like grip.

'Good evening, Commander Sanderson. I see you look a little more rested since we last met. Please sit in the back with me, we have much to discuss.'

Jack settled into the back seat with Petrov. The two guards got into the front and Petrov signalled that they should leave and then shut the glass panel that separated them. He turned to Jack.

'You look, how shall I say, a little bemused?

'Is it me or the transport or both? Let me deal with the easy part first. I have been asked to put a proposition to you to think about, but that can wait for now. You like the car? It is a Zavod imeni Stalina ZIS-115 limousine. To be precise. As you can see the ZIS's are hand-built high-end luxury sedans, your equivalent is the Rolls-Royces, I believe. What you do not know, however, is that our esteemed President Nikita Khrushchev detests the cult of personality of our late great leader Joseph Stalin and has recently changed the Stalina to its original name Likhacheva after its former director. They are now ZILs again. Strange how history changes so quickly.'

The car purred as it slowly moved through the Moscow streets. Jack had no idea where they were headed. He had assumed that he would be taken to a place of interrogation immediately. Under the fading effectiveness of street- lamps approaching dawn, he could see that the roads and verges were dusted with patches of white from an unusually light flurry of snow. Either side were zones of huge apartment blocks, rectangular barrack-like concrete slabs, grey and soulless. He sensed that it was to be a sunless, dull, misty and depressing day. They passed mammoth diesel lorries in convoy belching black smoke as they strained to carry their loads. Otherwise everywhere appeared to be deserted like a film set after shooting had finished save for the few cleaners scurrying about their business.

'I was wondering what you had in mind that was so important that you have chosen to flatter me with,' enquired Jack, as the ZIL slowed and stopped.

Petrov got out and handed Jack a long black leather coat, putting one on himself. He motioned to the guards to stay in the car and started to walk towards a bridge. Jack slotted in beside him.

'That is our famous Krymsky bridge. The first and only suspension bridge in Moscow built just before the last war. Beautiful, don't you think, even at this time of day.'

Petrov motioned Jack to start walking across the structure and followed him on the narrow side path. They reached the middle and stopped, looking down into the inky black waters of the Moskva river.

'It is known here as the 'Suicide Bridge'. Petrov pulled out a small pistol and pressed it firmly against Jack's rib. A look of horror spread across his face as he turned slowly. Petrov's face was alight with a huge smile and he pocketed the gun.

'I have deliberately brought you here because I don't want you to think that it is a way out. I want you to remember this short time together. I know you were only doing your duty when you dived into the water in Portsmouth. You had no choice. We knew Crabb would come, we were ready. We did not expect you. No disrespect, Commander, his notoriety was what we wanted to catch alive. He would have been a great coup. I respect your professionalism and your knowledge of our land and maybe our ideological problems. I am talking to you to save your life. Do you understand? '

'What do you want? Turn me into one of yours and let me loose?'

'No, no. My father was assassinated during the great purges in the struggle for power after the 1917 Revolution. My mother has no idea what happened to his body. She was a broken woman after that.

Fortunately, I chose to join the Party, albeit somewhat reluctantly from an ideological point of view. I don't struggle with the ideology but with what has happened since 1917. I worked hard, stood on nobody's toes, joined the navy where my father and uncle had started and followed the 'right' path. Eight years ago, it was suggested that my career would be enhanced if I moved into the security services by one of my late father's friends who has promised my mother that he'd keep an eye on me.'

Jack nodded as they walked slowly away from the bridge.

'I was working on a project about two years ago and stumbled across some archive material for the year 1919. It was during the civil war that raged between the Bolsheviks and the anti-factions after 1917 that I discovered what had happened to my father. As a senior rating in the imperial navy under Czar Nicholas II, he had been part of the raiding party from the crew that had taken over the ship in harbour. The mutiny was doomed to fail as it was badly planned and was easily subdued by the land forces that boarded the ship before it had time to sail. A good number of the crew were killed in the battle for the ship, but my father survived. He was taken into town with three of crew. They were summarily hanged in the town square and their bodies left there as a warning to others.'

'Prior to his death and presumably unknown to those involved in his summary execution, my father had chosen to join the Social Democratic Labour party, the Bolshevik wing not the Menshevik. This went down well with my application to join the security service because as you know it was this party that under Lenin, Trotsky and Stalin forged the Soviet Union you now see.'

Jack was fascinated by Petrov at this stage. The light from the obscured rising sun lifted some of the gloom that hung over the river. They strolled passed the car with the two guards who quickly acknowledged Petrov's presence with a click of the heels.

'So, what do you want to propose to me?'

'Actually, nothing !!'

'I couldn't talk to you in front of the guards. Eyes and ears are part of our society. I want to give you an outline of what we do here to spies so that you have a chance to survive. I realise that you are trained to cope by psychological training, but practice is never the same as reality. What I am saying is treason, I know. I want change here. If you survive and get home, it will be one small step in that direction. I will keep an eye on you, but you will never know. I am doing this for my generation that are sick of terror and subjugation. Sick of the genocide of Stalin. Tens of millions missing, slaughtered by, how did you describe it, his paranoia. Sick of not knowing who your true friends are. I am doing this for my young son at home. There has been a little thaw with Premier Khruschev but the meglomania is still there. Believe me, I am not the only one, there are thousands of us, KGB or no KGB.

'I am sorry to say that our time is over together, Commander. I have to escort you to your next home.'

The ZIL slowly moved from the curb as Petrov and Jack settled in the rear. Petrov then carefully explained what he had to endure for the months ahead in order for him to be prepared mentally and to survive. Anyone listening could believe that Petrov was trying the frightening tactics. This time the rear curtains were pulled so that there was no view to the outside world.

The ZIL turned off the main road into a large square through the central archway into a courtyard. The historical stench of death sent shivers through Jack's body. He knew where he was and did not want to contemplate the next thought.

CHAPTER 7

Lubyanka Prison, Moscow

With a slight sideways glance, as the guards manhandled Jack out of the car, Petrov said 'Goodbye'. Jack was approached by two more guards who stationed themselves on either side of him. He remembered that he had not returned the leather coat. A problem, possibly not. He recognised the entrance of the Lubyanka Prison. He knew it was one of Stalin's places for interrogation and murder. Moscovites joked that it was the tallest building in the world due to the depths of its cellars. He took a deep breath of the cool fresh air, probably his last for some time. As he stood motionless inside the entrance while his presence was announced, he looked around sensing the horror that others had been subjected to in this place. Below in the bowels of this building, four men whose names no-one knew or dared talk about had dispatched forty thousand of their countrymen each with a single shot to the back of a bowed head. The cells in which these murders took place were alleged to contain a pail of vodka and another of cologne. Each day for years, these executioners in turns would spend up to eight hours a day methodically killing 'enemies of the state'. Illiterates destroying some of the Soviet's

45

greatest intellectuals and functionaries. What, in reality, were his chances?

At the desk, a burly man, forehead sweating, smiled at him exposing twin rows of steel-capped molars. Outside these walls, there would be nothing special about this man who cycled to work each day. If not for his military uniform, people would think of him as an amiable village teacher. Here in Lubyanka, Ivan Sopel was an evil man to whom pain, and torture were inflicted with callous precision. He rose from his seat.

'Oh, by the way, you will not be needing this.' He held up the leather coat that Petrov had given him with a threatening smirk on his face.

'Follow me,' he barked. Those were the last words to be spoken to Jack for several days as the enforced silence now took over. His two guards followed as Sopel led the way down the first corridor to the right and down two flights of stone stairs. The silence was interrupted by the harsh sound of their boots on the cold worn granite steps and the clicking of Sopel's fingers as he passed several cells warning their inmates to keep away and stay silent. Each cell door was painted a dull grey, flaking and rusting in parts from the dank gloomy air. Each had small round spy holes. They came to a halt outside one such cell and the jangle of keys beckoned Jack into stopping. He was bungled inside, and the door slammed shut behind him. The bright central light flickered on. The gloss cream paint of the walls and ceiling shone back at him. He lay on the bed and pulled the rough horse-hair blanket over him. Within seconds he must have fallen asleep because the next thing he heard was the banging on the cell door and an eye at the Judas hole.

Orders were barked in Russian.

'Whilst you remain here, comrade, you cannot sleep during the day. You cannot sit on the bed or lean against the walls. You either walk or sit on your stool. We will be here to make sure you obey.'

Along the corridor, another warder shouted 'opravka'. This was the communal trip to the toilet block. Each person was given ten minutes. Jack looked at his companions, they, at him as they washed, shaved, and some cleaned their clothes. Whispers of communication were cloaked by the sound of water. This was followed by breakfast, hot water coloured by tea or coffee, daily ration of bread and two pieces of sugar. Breakfast was followed by a single file walk around one of the inner courtyards for twenty minutes. The rest of the day was a repeat. Lunch and dinner were equally awful. Soup made from rotten cabbage or entrails. Finally, there was another trip to the toilet block in the evening.

After that first day, on his return to the cell Jack was confronted by Sopel filling the entrance, leaning against the door frame of the open cell.

'Doctor wants to see you first thing in the morning,' he spat. 'Wants to check you over before we have our little chat.'

He moved to one side so that Jack could pass and as he did so, slammed his boot into the small of

Jack's back catapulting him into the wall at the far end. The key turned in the lock. Jack pulled himself onto the bed and covered himself with the blanket.

'Hands!' came the instant demand. 'No hands under the blanket. On the outside where I can see them.'

The bright light remained on throughout the night. He didn't know then that it was never turned off. That night was worse than the day. He had been woken up five times. 'Hands!'

'Opravka', the next morning, came as a relief. Not just because he was desperate to relieve himself but because of the intense light that invaded his privacy. As soon as breakfast was over, Sopel was upon him, escorting him upwards to the ground floor and a grim looking medical room occupied by a small bespectacled man in a white gown. After a superficial examination of his hair, skin, mouth and some pushing and prodding, he was dismissed back into Sopel's care. He was marched back down towards his cell but as he attempted to turn into his corridor, Sopel's hands were on his shoulders.

'No, no, my friend. Down one more flight this morning.'

On the next floor, the first few cell doors seemed much closer together. Sopel, with the help of the floor guard who had joined them, opened the third door.

'Strip,' he shouted.

Then the two of them squeezed and bustled Jack inside. It was the size of a small cupboard, about the width of a man's hips. Once inside with the door shut, it was almost impossible for the body of a man to change position or turn, and certainly not one of Jack's stature. This time there was no light just pitch blackness. Captivity training kicked in. Jack immediately started to relax his tense body. He began to control his breathing taking a long-measured breath in and out, ensuring that its pace became slow and shallow. His heartbeat followed this pattern. He moved his neck from side to side, up and down, flexing and stretching his fingers and hands at the same time, shaking them a little. He did the same with his toes, ankles and leg muscles. As time passed, he could feel his legs throbbing, his throat drying and the air becoming less easy to absorb without long drags that made him cough. The pain and fatigue in his legs spread and now became pins and needles spreading from feet to lower leg to thigh, and his own polluted air caused him to pass in and out of consciousness as the CO2 level rose. As he sank downwards towards the floor the walls wedged him, constricting his chest and lungs. For a moment he regained his composure and tried desperately to think of home. His mind raced from delight to delight in the effort to quell the pain. The uninhibited laughter from tickling the children, the kicking of their legs uncontrollably in their efforts to prolong or resist the pleasure. The seconds, then minutes passed. He lost all sense of time. He could not concentrate anymore and eventually closed his eyes. Then from nowhere he thought about Colonel's Petrov's leather coat. Had he made a mistake that could cost him dearly at the hands of a zealous colleague? Had he done it deliberately to make a point to Sopel? He could not think clearly, confusion had set in. He was beginning to realise that for all the training he been through, the reality was almost unbearable just as Petrov had said. He shook off the thought of not caring whether he lived or died. He knew dead people did not know they were dead. How could they? They had no awareness to figure it out. He was alive and going to survive. Some parts may give him excruciating pain but awareness, recognition and sensibility, all part of his consciousness, were his friends.

The cell door was unlocked, and he was dragged out onto the cold concrete floor. He was dowsed with two buckets of ice-cold water. His eyes involuntarily flickered open, his breathing quickened as he pulled in lungfuls of air, choking as he did so. He was hauled upright, moaning in painful protest but relieved at the thought of going back to his cell.

'Again,' thundered Sopel.

Jack kicked and screamed like a recalcitrant child, hopelessly and in vain as he was pushed into the space with the flat hand of Sopel crashing into his neck. Again, the door locked behind him as he buckled into the space for the second time, then the third and finally the fourth time. Each time, the cold water renewed his mental resolve to survive, physically each time his body rebelled more quickly to the torture, but each time, Jack sensed but could

50

not be sure that the time hidden behind the door was getting less and less. Whatever the truth it helped him to think so. On the last occasion, his legs started to swell, he could not control his breathing so easily and despite the severe cold he started to sweat. He made a feeble plea for mercy. It wasn't heard outside, but Jack immediately regretted that he may have given his tormentors the upper hand.

Moments later, he was dragged unconscious into the corridor and doused with more cold water. His head lolled as if he had broken his neck as they dragged him up the stairs, his swollen feet bumping into each granite step as they went and back to his cell shivering uncontrollably. He flopped onto the bed and covered himself with the blanket. Sleep came too easily, for how long, he had no idea.

'Opravka.'

The cell door opened, and the guard walked in.

'Opravka,' he bellowed from the cell door. Still no movement from the bed. He called his comrade and they hoisted Jack into a standing position. His eyes flickered open but unseeing, his legs crumpled beneath him. He was dragged again along the corridor and half carried up the stairs to the doctor's room. The door was barged open and the guards let Jack slump into the chair in front of Doctor Shigalev, who had sprung to his feet in surprise.

'Yours, comrade Doctor.'

Shigalev helped Jack onto the couch. This time the examination was somewhat more thorough. He then called Sopel, and on his arrival, motioned him into the adjoining room. Jack could hear them shouting at each other. He was not in a fit state to absorb the whole conversation but could pick out bits.

It was Shigalev saying. 'You're going to kill him, you idiot. Your masters in the Kremlin want a political denunciation of the West and all it stands for. This is a great opportunity for us. Denunciators and informers can go some of the way but not all of it.'

'Don't ever call me an idiot again, comrade Doctor. Perhaps, you do not realise that he told our KGB Colonel Petrov nothing. They had a week of trying before he was handed over to me.'

They were obviously disagreeing on the severity of the tactics. A weak smile came to Jack's face, a small victory for him, perhaps.

His inner strength was to be tested every day for what seemed like an eternity, his body slowly becoming detached from his mind, feeble in its protective responses. He had noticed that the new isolation torture cell was slightly larger and that he could manoeuvre his limbs a little more or was he losing the muscle and bulk of a fit man. He tried to concentrate his thoughts on the pleasures of his family life in England each time the pain and stress levels escalated, but as the days passed these thoughts of past times became more sporadic and less vivid. He could not hold on to anything long enough, save for the greyness of his future that seemed to spread like an invidious affliction. All his efforts seemed futile. Just as he was reaching out for more succour, he began to realise that Sopel had not attended his cell this morning. His routine today was changing, and for the better.

Doctor Sigalev attended Jack frequently over the next few days. Jack soon understood that with the healing of his body, he would soon be the subject of a show trial.

Sigalev, Jack soon reasoned, wanted to be more than a Doctor. He wanted to give Jack advice. Was he part of Colonel Petrov's eyes and ears? In the privacy of his examination room, Sigalev started to turn on various pieces of equipment that could create sufficient background 'hiss' that would prevent his words being transmitted in any intelligible form to whomsoever was listening in. He turned to Jack putting his finger to his mouth to order silence and shaking his head and started to whisper into Jack's ear. The smell of stale cigarettes on his breath.

'We have more Mental institutions than hospitals in Moscow. More Consultant Psychiatrists than medical ones. We know how to turn people into followers. To take away their dignity and to obey orders. We know fear is our best guardian. As far as the State is concerned, the past for you does not exist. You cannot escape from here or from your crimes against our State. I want you to listen and learn from me. I will try to save your life whilst you're here in Lubyanka. You have no rights, either for a fair hearing or a fair trial. You have no human rights.'

Jack listened, staring straight ahead, feeling Sigalev's hot breath. There was no emotion in his eyes.

'The President of the Court will have all the facts of your mission. I am telling you that you have to reject the use of Counsel for your defence. There is no defence. What right do you have for mercy?'

Jack nodded focusing on Sigalev's stern face as the Doctor continued.

'You must avail yourself of the right of last plea at the end of the trial. You should then submit yourself and your beliefs to the mercy of the Court and plead for clemency. Believe me, I have seen too many trying to fight for their rights or their cause. It never works. It just makes their punishment greater.'

Jack was about to respond but thought better of it. Was this man the last in line trying to break the psychological barrier. Did Jack have to withstand this last approach or was Sigalev genuinely trying to help? Colonel Petrov had warned him of the layers within layers, good guy, bad guy, all on the same side, all with the same goal., but he had also said he would be watching although Jack would never know.

'You will know,' continued Sigalev, 'what your last plea should be. It comes from within. Let your soul speak.'

Jack was surprised by this last sentence. It sat as a brave statement in a society where free thinking was considered subversive. Now Jack dismissed

Sigalev as one of the layers in the Soviet world of mistrust and suspicion. Jack was going to trust his instinct.

Several weeks had passed since Doctor Sigalev's advice. Jack was preparing himself for his right of last plea and each day, succoured by memories of his family back in England, he grew stronger and stronger. About noon on what Jack had calculated, from glimpses of the calendar on Sigalev's office, was his thirtieth day in this brutal asylum, two guards appeared armed with a clean grey buttoned shirt, grey flannel trousers and a loose fitting collarless grey jacket. They threw them onto the bed with disdain.

'Dress!!' came the instant order as they waited impatiently at the cell door. Jack did as he was told quickly and without argument. Once he was ready, he turned towards the door. One of the guards with pistol raised, grabbed Jack by the shoulder and threw him into the corridor and demanded he follow. They did not offer any explanation or answer his question. Instead of going upstairs towards the usual exit, Jack followed into part of the Lubyanka prison he had not seen before, down a dark cold and narrow passageway. Either side of him were cell after cell as far as the eye could see; some of the occupants had heard the clipped heels of the guards and pressed their colourless faces into the barred windows of their doors. Sightless eyes peered at him. Resignation at their lot, the image of death waiting to take them out of their misery. A slight shiver caused him to hesitate. The butt of the pistol caught him just above his right ear and he staggered into the wall to his left and fell onto the floor. A boot caught him under his ribs forcing the air from his lungs. Those watching this defenceless attack retreated into their own worlds for fear of the violence invading their space again. Jack was alone again.

CHAPTER 8

The Supreme Court Moscow

The trial of Commander Jack Sanderson started on the 22 June 1954 at the Supreme Court of the USSR. Jack was escorted into the courtroom and ushered towards a microphone. The courtroom was illuminated by three torch-like wall lamps. As a further reminder that this was an austere military court, next to him towering over him, from a raised step, stood a guard in full KGB uniform with his cap firmly pulled down over his head partially covering his eyes. Jack's hesitant gaze took in the rest of the light blue painted courtroom. On the wall above where the judges were sitting was the crest of gold emblazoned with the hammer and sickle in bright red. Below, in line behind the panelled dais, sat the three judges, two in grey tunic suites and the third in full military uniform. Their eyes from high above targeted Jack as he walked to his place.

On his level, the clerks and legal counsel sat quietly leafing through sheaves of paper. Opposite the judges, the remaining part of the court was arranged with tiers shelving gently to the rear with all the seats fully occupied. Jack caste a curious eye over them as he pretended to adjust the translation headphones thrust into his chest by his guard. What roles were they to play in the next few hour? He suspected none, other than the pretence of a fair trial, of civility and the due process of the law.

Jack had tried to prepare himself for this moment over the past few days, visualising in his mind the austere colourless court, the Soviet symbol of the hammer of the industrial proletariat and the sickle of the peasantry conceived in the Bolshevik revolution to confirm the unity between the different workers, the penetration of blue and brown eyes into his soul as he stood alone. Are they all trying to extract their vengeance to protect the system. The system where fear is their enemy as well. Would those here today understand his world if they could not understand their own? Finally, his eyes came to rest on the three judges. Do they know who were KGB officers, here in this room? he wondered. No-one ever knew exactly who whispered the final denunciation that would send one or all of them to their miserable deaths in solitude banished from this world in due course. The fear drove them to say things that their intellect, their innate moral code and their souls would normally reject.

Jack stood erect. He looked at the President of the Court who motioned towards the Prosecutor. He stood, pulled his robe over his shoulders, and started to address the court. Whilst Jack thought he would be able to comprehend each sentence and nuance, he nevertheless adjusted the headphones and the volume control.

The Prosecutors first voluble words emphasised Jack's position as Commander in the Royal Navy, a representative of his country and the West. The allegations came from opposing ideology, that was clear. Over the next hour, he set out to a hushed court a case woven by a fabric of half-truths, political motivation, of a naïve servant of his country, lulled and pressured into working for the British Intelligence. That? thought Jack would be part of his case too. He finally exaggerated the importance to the safety of the Soviet Union and the peace they sought for the protection and maintenance of their scientific achievements. It was clear that Jack was a spy caught in the middle of an act of espionage and thus without any hope of defence or sympathy. How could such a man be responsible for carrying out an act with reckless disregard for the rights of the Soviet Union. The only saving grace was that he had failed. They had lost nothing and nobody in Britain knew anything about the mission.

It was just after three o'clock in the afternoon when Prosecuting Counsel sat down. The President spoke next suggesting forcibly that Jack take advantage of the Defence Counsel who were sitting to his left.

'I refuse Counsel of Defence.' The murmuring grew louder around the court as Jack spoke again.

'I will avail myself of Last Plea,' he stammered slightly. Again, a feeling of disquiet sat heavily in his mind. Had Doctor Sigalev been his friend or was this the final mistake he was about to make that would take him back to Lubyanka and a bullet in the back of his head?

In his mind, he had convinced himself that there was no benefit in being arrogant, to charge them with the same double standards, to convince them of his good intent in the vision of a better world. That one would need a balance created by equality. He had realized that he would never be a pawn in the espionage game to be traded in the marketplace when the British had caught someone to barter with for one simple reason, he knew he had been posted missing presumed dead by his Navy.

At this point, Comrade Ulrich, the President of the Court, straightened his head after a huddled conference with his colleagues and drew in breath. He turned to Jack.

'This Court will hear your Plea. We will adjourn and reconvene later for an evening session.'

All rose and the three judges left the courtroom. Jack was escorted down to the holding cell beneath.

In Jack's Last Plea, he started by relating his autobiography, filling in all the gaps that the Prosecutor had omitted. Correcting some of the facts, he had been unable to believe some of the detail that the Prosecutor had access to. Had he been double-crossed? Had his instinct not to trust Matthew Johnson been right? It was too late to change tack now and what would be the point. No, he would continue and hope a chance in a future life would allow him to re-visit Matthew Johnson. He talked about the family he left behind that cold, damp April morning. Then he continued.

As a cadet, he had entered Dartmouth Naval College and how later he had fallen in love with the Russian language. He did not express his love of their history and culture and the fact that he had studied at University with the help of the establishment. He was going to carefully omit anything that would put his politics in the old Russian camp before the revolution.

From that date onwards, he'd became part of what we in Britain regard as the 'establishment'. Reluctantly, he admitted that at that time Britain had had the greatest sea force the world had ever seen and Britannia ruled the waves. He wanted to be part of this, there was no question in his parents' mind that he would not follow in the family tradition.

'I tell this court now, that was a mistake. I was 17, a child with a child's intellect. I took this path deceived by the glory of the past and the power for the future. I now accept that the past cannot be crossed out as by a pencil. It is something I have to live with. However, you must believe me now that you know that I have never been in a combative situation in any war or skirmish, that my only role in the navy has been as a diver, mostly in the rescue and recovery of ships and personnel. This present episode cannot be wiped away. I must admit to my roll. However, I was only involved to help my old friend. Which of you, comrades, would refuse such a role? I do ask for mitigation. I have told you the truth.'

Jack took a deep breath and studied the faces of the three judges. Not a glimmer of sympathy could be gleaned. He finally said, 'Anyone of us can be deceived, but should that deception cost a life?'

He knew that many present today would have lost friends, family and work colleagues to deceit and could possibly lose them tomorrow or the next day. Premier Khruschev had not followed Stalin's paranoia with such vigour, but his position depended on total regard to his own safety and was probably always looking over his shoulder. Jack took a sip of water to reassess the atmosphere around him. Had he further endangered himself by assuming a lack of inner strength and commitment? A nervousness overcame him now as he was not sure that his assumed role of deceived Naval Officer had been strong enough to save him from immediate death, but he had now done all he could. He bowed to the court indicating that he had finished.

He was marched back to his cell flanked by two guards. They were halfway across a courtyard when they were approached by Colonel Petrov and he was taken to another interrogation room. Leaving the guards outside, Petrov took out of his tunic pocket two English newspaper cuttings and handed them to Jack.

'I'm sorry but now we have closure. Read them here. I will wait, then hand them back.'

CHAPTER 9

Lubyanka prison Moscow 1956

Jack took the first page and started to read. It related the events that took place on Sunday 9 June 1956. It read like an interview but captured a devastating moment in Jack's life. His hands were shaking as he fought to gain control of his emotions for the first time since he'd attacked Petrov on board the Ordhonikidze.

John Randall was staring out across the waters off Pilsey Island Chichester in Southern England in the direction of Portsmouth, shielding his eyes against the intensity of the morning sun as it rose casting blinding reflections of yellow light over the water's surface.

'What are you looking at, John?'

His two companions tried to focus in the same direction.

'Not sure, could be anything. Look over there, three or four hundred yards away'.

He pointed eastwards from their small boat in that direction as it pitched and rolled in the swell of the incoming tide. John Randall and his companions had been at sea for several hours that Sunday morning. It had been a good summer and this Sunday was no exception. Their fishing trip had not been particularly successful, but it had been fun and relaxing.

'Come on, lads, let's take a look.'

He started the outboard motor and slowly glided away from the sandbank, steering towards the object. The swell kept obscuring their vision but as they neared it, all they could make out was a bloated black shiny surface about the size of a large seal.

John killed the engine and the boat drifted slowly towards it. The object appeared to be clothed in a diver's suit. As they drew closer, they realised to their horror that they were looking at a headless corpse.

'Come on let's get it aboard.'

John leaned over the bow and pulled the object alongside. As he attempted to lift it, seawater spewed out of the top of the diving suit. It carried with it several fragments of flesh and bones. The smell made them wretch and hold their breath as they struggled to pull the dead weight aboard. The suit kept slipping spilling more of its contents into the sea and the bottom of their boat. Eventually they succeeded and laid it to rest by their feet. It was apparent that the body before them had no head and no hands.

They stared in silence unsure what to do next. John started the engine and they headed towards shore.

'It's going to be difficult to identify this one.'

CHAPTER 10

England 1956

The second article followed on.

*An inquest took place on Wednesday 26 June 1956.
The pathologist, Dr King, read a report and confirmed his
original findings. He produced evidence of the physical details
of the deceased and the clothing.*

*Next to give evidence was Gordon William Bostick, an
officer from the Admiralty in London. He confirmed that
deceased retired from naval service in 1955 and since that time
he had not been employed in the service of the Royal Navy nor
done any training.*

Had anyone been there to cross-examine
Bostick, they would have discovered that was not the
whole truth, thought Jack momentarily.

*The deceased was still a listed member of the Royal
Naval Voluntary Reserve.*

*The deceased's service record as a diver of some reputation
and gallantry was read out by Mr Knowles. In support of the
pathologist's findings, he described how when working in
Leghorn in Italy in 1944, he had been ordered to find limpet
mines attached to the hull of an American cruiser. As he wase
going down, a tug passed overhead causing water turbulence
and had thrown him against the protective barbed netting so
causing the injuries that had been described earlier. He also
confirmed the deceased's preference for a two-piece suit without*

hood. Mr Knowles described the smallness of the feet and legs and the colour of his hair.

In summing up, the Coroner said, 'I think it would be beyond all our ideas of possible coincidence if all these facts were put down to sheer coincidence. I am therefore satisfied that the remains which were found in Chichester harbour on the 9 June were those of Lieutenant Commander Lionel Crabb RNVR.

Jack looked up at Colonel Petrov and handed him the papers.

'Thank you.'

Petrov opened the door and turned to Jack. He clicked his heels together and bowed ever so slightly.

RUDI STANIK

CHAPTER 11

Monday 23 April 1941 Stalingrad Russia

As evening of the first day fell, the train came to a halt. Ahead the tracks had been bent and twisted from the last German field gun barrage; smoke still rose lazily from the burning sleepers. Nobody moved. Outside the officers were talking animatedly with the driver and guard. With a juddering and clanking, the carriages started to move backwards and came to rest in a siding hidden by the framework of a shattered factory on one side and the vast open land to the west on the other.

'Vne,' shouted the officers running through the train carriages. The Frontoviks, as they were called by those knowing that their destination was the front line in the defence of the Motherland, quickly gathered their kit and climbed out onto the tracks falling over each other so as not to be last to line up.

'We are not going to be able to get any further. The rest of the way, we march.'

Rudi was scared for the first time. It was an intellectual fright, a fright of what may happen as soon as they made their way back up the line. The noise of planes overhead, the even snarl of their engines became overwhelming, then as they banked away the noise faded. He shivered and looked at the faces around him. Clearly, he wasn't alone as he fought to control himself. He wasn't going to die in this cesspit of carnage.

Within seconds some distance to the south east of where they were marching, the faint sound of whistling could be heard above the relative silence. The first bombs exploded. Rudi grappled with his helmet straps, his heart rate exploding in his chest. He was jolted into a kind of emotion prompted by danger that he had never experienced in his short life so far, He realized he was trembling as he watched the smoke rise ahead of him, followed by a shockwave of exploding bombs. From now on that dread gripped him each time he heard the whistling of impending destruction and death. The senior officer ordered them to move away from the tracks, running after him, they all made a sharp turn into a bombed site of a former warehouse reduced to mangled steel and concrete. Amongst the debris they sought protection of a sort. They were all now spread out over a large area and communication was almost impossible. Flares appeared in the sky. In the short time they had been together that was a signal to stop and take cover. Half the recruits, petrified, kept running away into the open again; Rudi remained hidden along with two others who had dived undercover of a large concrete slab.

A German Stuka roared overhead and there followed a long burst of machine gunfire as it strafed those Frontoviks running into the open. His eyes caught their arched backs and then the cries as they fell and breathed their last. Another string of bombs started to whine down. Rudi had the feeling that as it got closer the back of his head would explode and his time had come to leave this world, but then the noise of the continuous whistle started at a high pitch and slid down the scale until the earth shattered around them. Rudi lay face down under the concrete canopy with the brim of his helmet in the dust, as close as he could get to the bottom of the hiding place and held his breath. The heavy rumble of the detonation sent shock waves through the ground blanketing the whole area. He lay there motionless. His breath had been taken away, his chest was constricted and tight, dust and earth covered his face and invaded is nostrils and ears. It took him a while to realise that he had not been hit, a few scratches from the concrete that had exploded around him but nothing more than superficial. In the silence that followed Rudi rose out of the concrete canopy.

A long row of flares was still burning in the sky seemingly stationary instead of falling. For an instant, Rudi thought that they were directly above him but, on clearing his eyes, he realised they were moving to his east, away from them. He could not see any other signs of life. He shouted. Silence, but he noticed a waving hand and moved towards it.

Another bomber roared overhead; another string of flares ignited casting light directly over the top of him and his two fellow Frontoviks.

'They're going to get us this time,' howled one of his comrades.

They dived under the concrete canopy for the second time. Rudi began to shiver slowly at first, then in bigger convulsions as if he had just resurfaced from ice cold water. He shook uncontrollably all over, his knees banging against the concrete dust and his arms flailing against the canopy above. There was no direct hit, but Rudi went on shaking until the flares dimmed and silence returned. He turned self-consciously as the trembling began to subside, to find he was not alone in being so petrified when he saw the eyes of his two comrades; he felt their fear too. For the next few minutes, they talked the terror out of their systems. Finally, with their courage returning, they crawled from under the debris and slowly got to their feet. Grabbing their guns, they stumbled over the ground to where they last saw the senior officer and some of the other recruits.

Their first sight was the senior officer's binoculars swinging silently to and fro from a fragment of steel hanging from a concrete post; below perched at an unsteady angle sprawled the top half of his body, his legs lay detached several feet away. Rudi doubled over and vomited. In front of him, bloodied and vacant were the staring eyes of another man. He jumped back and fell heavily on his side, then ran as fast as he could away from death, away from this city and the carnage of war, away from his two comrades. It was only when he could run no more that he was forced to stop and look around.

Behind him was Stalingrad. He was alone and lost in the middle of nowhere, all he could see was the faint glow of the fire that engulfed the outskirts of the city he had just left that were dancing on the still water of the Volga. Within minutes, he heard the crackle of gunfire in the distance to his right. Not knowing whether it was friend or foe, he lay still against the cold damp ground; for a moment the earthy smell from the long blades of grass, still growing in this chaos, comforted him. He lifted his head slightly and looked ahead towards the river. A shower of bullets disturbed the night air, as over the bank, to his left came hundreds of German soldiers charging across the field firing at all angles before them. He felt a sharp pain momentarily and collapsed into unconsciousness.

CHAPTER 12

Moscow Soviet Russia 1941

Rudi Stanik was 22 at the end of World War II. He'd grown up not knowing anything other than absolute faith in the Soviet system, apart from stories quietly spoken behind closed doors by his mother and father. All able-bodied men were eligible for conscription over the age of 17. He had deferred his entry into the Red Army for as long as he could under University dispensation.

On Sunday, mid-April 1941, a letter was posted under the door of his apartment. The next day, carrying a bag with spare clothes and underwear, Rudi set out for the collection point. The sun was rising yellow over the six golden onion domes of the Cathedral of the Assumption secured behind the Kremlin walls. Almost at a run along Kadashevskaya Nab, Rudi pulled up his collar and adjusted his cap against cool morning air as he continued along the embankment recently reinforced to contain the Moskva river and then crossed the newly constructed bridge towards Lubyansky Proezd and took a right onto Myasnitsaya Ulitsa.

Minutes later he stood outside the rusting unkempt railings surrounding a bleak sober military style building. Those already there did not acknowledge his arrival, they kept their heads down, no smiles, no eye contact. Normal human social interaction had already been banished from these young recruits. Inside the building behind a tattered wooden desk sat a large man with his arms crossed over his belly. The buttons on his uniform strained to keep his bulk enclosed. Rudi stood before him motionless looking straight ahead over the top of the man's peaked cap.

'Imya Vozrast Adres,' barked the officer.

'Rudi Stanik, 19. Recently changed address.' He handed over confirmation.

'Tam.' The officer motioned his head to his left.

Rudi walked towards the long table eyeing the ammunition pouches, shelter cape, ration bag, cooking pot, water bottle and a tube containing his personal details. A rough looking bearded man with a scar running down one cheek dressed in a ragged stained army uniform threw a set at him which he just managed to catch against his chest.

'Dobro pozhalovat v Frontoviks.'

Rudi looked blank but said nothing. He had no idea what 'Frontoviks' meant and was too scared to show his ignorance. He was then ordered to line up with the other comrades and marched back passed the Kremlin to Paveletsky railway station.

Some Moscovites looked on, others ignored them. Most of the young children watching them pass, waved and cheered. After several hours of travel crammed into ancient wooden carriages that rolled and bucked over the tracks, Rudi had his first cigarette much to the amusement of the new recruits in his compartment as he made the mistake of inhaling after a long drag and coughed until he was out of breath.

'Polegche ponemnogu. Take it easy, little by little!'

'Why didn't you warn me?' he stuttered with his head swimming.

'Here, have the rest for later. You'll get used to them and they will stem your hunger and dream away your stresses.'

Rudi nodded and closed his eyes. He could not sleep despite the little he had had last night, troubled by fear and dread of what may come and kept listening to the babble of conversation around him. At one point, he couldn't help but concentrate as one of the senior officers in the carriage raised his voice to take charge of the conversation.

'Comrades, the Germans are here to impose their way of thinking on us. This is not just a war between two states or two armies but an ideological conflict between Bolshevism and National Socialism and also the racial differences. They think of our Motherland as belonging to the ice age, having no intellect and racially inferior, calling us 'sub-human', if you like. Hitler's main quest is to gain control of our natural mineral resources and our seaports in the south to assist his aspirations for colonial expansion. They are waging war with unprecedented, unmerciful and unrelenting harshness. They will show no compassion or mercy towards any of you.

It will be better to die than be caught. Cowardice in the line of duty is unthinkable. White flags are untenable. Holders will be shot by both sides. Remember you are fighting for our leader and saviour, Comrade Josef Stalin.'

The clapping started sporadically and spread throughout the carriage rising to a crescendo of noise. Rudi watched, fearing all eyes would be on him if he didn't tow the party line and reluctantly put his hands together.

'Furthermore, comrades, you will remember that we are proud of our Soviet empire. There will be no chivalry ahead of you. No mercy at their hands on the grounds of humanity. You will be looked upon by the Nazis, not as a soldier, but as an ideological enemy. There, my friends, is no better reason to give your life for the Motherland'.

The underlying fear that Rudi had before, about never returning home, made him shiver. One days training on how to handle a rifle and carry a uniform proudly was all he had against a fanatical well-trained enemy.

CHAPTER 13

Stalingrad 1941

The harsh prodding of the bayonet stirred Rudi. Standing over him he recognised to his horror the giant figure of a German soldier. The jabbing continued until Rudi slowly arose from the earth leaving his gun on the ground, blood from his head wound still trickled down his face slowly congealing around the stubble on his chin. The German ordered him to hold his hands high above his head whilst he patted him down ensuring Rudi had no further weapons concealed in his tunic. Satisfied, he pushed Rudi towards a column of fellow Russian Frontoviks, heads bowed, dragging their heavy mud ladened feet towards away from the Volga river.

Rudi had always feared the first moments of capture. Would it be a bullet in the back of the head just where to stood? Stories from those who had survived the first wave of the German onslaught of Operation Barbarossa told of the excesses of the German advance across Russian soil. The raising of villages, slaughter of the peasant population and the ruthless shootings of surrendering soldiers by the Wehrmacht soldiers under their Nazi commanders.

Rudi was lucky enough to escape the arbitrariness of those first moments as a POW as the troop carrier to escort them west failed to start. Despite several attempts by the Germans to find the problem, nothing happened. Rudi tried to suggest that he could help but was butted to the ground. Eventually an officer intervened and hauled him to his feet. Rudi explain he was an engineer.

'Let him try!'

Rudi was released and pushed towards the vehicle. He looked around; all the faces of his comrades were upon him. He could feel their eyes staring into his soul. Collaborating with the enemy was a death sentence. Who amongst them would extract vengeance and when? The thought was wrenched from him as a bayonet pierced the flimsy army coat and felt a trickle of warm blood ooze into the fabric. He also knew that failure was not an option as he peered at the Maybach HL230 V12 engine. He had seen others like it before in another life at University so within minutes the engine coughed then began to purr and with it, Rudi's escape from death was postponed as he was force-marched across Soviet soil towards Germany. His first few days were as terrifying as the short combat encounter Rudi had already been part of outside Stalingrad, but he kept his mouth shut and his eyes wandering over his fellow prisoners, just in case one of them harboured mistaken ideological feelings of revenge.

It was on the second day that they spent the night in specially furnished pens enclosed with barbed wire and guard towers with machine guns.

All night long the sky was illuminated with flares and the drone of aircraft engines followed by the distant whistling as barrages of bombs and incendiaries fell on Stalingrad. The next day, Rudi could see the column of prisoners stretch from hill to hill disappear into the horizon. He watched in horror as the Germans reduced healthy people into a state of helplessness and death. The column of hungry, exhausted, pitiful men shivering from cold and damp marched on. The sound of gunfire had become so familiar, he never flinched now. Those still alive but not marching were dispatched by a single pistol shot. A prisoner that had talked to earlier in the day sat down at the rest stop next to him unable to get up when the order came. Rudi tried to pull him into a standing position in vain. A horse drew alongside, the rider's whip slashed into the defenceless man's arms that covered his face. He remained motionless. The shot from the escort's pistol blew the prisoner's head apart spraying skull bone, blood and grey matter over Rudi and others marching passed as Rudi joined them. The horse reared, the officer reined the animal around and disappeared towards the front of the column.

Rudi's loathing for the Germans and the Reich increased with every step he took westwards but increased his determination to stay alive. The remains of the butchered Russian population had seen what was happening to the prisoners. The survivors of the German scorched earth policy of the early days of Operation Barbarossa in 1941 and the treatment of their comrades in arms had caused the remnants of the civilian population to disappear into the swathe of wasteland that once small holdings gave life to this land that surrounded them.

As they continued west, the policy of brutality and starvation gradually thinned the ranks of the POWs, but it became apparent that the burden was too great for the Reich to carry. Rudi saw thousands of tons of food being transported west whilst he and his survivors were forced to survive on rations so meagre that men including himself foraged for grass or any other sustenance under threat of a bullet in the back. One of Rudi's comrades stepped a few meters off-line to grab a morsel to eat. A bullet exploded in his chest as the first piece of food for two days entered his stomach.

Finally, as the winter weather worsened and the German advance into Soviet territory halted as supply lines became impossible to maintain, orders arrived to transport existing prisoners by rail to Germany. Rudi and a hundred starving comrades were shoveled at gun point into the vast bowels of long wooden slatted wagons. Soldiers, some completely deluded and broken, others bleeding from their wounds fell upon each other as they stumbled to avoid the jabbing bayonets.

Over the next few hours, the bottom of the wagon red with blood gradually turned black. The warmth of living bodies started to dwindle as the mornings brought more deaths of his comrades. After five days, Rudi, his eyes half closed and his body shivering, sensed that the train was slowing. It lurched to a halt. Focusing, he saw that all but three faces had turned grey in death. He knew he was one of the lucky ones. Strong men, beaten and humiliated, had an ignominious end. No valour, just death from infected wounds, cold, hunger or thirst. It did not matter now, no one here cared. Before he and the other survivors were ordered to throw the skeletal bodies onto the platform, they picked at their dead comrades taking anything that might help another day's survival; clothing, rags to wrap around their hands, another pair of socks, anything would do. There was no time for respect. Whips cracked above their heads. Non-cooperation would result in instant death as the rigid forms were thrown onto the snow dusted concrete below them. The guard dogs barked, sniffed and chewed at the broken mass of humanity that piled up beside them.

Rudi was ordered with the other survivors to line up outside the station. Some had difficulty in walking the short distance and stumbled in and out of the ragged line. Dogs pulling hard on their leashes, snarled and snapped at their legs drawing screams and blood in equal measures. As they stood there waiting, in the distance, the wretched sound of other dogs howling hung in the cold air.

'What do you think is happening over there?' whispered Rudi to the man hunched over standing next to him. A whip caught the side of his arm. Rudi staggered backwards and forced himself to regain his place in line.

'Silence, you little Bolshevic scum. That is the moaning and groaning of your comrades. All 80,000 of them in their transit camp. Unlike you, they are starving to death. We cannot waste resources on those unwilling to fight to the death like real soldiers. You will be joining them soon enough when you have paid your dues to the Reich.'

Colonel Dorsch smiled and turned on his heels and strutted to the head of the line and took his seat in the Jeep. The vehicle then headed back along the line and took up a position behind the last prisoner. The column started to move forward down a long straight road flanked by tall poplars denuded of their leaves but with branches covered with the melting of the last flurry of snow that had fallen the previous night. It was impossible to linger underneath them, but Rudi and some of the lucky ones managed to catch the drops of ice-cold water as they fell into open mouths and wind-scarred faces. At several points along the way, the prisoners were allowed to rest and wander away from the road into the fields flanking each side of the road. Foraging for anything to eat, Rudi and several others found a few potatoes, that even in their raw and almost indigestible state tasted like the finest banquet. Rudi thought that this was unusual behaviour from their captors. It was later that day that Rudi was to learn the reason. He and other POWs were going to be part of a massive slave labour army to bolster the Reich's military output as the strain of global conflict increased. A day later, they stood in the remains of the once thriving town of Karglinsk. They approached the railway terminus that had once served the inhabitants, but now lay abandoned and silent, only inhabited by wild dogs and rats that had picked dry the bones of those left behind. The peasant population that survived the Nazi advance earlier that year had vanished into the surrounding countryside.

'You are being transported to our coalfields in the Ruhr and in the meantime, I am responsible for getting you there alive,' announced Colonel Dorsch.

CHAPTER 14

American Zone Europe 1945

Rudi out lived the brutal conditions of the coalfields in the heart of the Ruhr industrial powerhouse of Nazi Germany which witnessed the deaths of three quarters of his fellow Russian POWs. The camp nearby where he was incarcerated was liberated by Americans in the spring of 1945. Weak and undernourished, he had survived against all the odds.

After the formalities of identification had been completed, Rudi was taken to a holding camp by the Americans to recuperate. He was forced to share a small cell with another man who spoke the English language with an American twang but was also fluent in Russian. The man looked in remarkably good health for a fellow prisoner, but Rudi said nothing. Unaware that the man was a 'plant' and would be gone the next day, every detail about Rudi, his family and life in Russia and as a POW was carefully noted. This was the American's tenth assignment in a matter of days. The Russians were indeed impressed with their man and he was expecting to be paid a fair reward for his work.

'Please sit down, Stanik,' the American Captain said fingering an open file in front of him.

'With this information about you and your family I have here from my Lieutenant, I'm afraid you cannot stay this side of the fence, so to speak. Whether you like it or not, we have no choice but to turn you over to the custody of the Soviet authorities now we are satisfied with your ID and status'

'There is nothing left for me back home. I will not be going home, believe me. Nobody knows if I died or not, except you.' Rudi hung his head in despair.

'I am really sorry, but your file has already been delivered to the Soviets. I have no choice now. I cannot hide you and pretend we have lost you or you've escaped. I'd be court-martialled.'

Rudi was now aware that his loose tongue had cost him dearly. Who was this Lieutenant that had cost him his freedom?

Within days, Rudi was handed over to an officer of the NKVD, the Soviet secret service. As he was taken to the interrogation room, Rudi noticed another man in the office adjoining handing over files, he could not be sure, but the man looked very familiar despite being well dressed. The same small stature, bearing, similar in many ways. Yes, he was now certain it was the same Lieutenant. Clever bastard, he thought to himself. Rudi's attention was drawn back to the officer in front of him.

'We have your file from the Americans. Do you have anything to add?'

'After three years of hard labour, starvation and brutality, why am I imprisoned again?'

'Comrade Stalin required every Soviet soldier to fight to the death or face summary execution or imprisonment. Order 227. You failed in your duty, Comrade Stanik. You are a traitor, especially because you worked for the Nazi war machine.'

'But I had no choice, other than dying.'

'Exactly. You made the wrong choice. You helped the enemy instead of dying for the Motherland.'

In prison, Rudi was isolated from other prisoners and did not know how many of his comrades had also been arrested. Years of struggling as a POW to stay alive had taught him strategies to cope with isolation, using his head by resorting to his love of engineering by designing metal structures, solving mathematical problems, imagining and counting steps between the places he had been in the last few years. All of this had given him the strength to carry on.

Rudi thought he had seen it all whilst in the Reich's custody, but this was an altogether different situation. The NKVD wanted a confession and that meant only one think in his mind, torture and the infliction of pain. This was going to be difficult to bear. He could cope with being beaten, pistol whipped, even shot at, and deprived of sleep, but by his own countrymen. That was intolerable. After every session of coercion, he stood firm denying any wrongdoing.

'Here, look at this,' holding back his hair and pointing to the head wound from the Stalingrad capture.

'Show me where that is cowardice? Where were you during the fighting. Safe behind these walls. You are the ones who should be this side of the table,' shouted Rudi. 'You'll get no confession from me. I am immune to your pain. Ever worked in a coal mine, you lazy bastard?' *Not sensible,* Rudi momentarily thought to himself, but it was too late. The interrogator's hand swung across the table knocking Rudi off the chair. He clattered to the floor, unable to save his head from crashing into the concrete floor with a fearful thud, his hands firmly strapped behind his back.

The trial lasted five minutes. Rudi was sentenced to twenty years in a labour camp for, as the judges put it, 'not serving his country more faithfully'.

CHAPTER 15

Moscow 1945

Battered and bruised, Rudi was herded into an overcrowded cattle car. He managed to find enough space near the door and sat down. His eyes wandered carefully over his fellow prisoners; young and old, expressionless, resigned to their fate. He learned not to stare, not to attract attention. He fingered the back of his head, the swelling had subsided, but the tenderness remained. His other wounds from beatings in the confession cell were hidden and refusing to heal. The rations were minimal, water amounting to two cups a day and salted fish, their stable diet. Gradually over the next three days, Rudi's body began to give out, physically. He realised he was suffering from dysentery. He could not retain any liquids and eventually lost consciousness.

He was delivered to 501 Labour Camp and immediately transferred to the hospital. Most of the doctors were prisoners themselves but the local town of Salekhard supplied others that may be needed from time to time. In Rudi's condition, it was the town's doctors who treated his unattended wounds and brought his strength back, stronger than he had felt for years. After two weeks he was released into the camp. Siberia was cold, very cold like nothing he'd experienced in Moscow. The damp smell of vegetation hung in the air. The gates were shut behind him. The evening was entering its last phase before night as he walked towards the hut he was expected to report to, but natural curiosity got the better of him as he walked along one wooden fence and along the next and completed the rectangle. 501 was typical of many within the Gulag system. He was careful not to step into what looked like a no-man's land barrier of twisted wire and post, a meter or so inside the tall wooden fence he had been following, remembering stories from the hospital of the guards firing on sight, no warning. The watchtowers at each corner appeared to Rudi to command unlimited views of the whole of 501. Any thoughts that Rudi may have entertained of escape vanished without trace as he surveyed the place.

Once he had found the barrack hut he had been assigned to, he entered immediately shutting the door behind him to preserve the heat from the wood burning stove that stood in the middle surrounded by two tier beds attached to the outside walls. The floor was covered with mud that seemed not to dry. Most of the inmates appeared to be asleep in their ragged torn coats, never having the strength or willpower to take them off. One lightbulb fought to illuminate the scene through the steam rising from their damp clothes.

Rudi's resolve to survive at all costs had returned. Those in the hospital had warned him that the criminals amongst inmates were used to getting their own way. In the space Rudi had been allocated, sitting on his straw mattress half covered by threadbare blanket was a young man, dry and warm, as if he'd spent the day lazing in the hut. He looked better fed and cleaner than most of them.

'Not working today, day of rest, eh?' said Rudi jovially.

Eyes flickered open and heads rose as others in the hut took notice and feared the worst for this newcomer who had just walked in. He clearly did not understand the way things were in Camp 501.

'Need some money from you, Comrade, for your rent,' he demanded reaching out and pushing Rudi by the shoulders, thinking he was an easy touch like most of the other prisoners had been.'

'Sorry. No go. I paid my dues at Stalingrad.'

The war veterans in the barrack gathered round the bunk, keeping their distance, expecting to have to wade in to protect their fellow soldier. What they didn't expect was the quick stamp of Rudi's foot against the knee that sent his opponent backwards, followed by a two-handed blow to the face that knocked the man to the floor. Rudi grabbed the man's overcoat and rammed his head into his knee as he pulled him upwards. As he tried to get up, Rudi leant over him, taking his blanket. He made an enemy, but importantly laid down a marker.

'I told you, no rent. Now leave me alone. Next time you might not be so lucky. Right.' With that he lay down and closed his eyes in mock sleep.

His first few days were spent stacking rails, sleepers and equipment onto caterpillar lorries that belched black smoke into the cold air and then following on foot out into the wilderness and then unloading the cargo. Day after day, the routine was monotonous and backbreaking hard. Several politicos were already reduced to muttering bent forms unlikely to survive for very long.

'Stanik, come with me,' shouted one of the guards. It was his fifth day of unrelenting, punishing, physical work.

The air was freezing, the light seemed grey despite the snow lying trampled and brown. It was a forbidding, unforgiving land where Rudi was now part of 'Transpolyarnaya Magistral' railway project. He entered the outer office and shook off ice particles that clung to his overcoat and cap. He knocked and waited, standing to attention.

'Yes, come in,' came the booming voice of the camp Commandant, Colonel Barabanov. As Rudi entered, he was invited over to a table where the Colonel was surveying a large map and some detailed drawings. He picked up a file. Rudi recognised it as his. He could see the number, his number, still the same from the American release camp, 280646'. The file that the American Lieutenant compiled.

'Stanik. I see from your records that you studied engineering in Moscow.'

'Yes, but I didn't finish my studies. I went to fight for the Motherland.'

'Not for very long., I see.'

The Colonel smiled. Rudi relaxed a little.

'Well, you are now part of the 501 now and I have my orders to build this railway eastwards from one deep water seaport, Salekhard, towards here.' He pointed to a town called Igarka, another deep-water seaport.

'Twenty eight stations and one hundred and six sidings. What do you think of that? The Transpolar Mainline.'

Rudi wasn't sure he should answer. Was it a statement or a question?

'Come on, answer me. I'm not NKVD, you know.'

Rudi looked closely at the map.

'Am I a prisoner or an engineer?'

Colonel Barabanov looked into Rudi's eyes and was silent for a moment.

'You're both, but now I am asking you as an engineer. You understand?'

They were alone. Rudi nodded slowly.

'If you want my opinion, it is not feasible. How are you going to cross the Ob. He took the ruler and measured. It looks at least two kilometres wide here.' Rudi was now the one pointing. 'Ferries in summer but.......'

The Colonel interrupted.

'Yes, true but when the freeze comes, we will span on the ice using special crossties that our engineers have designed. Look.'

Rudi was now thinking that this project was that of a madman and his life along with tens of thousands of other Gulag prisoners, mostly political ones he'd now realised made up the majority, would be an epitaph to the megalomania of Stalin.

'I know what you are thinking.'

Rudi stiffened expecting to spend the next few days confined to the camp's prison.

'It's madness. Well, maybe, it's going to be difficult but, whilst you were away in Germany most of our industry was relocated to this part of the world, Western Siberia. We are used to living and working under these conditions and we must make it work.

'I have my spies, you know. Inside the camp and beyond. Other prisoners already respect you. You are strong now and with your engineering background, we will be able to make progress. I need a section boss. You'll get extra rations. I want men like you, so what do you say?'

'May I ask a question, Colonel? Actually, it's two questions.' Barabanov nodded. Rudi hesitated.

'Firstly, can you confirm that a Lieutenant, not a member of the NKVD, compiled the information in that file and does it mention my parents' arrest?'

Barabanov studied the open file in front of him, scanning and turning the pages quickly.

'Yes, to both questions. It reveals matters relating to your parents. That was a mistake, a big mistake if you want the truth irrespective of whether they were guilty or not. Anything else, you want to know?'

'I know this may be impudent, but did you volunteer for this job, Sir?'

'Stanik. No. I was ordered to take command here. I had no choice. None of us have any choices, we do what we are told, as you no doubt realise by now. I have seen many brutal things that I do not like. You could say that I too should be one of you for even thinking such thoughts. I believe that there is another way to use slave labour that will achieve better results. I expect you to think like me even though we are on different sides of the fence.'

Rudi was dismissed and returned to the barracks to prepare for the next shift. Weeks moved into months and months into years. Deaths, not from brutality but from illness, became a regular event. Barabanov was as good as his word and Rudi escaped the worst excesses as his food intake as a section leader allowed him extra rations. Progress was slow. Building a railway in winter was hampered by severe cold, permafrost and worst of all great food shortages. In the summertime, the terrain became bogged. The prisoners suffered from disease caused by mosquitoes, gnats, midges and horseflies. Rudi's complaints about lack of power machinery went unheeded. His team was decimated by illness and Rudi spent several weeks of treatment for blood poisoning from insect bites made worse by irritations from lice infestations. The planning of escape albeit just a fantasy became a respite from the pain and drudgery of existing in this hellhole.

Then one morning, without warning, the prisoners awoke to find that instead of the usual shouting and barking of orders for the day's work, there was an eerie silence, just the sound of dripping water as the ice melted on the barrack roofs. Outside the train engines were silent, no steam and smoke rising from their bellies. The project had stopped, and the gates were flung open. Colonel Barabanov and the troops guarding the 501 Labour Camp disappeared overnight. It was a strange and uncomfortable feeling that overtook Rudi. There was no outward pouring of emotions amongst the survivors. How could there be? They were left to fend for themselves, isolated in this frozen wasteland. Many more would die before reaching and finding their former life, even if they chose to do so. What could they do? Families had been broken up and who wanted to be associated with a former Gulag inmate? Rudi made the difficult decision to try and rebuild his life but first he had to find his way west towards Moscow.

JACK SANDERSON and RUDI STANIK

CHAPTER 16

Journey to Siberia Soviet Russia

'I, Rudi Stanik, a citizen of the Soviet Socialist Republics, entering into the ranks of the Red Army of the Workers and Peasants', take this oath and solemnly promise to be honest, brave, disciplined, vigilant fighter, staunchly to protect military and state secrets and unquestionably to obey all military regulations and orders of commanders and superiors.......If by evil intent I should violate this, my solemn oath, then let the severe punishment of Soviet law and the total hatred and contempt of the working class befall me,' recited Rudi quietly in a voice tinged with irony and loathing.

Jack Sanderson looked around at his fellow prisoners, all of whose attention was focused Comrade Stanik's words, he was about to say something when barked orders rang down the marshalling yard and soldiers began herding them into the cattle trucks.

'Is this our fate, you and I being together,' muttered Rudi as he put out his hand and hauled

Jack into the wagon. They looked around. The first on board had helped themselves to space by the open windows. Jack, who had found a room on the floor, enough for the two of them, listened to the mutterings of the younger man next to him. *Fate*, who knows, Jack thought to himself as his attention was drawn elsewhere.

'There was only one slop bucket in this pigsty of a cattle truck. We need another.' Shouted one of the prisoners as he attempted to relieve himself through a narrow opening in the side opposite the door.

The scream that followed, pierced the atmosphere like an arrow finding its target. Looking out, Rudi saw a bayonet wound with bright red blood pooling on the tracks beneath. The man was pulled back inside as attempts were made to staunch the flow from the wound.

'He'll not last the night,' said Rudi turning to Jack. Jack nodded agreement then stuck out his hand.

'Jack Sanderson. I heard your name, Rudi Stanik, when you recited your Oath to the Red Army.'

'How did you know it was for the Red Army?'

Jack smiled. 'It's a long story of a Russian speaking Englishman caught committing an act of war. What about you, Rudi Stanik? We've got a lot of time and I sense you're not, how shall I say, a believer in the current system that has invaded your Motherland.'

There was a long pause as Rudi studied Jack closely, then a smile flickered momentarily across his face.

'I love my country and all that it could be again.' He hesitated and cast glances at the other fallen souls around him. 'I have a sense that I spent a lot of time crying when I was a little boy growing up in the 1930s. It was a bad time for us, not just me but everyone living under Stalin. Families lived in fear of the dreaded knock on the door. It was a harbinger of a journey that would end here in a truck like this on its way to a slave labour camp,' whispered Rudi hardly moving his lips for fear of others around him.

'I studied at the University in Moscow, engineering, mechanical. Dad always said he wanted a proper engineer in the house. There, we were made aware every day that the State came before everything. The leadership had a clear goal of trying to destroy personal ties among private citizens and to create an atmosphere of distrust and fear. Your friends were encouraged to denounce their enemies whenever they felt there was a threat. Did you know that one in twenty, at least that's what I've been told me, were arrested just before the outbreak of the war. That's unbelievable if it's true.'

'Yes, I knew about what we called 'the Great Terror' in the West. What happened to your family?'

'I don't know exactly.' Rudi lapsed into a melancholy state and Jack gently touched his arm.

'I'm sorry, didn't think,' sighed Jack.

'No, it's all right. It was my first term at the University. I came back to our apartment. I opened the door and was taken aback by the smell of stale sweat, boots and tobacco. Our only two books had the pages ripped out, the pages were scattered about the floor. Cupboards had been flung open; clothes were hastily stuffed back in drawers. I had no idea what had happened. My heart froze in a dreadful premonition of tragedy. I still believed in the justice system and that they'd come back.' Tears ran down Rudi's face.

Jack said nothing and waited for Rudi to continue.

'Mum and Dad worked in a tractor factory. Mum was in charge of invoices in the office and Dad worked as an engineer, actually he operated a lathe but always liked to say he was an engineer. Dad was a very popular man amongst the other workers. After they both disappeared, I went to the factory. Nobody was prepared to talk to me. They were petrified of further arrests.'

'So, what happened?'

'I was at the apartment clearing and packing. The state said I had to move as it was too large for one person. Two rooms, cooking behind a curtain and a washroom down the hallway, too big!! Anyway, there was a knock at the door. I opened it. A man I had never seen before, stood there. His finger across his lips telling me to be quiet. I checked the hallway and pulled him inside and closed the door. He told me that the head of Dad's work unit had become jealous of Dad's popularity and concerned that his job would be taken over by Dad. That man put several articles from the factory in Dad's work bag and denounced him for stealing and for good measure told the factories propaganda liaison office that he had heard Mum and Dad making jokes about Stalin. I've not seen them since. Complete lies all of it. How could those two lovely people become 'Enemies of the State'?'

Rudi took several moments to recover from the futility of it all.

Jack said nothing. They had not moved an inch in hours now. It was getting cold as the sun began to fade and the evening breeze penetrated the slatted wooden wagon.

'I am so sorry. I thought I knew but I am beginning to feel that my education was a waste of time, lying here at the bottom of the human pile. Was your education a waste of time, Rudi?'

'My education? Yes, I suppose it has been, now you ask. The only benefit I gained was a delay in conscription into the Red army and the prospect of living a little longer, but that was soon to become a myth.' Rudi hesitated. 'No, actually,' remembering the German troop carrier he brought back to life and the railway fiasco.

'However, I endured, as a POW, the brutal conditions of the Nazi coalfields, witnessing the deaths of three quarters of my fellow countrymen. The camp where I was imprisoned was liberated by

Americans in the spring of 1945. I had survived against all the odds.'

'That was a long time ago. What happened next to bring you here,' enquired Jack.

Rudi related his experience with the Americans and being convicted for 'not serving his country more faithfully'. The brutal and harsh regime in Labour Camp 501 and the vanishing army of soldiers guarding the camp without warning after he had served ten years of his sentence. Jack didn't interrupt after hearing about the detailed circumstances of Rudi being handed back to the Russians and Colonel Barabanov's revelations surrounding Rudi's suspicions about the American Lieutenant. He'd wait until Rudi had finished his story.

'I thought, really thought, that I was free again after they opened the camp gates and left us to fend for ourselves. How wrong can you be? Look, here I am again sitting next to you.

'Several of us, in fact they were all ex-veterans, gathered what supplies we could and made our way along the course of the railway line that we'd been building towards Novilsk. From there I made my way to Moscow, begging and scrounging along the way. No-one had told me that the Camp had been abandoned under a mass amnesty from Comrade Khrushchev. What happened next was a typical example of Soviet life even now. I had no papers, no friends and no life in Moscow to help me. I wandered the streets sleeping rough in doorways, avoiding anything and anyone that looked official.

Nothing had changed. People were still afraid. I don't know who or why but in the middle of the night a couple of weeks ago. I was taken to a police station and subjected to several hours of intermittent interrogation.

'The Commissar of the Police station told me that he could find no paperwork that released me from my original prison sentence and that until he had anything official in writing I must remain in custody. He wiped his hands of me by escorting me to the station and into your company. There you have it, Jack.'

'I'm sorry, Rudi. You mentioned an American. Tell me about him?'

'I shared temporary accommodation with him after the Americans freed our German POW camp in the Ruhr. It was such a relief to be free and for a long time, I suppose, I was pretty animated. Told him all about my life before the call up to save Stalingrad. My parents' disappearance. He was a good listener and his American accent lulled me into a false sense of security, looking back.'

Rudi told Jack about seeing him handing information the NKVD. Rudi was sure he was working both sides and hated him for handing him back to the Soviet regime.

'Can you describe him for me?

'Interesting,' said Jack. Rudi looked at him quizzically.

'Well, I have had a lot of time to think about what happened to bring me here.'

Rudi listened intently as Jack told him the details.

'It seems both of us are here because of one bastard, Johnson.'

CHAPTER 17

Moscow same day

After hours of waiting, a whistle at the end of the marshalling yard, heralded the juddering and jerking forward motion of the train. The slop bucket in the corner tipped and rolled across the floor coming to rest at Jack's foot. He picked it up and stumbled to replace it, as the train gathered speed lurching from side to side traversing the points exiting the marshalling yard. Jack counted fifty others in his wagon, twenty-one wagons excluding the guards' carriage, total over a thousand prisoners.

Jack and Rudi stood to look through the ill-fitting wooden slats in the dying yellow glow of the setting sun of this November evening and watched the city lights fade as the train headed east. Jack held the bars of the window space with his mittened fingers. The chilled air coursed through his hair. He had devoured every aspect of his surrounding since being released from his Lubyanka cell. He accepted that it was going to be a lifetime before he was to see the skyline of a city again.

It happened so quickly. Two days ago, Jack's cell had been his home for the foreseeable future. He reconciled himself to the future albeit bleak and pointless, waiting for some political change or a pawn in some covert game of chess to move in his direction. Instructions had come to pack his meagre belongings and now his future was being lost in the vast wastes of Eastern Siberia.

He looked to his left and then his right as the wagon banked to take a curve. The cattle trucks groaning and whining as they were pulled by this immense iron maiden of the Soviet railway system. Grit and smoke billowed from it stinging Jacks face as the wind caught it. The night sky gathered overhead, grey and heavy. There was no more to be seen. Jack returned to his place on the floor casting his eye around, careful not to linger too long on any one face from fear of reprisal. Sullen sunken eyes followed his. Who were these souls? What was their crime? He had never understood man's inability to reason rather than to fight. To talk rather than act.

His last meagre meal of soup had been hours ago at lunchtime and now he had to endure the pangs of hunger. Until his capture, he had been a man of routine and so his stomach expected action three times a day but now he had learned overcome that expectation, but he could still feel inside the continuing battle. Jack vainly tugged at his collar hoping somehow it would extend and give him more protection against the gathering cold. He attempted to lie down and get some sleep, but it would not come. He was too cold and too uncomfortable. He listened to the rhythmic tune of the wheels over the joints in the rails hoping that sound would hypnotise him to sleep curling up further into a near foetal position remembering the comfort he gave to his two children, Susan and Nicholas, when they needed help to overcome some nightmare or other.

The train continued its relentless progress east through the night, its cab occasionally illuminating the sky with the red glow of its belly fire as men up front tried to quench its thirst for coal and more coal. Sparks, smoke, and steam gushed from it as it kept up a full head of steam. The occasional station light illuminated the length of the train as it passed and faded casting shadows across the interior of the wagons. Jack searched the faces, some young, some old. Mostly faces of neglect and suffering of hope vanishing. Jack had tried to keep himself fit and his mind active since the terror treatment in Lubyanka had stopped. Secrecy was one rule he had stood by save that Rudi and he had unburdened themselves of life's strange fate that put them together.

He clutched the bottom lining of his coat checking that the magnifying glass was still there. He checked this several times a day. He had pilfered it from one of his former colleagues who never returned one day. His eyesight had suffered at the hands of that bastard Ivan Sopel, the constant beatings, under nourishment, the lack of rest and sleep, there wasn't just one cause but accumulation of many. His eye glass gave him another window into the real world when he had the chance to secrete written material away to read later. He was not aware of sleep but must have dosed off because he was startled by the squealing of brakes as the old wagons slowed and finally juddered to a halt. Next came the wrenching of the bolts on his wagon and the door was rolled back. The first light of dawn's deep crimson sun blanketed the station and surrounding building casting black shadows in its wake. The light had a metallic jewel-like quality. The snowfall of the previous night covered the platform and the roof tops. The morning air, not cajoled and pushed by the violent winds that can inhabit these lands, filtered into the wagon dispersing the smell of urine from the corner bucket. The tick, tick of the cooling metal brakes, the hiss of excess steam exploding onto the platform edge and the sounds of uncomfortable men trying to raise themselves from the floor, held his attention momentarily.

Every prisoner was made to line up on the edge of the platform. Rudi and he stood side by side. There were many more than a thousand men on this train. Far more than he had thought when they left Moscow, some of the trucks must be hideously overcrowded. Ahead of the men under the station awning stood several trestle tables. Each had a large tub that was steaming in the cold air. In file they attended the table, taking a spoon, bowl and piece of black bread. They stood facing their wagons and ate in silence. Fish, potato and black cabbage soup, as far as Jack could tell. His spoon searched the bowl for any protein he could find, the morsels he did find he sucked and savoured as if a fine fillet steak. He finished the bowl and licked the inside dry. He broke the bread in several small pieces, putting half in his pocket for later.

Moments later all the prisoners were on board again. Jack and Rudi held their positions against the side of the wagon as the train pulled slowly, wheels skidding on the snow laden track as they sought traction. For the next few hours Jack could see nothing except bare landscape that lay out in front of him for mile after mile into the distance. Now and again stood a solitary house amidst a clutter of dilapidated outbuilding and a cluster of trees which appeared to offer scant protection to the elements. His heart sank at the desolation.

Jack realized that he may have spoken too much since the train had left Moscow. He decided now to hold his own counsel. Was Rudi a plant? No, it could not be possible. Silence better be his mantra from now on. Better protection ultimately, he'd realised. The only ones that did make conversation were a father and son perhaps. They seemed to resemble each other and had huddled together the previous night for warmth and comfort. As morning passed into afternoon, the skies darkened, and flurries of snow drifted through the stats and settled on the wagon floor. They remained there as the temperature dropped below freezing. There were no more stops that day.

The 'father' started to cough, quietly at first as if trying not to disturb anyone, but gradually it became louder and louder and uncontrollable. Rudi got up and shuffled across the floor towards the floor near the wagon edge and scooped up some fresh snow from the floor in the palm of his hand. He cradled it as it began to melt. He placed a few drops onto the old man's lips as he was lying in the younger man's arms. The old man's lips opened slowly, and he took the water. He put his comforting hand on the old man's shoulder. He looked up and a glimmer of a smile formed as he took the offering of a small piece of bread from Jack.

'He's going to need more warmth to survive this journey.'

The younger man looked at Jack plaintively.

'Thank you for helping my uncle.'

Jack and Rudi both nodded. They looked around at the rest of the faces. So far, beyond the abject, downcast, and shabby appearance, everyone else looked to be in tolerable health. The younger man gathered from the floor as much unsoiled straw as he could find and made a thicker mattress for the old man and lifted him on to it, covering his sides with the excess. *Family is an extremely strong bond in these fragile times*, thought Jack. Jack found sleep easier as the wagon rolled from side to side, letting night descend upon them as the darkened wilderness outside slipped by. Morning broke with snow driving hard from the east. Jack lay watching the flakes pass the open slats silhouetted against the dark grey sky. He turned over to free his leg from the weight of another poor wretch laid out across the wagon floor. He stirred. Jack looked across at the old man's face. It was white with the wrinkled skin pulled tight across the facial bones. A faint smile crossed his eyes. He had survived the night. Jack got up slowly and stretched, working the circulation around his body. He felt the blood tingling his fingers as it warmed them. He carefully picked his way over an array of inert bodies towards the window. The frost on the bars glistened under his breath. The train had started to enter a forested area and the wind that had blown constantly across the plains was now trapped by the density of the trees and had died significantly. He found it easier to look although there was little of significance to be seen. He stayed there over several minutes aimlessly looking unfocused at his surroundings. His attention was gained by a punch on his shoulder. He turned to see Rudi's concerned look as the young man approached them.

'He's going to die soon.'

Jack put his arm round the young man.

'It is, perhaps, a blessing. He would never survive where we're going.'

The young man turned back from the opening and looked at the crumpled heap that was his uncle.

'What can we do?' he questioned.

'Wait and watch and one day our time will come,' was all Jack could volunteer.

Both men had watched out of the slatted openings as the train slowly making its way up the gradient. The trees thinned and another track appeared parallel to theirs. The morning sun had filtered through the clouds; yellow tinges of light caught the snowdrifts making them slightly luminous. The routine of a food stop was approaching as eager heads peered out at the approaching platform.

After half an hour, they were on their way again. This routine was to continue several more days. With each passing day, Jack and Rudi watched as their companions became less animated but more restless. The stop on the fifth day had taken longer than usual as the train had arrived early. The extra waiting on the platform had melted the snow so that it had filtered through the felt boots that Jack was wearing and he began to feel the cold creeping through his body. He sat down to loosen them, ready for another wretched night.

CHAPTER 18
Siberia Soviet Russia

As he looked around, one of the men who announced himself as from the real Russia, the Ukraine, much heavier and stronger than the rest, emptied the lavatory bucket contents out of the opening on the side opposite the door as the train gathered pace out of the station. He had turned it upside down between his knees and was making holes in the side near the bottom with a file he had taken from inside his coat lining. He was striking the blunt end of the file using his boot as a hammer. The operation had taken quite some time and when had finished, he stood up, towering over most of his companions.

'We shall have some warmth tonight,' he announced in a deep satisfied voice.

Murmurs of approval spread around the wagon. He knew that most of his companions would have some form of cutting implement hidden about their person. Life in prison had taught him and others their importance. Everyone was told to scrape the straw to the sides of the wagon and attack the wooden floor. Two hours later there was sufficient wood to last for a few hours. The unbearable cold came in the early hours of the morning and it was agreed that they would wait until late, when most of the train's complement of guards were dozing in their carriage at the front of the train, before they lit the straw base. The thick metal of the bucket would retain some heat thereafter.

The old man was given more than his fair share of the space around the fire as the kindling was set alight by a shaking hand. The red glow of the flame lit up the weary faces of the fifty men, their eyes transfixed by the flickering light. Soon the heat was being felt by all. Sleep that night would be delayed. The snow that flickered through the openings, now partially obscured by the interwoven straw to retain the heat inside the wagon quickly melted to water. One bowl stood within the flames with water bubbling away and being replenished as each man in turn drank some of the warm water cupping his hands around the bowl lingering longer to soften the mittens that had frozen earlier. The men had done their best to obscure the scratched and splintered surface of the wooden floor by redistributing what was left of the straw. The wagon listed from side to side rocking its cargo of prisoners gently. The men gradually fell asleep inhaling the scent of smouldering wood as the fire began to dwindle to reddened embers.

During the long, lonely night, the terrain outside began to change as the train entered a mountain range. The track became more uneven and no longer straight. The old wagons started to lurch and buck as they were dragged unwillingly through the foothills. The fire bucket in wagon number eight, no longer stood where it had been. Still burning imperceptibly, it had been shaken to the side of the wagon and had now spilt some of its smoking contents onto the straw. Within seconds the corner was ablaze. Shouts of help were useless. Men shed their coats and attacked the flames, beating them in vain, as they spread around the sides of the wagon and over the floor, crackling and spitting as they gained a hold of the splintered wood.

The huge Ukrainian was already attacking the barred openings with a wooden bench. He was joined by others as the battering ram began to bend, finally ripping the bars from their bolts. The Ukrainian was the first to jump and disappear into the darkness as the train slowed. The rest pushed and jostled each other to freedom, jumping and being lost in the night, as the fire spread, engulfing the wagon and spreading to another. Men trapped by the flames vainly sought the courage to plunge through the fire and into the unknown. By now, the guards at the front of the train realised what was going on and ordered the driver to stop. Violently the brakes took the hold, sparks from the wheels added to the confusion of the night as the train skidded and rocked on the tracks. Shouts and gunfire echoed through the night as the Commissaire of the guards ordered one section to stop the fire spreading, and his section to follow the escaping prisoners. The bolts on the adjoining wagon were wrenched apart and prisoners stumbled out, coughing and rolling in the fresh snow to kill the flames.

Jack and Rudi lay still against the side of the track shielded from the guards by the wall of flame that now took hold of the floors and sides of both wagons. Jack's snow-covered coat was still damp, protecting them from the heat as they huddled together listening in horror to the shouts of others around them being burned alive and those who escaped being mown down by machine gun blasts from the guards who were trying to make sense of who had escaped from those that lay in the snow around them and the others still trapped in the inferno. Dogs and guards with flashlights ablaze disappeared into the night following the tracks of the escaping prisoners. Jack lay an arm across Rudi body holding him still as they lay amongst the dead bodies of their companions judging the right time in the chaos to disappear.

Within an instant of hearing the last of the search party's shouts upon finding another prisoner, Jack and Rudi rolled down the bank on the far side from the remaining guards who were battling to prevent the flames from spreading further, and as they descended through the snow away from the tracks, Jack grabbed a fallen tree branch and followed Rudi's path, raking the snow over the footmarks as they both disappeared deep into the forest. Eventually they judged that chaos was far enough behind them to rest. The snow began to fall again. Only the dogs could find them now and they needed handlers. Was it too much to hope that they would not be missed?

CHAPTER 19

Siberia Soviet Russia

The cold Siberian night froze them to the core as they huddled exhausted together in the lee of the valley protected by the tall pine trees and ground shrubbery. They watched the falling snow cover their tracks. The sounds of the guards with their barking dogs, split into several search parties, kept them alert long enough to realise that it was not capture that was their enemy, but survival in this inhospitable landscape without adequate clothing, food or water.

Falling asleep was not an option in this environment, they must keep moving even by day as the pale morning light threaded its way through the ceiling of pine branches above their heads.

The remnants of the bread and the fresh melted snow gave them enough strength to make their way east. It was early evening of the first day of their freedom that, having decided to follow the railway line well away from last night's crash site, they came upon several small houses. They sat undercover of a dilapidated wooden cattle shelter on the slope of the hill looking down upon the hamlet and waited until it was dark enough for them to approach undetected.

Jack and Rudi, shuffling and falling through the deep overnight snowfall, came upon a small outbuilding. On opening the door, they discovered that it was the home of the several sheep and chickens. The stalls were plentiful with hay and it was only a short distance to the house. Rudi left Jack and approached the building. He tried the rear door; at first it would not move, but with a lift of the handle and a gentle shoulder nudge, it eased open bending its elderly hinges. He waited for any reaction from inside. There was none; whoever was upstairs must be dead to the world. He looked around. There was a line of vodka bottles next to a table, one of which was still open with a few dregs left inside. He lifted it to his lips and savoured the warm feeling as it slipped down his throat. Milk and dry bread were all he could find as he grabbed one of the vodka bottles. The food was consumed in the company of the inquisitive occupants of the barn. The vodka would be for another time.

They were awake before dawn of the next day and continued east, heads down against the swirling snow; slow but steady progress was being made. The railway tracks must lead to the next settlement but how far, they had no idea. The line passed a lake several miles long, frozen, forbidding and leaving little protection against the rising wind that had started to blow gently over the last hour or so. At the end of the lake, they could see in the distance, hills rising steeply and disappearing into the grey sky above. After several hours, they soon came to a long tunnel which gave some respite from the freezing conditions. As they exited, they saw ahead of them the outskirts of a town which they later discovered was Skovorodino. It would have been foolish for them to be seen so soon after the railway fire. They decided, even though the town looked deserted in the fading light of the late afternoon, that it would be better to turn back and search for a more permanent home in the forest near the lake. Rudi confirmed Jack's thought that this was probably old White Russian country and that there was no love lost between the indigenous locals and the current regime, but they must still be on their guard. There was always suspicion lurking somewhere.

The tree-lined slopes of the western tips of the Stanovoy Mountains could make an ideal place to lie low for several weeks. It would be close enough to Skovorodino. In the meantime, they occupied abandoned huts that traders of years ago had built that had long been left to the elements. The moral dilemma of stealing to overcome hunger and deprivation soon settled into a normal way of life until Rudi found work and eventually, with a new lakeside hut as home, a semblance of normality returned.

'Where's that bottle? Now we shall we toast our freedom, Rudi'

Jack searched the hut, then remembered where he'd hidden it for such an occasion and popped the top.

'Za zda-ró-vye', said Jack raising the bottle and taking a slug.

'To your health', replied Rudi, translating, using his new knowledge of English

Rudi had found work with a local farmer, unconcerned about his lack of paperwork and strange accent. He made sure that the farmer had no room for criticism and the two of them seemed to get on well. It soon became apparent that the farmer's sympathies lay with Rudi's past, and whilst he only hinted at, the man still bore allegiance to the former monarchy and the Russian Orthodox religious worship, a dangerous combination under Stalin and even now under Khrushchev and therefore only spoken after excessive rounds of vodka and only to Rudi, the new stranger in his life.

One day he put his huge hands-on Rudi's shoulder and led him to a pen. There, huddled against the fencing, were two dogs.

'Meet Shuska and Theosk. They're yours and that sledge over there. You can't live here without them.'

Rudi was overcome with emotion and didn't know what to say. He just hugged the surprised old man.

Hours later, Rudi arrived home singing loudly after celebrating his good luck with rather too much vodka lolling on the back of the sledge with Shuska and Theosk at the helm. Jack was on the veranda and almost fell off his chair at the sight as Rudi rolled onto the ground and righted himself.

'Two more mouths to feed but company for me and for you,' slurred Rudi.

Then Rudi and Jack became accepted into the little community slowly even though they remained reclusive for Jack's sake. It was one night, after Rudi had accompanied the farmer into Skovorodino to the local market as usual on the last Friday of each month, that he returned excited by a chance conversation with fellow farmer at the market who under the influence of his third vodka, produced a crumpled piece of paper from his pocket.

'You should look at this, Rudi. Get out of this place. No place for someone so young, like you.'

Rudi looked at the farmer and almost forgot himself for a moment as he read but recovered and said life was good here for him as he crumpled the paper and threw it on the ground. *Watch your back, Rudi*. Jack would have been proud as Rudi watched the farmer walk away as he bent down and retrieved the paper and put it in his pocket. He was sure these people, who'd suffered much under the communist excesses, were genuine and would not report him,

'Jack, Jack,' he shouted excitedly. 'I've found a way out.' Shuska and Theosk barked their arrival home as Rudi stumbled in. Rudi fumbled in his pocket and pulled out a paper.

'Look, look.' Shaking the grimy looking paper furiously in Jack's face he pointed to the advertisement.

'From winter to summer.' He repeated as if Jack could not read himself.

Jack took the paper from Rudi's grasp and read the advertisement and a smile filtered through his tired face. He pulled the cracked glasses from his nose and Rudi saw that a tear had started to roll down his cheek. Jack lifted his mittened hand and stroked it away.

'But how can we do it, we have nothing but each other, no money only the clothes we wear.' He sadly put the newspaper advertisement down and lowered himself onto the stool next to the table.

'Jack, my dear friend, we need to do this together or not at all. I owe you more than you will ever know. You have a duty to your family and your country. I have enough for both of us. You know I don't have anything here in Russia to look for, but with you, I can start again and live in freedom. Each time I go into Skovorodino I watch my countrymen, strong healthy man, but oppressed by constant fear. When the fear grips you, it is with horror that you notice that as a human being you cease to exist. Like autumn leaves in the fall, all my good qualities are fading and being torn away by that fear. It is only when we talk together, here in our meagre surroundings, that I resolve to fight to retain my self-respect. You taught me that, you gave me hope.'

'But I fear that I have made you dissatisfied without being able to respond to those aspirations that I've given you,' said Jack cradling his chin in his hands and leaning forward onto the table.

Rudi got up from his seat and put his arms around Jack and they remained motionless for several minutes.

'I owe you my life as a person. There is no greater gift that can be given,' said Rudi pulling back and staring into Jack's eyes. Jack smiled and nodded gracefully.

It was a father-son relationship born out of necessity even though there was not a great deal of difference in their ages, fragile at first but now stronger and blessed with each other's need for each other. Rudi remembered his father and mother silently.

'The ship sails from Vladivostok at the beginning of December. No visas are required as it will be at sea for the whole trip lasting twenty days. How do you propose that we escape from a ship that does not dock anywhere?' posed Jack.

'I don't know the answer to that.'

'Oh, Rudi, the innocence of youth,' said Jack with a sadness of the realisation that this idea was just that, an idea and in his view had little hope of success, although he did not want to stifle Rudi's obvious excitement.

'We need to see the ship's itinerary and how close she sails to land,' said Jack.

Rudi could see a change in Jack's face hidden from all but him. Was he beginning to snap out of his resigned existence? It did not matter, Rudi wasn't about to give up just yet.

'I will go into town next week and find out all the information we need and whether there is any chance that we can buy two tickets.'

Jack smiled. Later he looked at himself reflected in the faded and scratched mirror that had once seen some other stranger's image. He pulled back his hair that had fallen over his brow. '*You look much older*', he thought to himself. Time and torture have reaped their lousy reward. Life in this remote place had helped him regain some of his strength, but he still suffered from the pain of deprivation that he had almost succumbed to whilst in Lubyanka. Whilst Rudi was at work, Jack had carefully exercised, unseen by the rest of the world, and hidden by the forest in this virgin landscape.

Throughout the ensuing hours, Jack let Rudi talk animatedly and enthusiastically about how he would live in the new world beyond these shores. For the first time, as far as Jack could remember, there was more than a sense of joy in the cabin. Could Jack wrestle away the sense of foreboding that had gripped him initially? Could Rudi coax Jack out of his inertia? Rudi was now determined to see Jack retrieve his purpose in life.

'Remember our first long conversation, Jack?'
'Of course.'
'Well, don't you still have a score to settle?'

Jack studied Rudi's face. For the first time in ages, Jack felt the strange feeling of revenge stir deep inside his mind. His blood coursed through his body fueled by adrenalin and his heart rate rose.

'Right!' he shouted across the still waters of the lake.

Rudi smiled.

'You need to set out a training regime that would make us much fitter than we have been for a long, long time.'

The summer sun and the warm summer days had melted the snow and ice that predominantly covered the landscape and made the water in the lake temperature tolerable, but still very cold and would not freeze again until after their ship sailed.

It was the lake that held the key to their success although at this stage they had no idea exactly how they were to escape. Jack cooked the evening meal and both men moved onto the small terrace overlooking the lake that Jack had constructed soon after they arrived. The sun was still high in the sky but as usual was casting long shadows over the mountains that kept guard around the shores of the lake. Jack pushed aside his empty plate and pushed back of the chair to raise his legs onto the terrace rail. He lit his pipe and smoke spiral gently upwards in the still evening air. Jack admired the unbounded enthusiasm that was spilling incessantly from Rudi's mouth. Neither noticed the sun falling slowly behind the mountains and the cold that set in. It was only when Jack's pipe refused to ignite that both of them realised that they were shivering, and it was late. Whilst Jack's knowledge of Russia and the Soviet Union was exceptional, there were specific gaps that need to be filled.

'Rudi, you need to use your time in Skovorodino each Friday gathering all the information. We'll need maps, train timetables, clothes, official identity papers and most important of all those tickets. I'll train both of us to endure the rigours of what is clearly going to be an enormous task.'

Rudi's absence from the drinking hall after the cattle auction became a habit which did not arouse any suspicion in the mind of his employer. In fact, his employer was grateful for the fact that Rudi was not drinking and was therefore capable of getting them both home safely. It was rare that his employer could remember much about the day's events after the copious quantities of vodka that he had downed.

Rudi had become a regular visitor to the State library in town gathering books for himself and Jack. He had befriended Maria, the assistant librarian, and it was she who found most of the information within the library that he required. At first, Rudi was hesitant about letting Maria have too much information, but as the Fridays went by it was obvious to him that Maria was beginning to like him and enjoy dealing with his questions. Friday afternoons were becoming important to her. She, like Rudi, looked forward to the moment when they could talk together. She had altered her shift so that she would be at the library every Friday afternoon. She was falling in love with this unusual youthful man about whom she knew very little but couldn't stop think about in her moments of solitude, but she was getting very curious about his motives for the collection of all the information. This evening he'd suggested they walked together after she finished work. She leapt at the invitation. Now she hoped that she could find out all about Rudi Stanik.

CHAPTER 20

Skovorodino Siberia USSR

Maria was born into a hard-working relatively prosperous peasant family in a small town north of Vladivostok in the far east of the Soviet Union. Her family successfully farmed about a hundred acres and sold their produce in town. Despite having an inquisitive mind, education was not high on her parents' agenda although she attended the little school. The little school tried to cope with all ages but didn't receive much enthusiastic support from the community. Maria was therefore left to educate herself from the meagre supply of books she found at school and that her teacher had hidden away hoping the authorities would not consider them subversive.

By the mid-1930s their farming enterprise was not acceptable under the theories of Bolshevism and the state forced them into 'Kolkhoz', a collective farm, and confiscated their land. Very soon her mother and father were reduced to having to survive on the meagre rations that they were allowed to retain from the farm's production. Matters became desperate after the summer of 1935 when the crops began to fail all over the region. Still, they were forced to hand over their quota leaving nothing left to survive on. Peasants died of starvation in the village and throughout the region and it was only later that Maria learnt that at least five million Soviet citizens died in those famines.

Desperation to survive set in. Her mother and father set out at dusk each day searching for scraps of food. Each day they were rewarded with something to eat. It may have been that they became too relaxed or were reported or maybe it was just bad luck, but one night they did not return. Maria frantically searched for them in cornfields, the wheat fields, knocking on doors of neighbours in vain until finally exhausted she returned home to find the local commissar sitting outside their farmhouse playing with her dog, Ilyish. He stood immediately towering over her. She brushed a wisp of her long blond hair behind her ear and smiled at him. He regarded her impassively, afraid to utter the words he knew would shatter her world forever. She sensed he was the harbinger of bad tidings. She was not afraid. He bent down so their eyes met. He gently put his hands on her boney shoulders.

'Maria, some men from town came here today, checking the collective's contribution to the state's agricultural economy. They wanted to see the land and the crops. Your mother and father were caught looking for food. I told them many were dying from starvation. It meant nothing to them. They arrested them and took them away. I'm so sorry.'

Tears burst uncontrollably from Maria as she buried her head into the Commissar's coat.

'When will I see them?' she eventually managed to ask.

'I am not sure. You have to come with me for the moment.'

'What about Ilyish? He'll be lonely without me.'

'I'll look after him,' he said. 'Here, I'll put him in the car with us.'

She gathered her favourite dolls and clothes and wrapped them in paper and tied them with string. Lingering momentarily by the front door she looked longingly at the threadbare bits of furniture around the hearth where the three of them had spent happy times before the madness of 'Kolkhoz', playing games before the log fire, her father drinking too much vodka than was good for him and slipping into a noisy sleep. Finally, the Commissar shut the door and took her hand as they walked slowly into the centre of the village where a black car awaited them.

Holding Ilyish on her lap, she was driven to Vladivostok. The Commissar took the dog from Maria after she hugged him one last time before she was escorted up the steps into a large austere building surrounded by a brick wall with rusting iron railings perched on top. She looked over her shoulder one last time at Ilyish with sad longing in her eyes. The dimly lit hallway was populated by a slovenly dressed woman slumped in an armchair with her feet resting on a small foot stool in front of her. Her eyes were half open and at the sight of Maria and her escort she stumbled to her feet straightening her crumpled full length woollen skirt and bowed her head in supplication. They marched passed and climbed the stone staircase to the first floor.

Her escort, a slim man with steel rimmed glasses and crisp NKVD uniform told her to wait outside the glass door of an office marked 'Superintendent'. He knocked out of courtesy and entered closing the door behind him.

'Her name is Maria. She is now under your care until she is eighteen. She's bright and once over the shock of losing her parents should prove a worthwhile addition.

'What happened to her parents?'

'Caught stealing from the collective. No interrogation is necessary. There will be no trial. It's an automatic ten-year sentence for being counter-revolutionaries. They will be taken northwards at dawn tomorrow. I believe they are destined for Komsomolsk but that's of no concern to us.'

Maria stood patiently outside the door. She was ten years old and now orphaned by the State.

She was never told what happened to her parents after they went missing. She never knew that they had been taken by open cattle truck in freezing conditions northwards to the notorious Komsomolsk labour camp where they were immediately separated and died of loneliness and starvation within days of each other, never knowing what had become of their beloved Maria.

CHAPTER 21

Skovorodino Siberia USSR

Maria was sitting in the office as usual, one Friday, when Rudi arrived. He looked around furtively to see if other eyes were prying and satisfied that there was no one in the library and that the office door was firmly closed, he smiled at her as she approached. To her surprise, he took her in his arms and kissed on the lips. She hesitated and pulled away looking around. Her eyes were sad. Rudi could see that she had been crying.

'What's the matter?'

'Oh, it happens now and again. Something triggers a memory. Today, it was the lonely whistle of the factory beckoning the workers to change shift.'

'Come here,' said Rudi putting one arm around her waist and stroking her blond hair with the other. 'We have plenty of time. Tell me about the sadness, only if you want.'

They sat together holding hands on the couch. Rudi had always been mesmerised by Maria's deep blue eyes. Today they started to shine again as she relaxed into him.

'When I was sent to the orphanage, I missed mum and dad terribly. At night the lights from next door used to make the lace bedspreads look like snow. I used to shiver and hold my teddy bear tightly to my chest. I was not the only one. There were sixty of us lined up in this dormitory. I used to lie awake listening to the sighs and murmurs of the others. The crying had stopped. They'd got used to the routine.'

'Were you ever….' Rudi hesitated.

'What hit, beaten, abused? Yes, not to begin with only when we were old enough to work outside the orphanage. It's funny really, but the doctors used to try to make you older than you were. I was ten but they made me thirteen within weeks because I had been used to working on the farm and in the fields and was thin but strong.'

'So, they put you to work?'

'Not immediately. There was some edict that demanded we attend school. I loved it because I could forget the past and the present for those few hours in the classroom. I used to help the little ones as well as teaching myself from books as much as time let me. Do not forget, Rudi, this was a NKVD place. They thought the State was best at parenting. They provided food, clothing, education, something most of the peasantry couldn't in those days. It was their 'moral' system, weak familial links and strong collective ideals.'

'Were you ever allowed to talk about your parents?'

'No. Once inside, that was it. Some kids are made to feel ashamed of having parents who are 'enemies of the state' and disconnected from them altogether. We were especially susceptible to propaganda from the Soviet regime. We had no parents, no alternative views or values.'

'So, what did you think?'

'We were told, and could see for ourselves, that had we been in any other country, we would have died of hunger and cold. I had experienced hunger, so I suppose to begin with I believed them. I'm not sure whether I was taught to feel and think and discover life, or whether I learned not to and just accepted everything I was told. Over time, it worked, only fragments of my childhood lingered and day by day they began to fade, just as the regime wanted.'

'What changed? The Maria, I know is a very different person.'

'After dishwashing, working on a local farm, I was sent to work in a textile factory. That's what changed me.'

'How?'

'A brigade of us from the orphanage, were marched each day to the factory in all weathers. Some of the girls were eleven, but if they were boys, even younger. After we'd got used to the routine, we were forced to stay at the factory. We worked shifts of twelve hours a day, seven days a week. There was also a night shift. The noise was intolerable at first, but we got used to it. I remember the whistle, that meant on or off, depending on your gang. Those terrible conditions, the beatings for being late or not keeping up with production schedules. That is when I stopped believing in the system. I'd seen the propaganda images so had the others. It was such a lie.'

Maria turned to look Rudi in the eye and gently put her hands either side of his face.

'I stuck it out for the next few years until I was eighteen. They tried to tell me that I was only fifteen to keep me longer, but I had the paperwork. Can you believe it?'

'OK. At eighteen or was it fifteen, you left, just like that. Nowhere to live and nowhere to go? That's a hell of a gamble you took.'

'Never entered my head. I just had to find a way out. Anyway, that's enough. Later'

Rudi bent and kissed her.

'You can't, here,' she said with embarrassment.

'There's nobody here to see.'

He kissed her again on the cheek, clutching her shoulders and letting his hands fall slowly evocatively down her arms to her hands. She stepped back. He had always assumed she was slightly smaller than him, but today he realised that she was an inch or two taller but still effortlessly slim and small boned.

'Later.'

She grabbed her coat and the papers she had promised to find for Rudi, and they left the building together. Maria's house was some way from the library, but fortunately closer to the market hall where Rudi would have to retrieve his employer later that day.

'The owners are away at the moment, so we will have the house to ourselves,' volunteered Maria.

Rudi picked up Maria and backed into the bedroom and laid her gently onto the bed. He kneeled softly on the mattress next to her and unbuttoned the front of her dress, kissing her tenderly on the lips. She closed her eyes. She had imagined this moment many times as she had lain awake at night thinking of him, using her own fingers to pleasure herself as if it were him. He cupped his hand over her pale but firm breast and fondled her nipple. It grew slowly under his caress. She groaned with pleasure at his touch and he kissed her, his tongue moistening her lips and exploring her mouth. Her skin tingled with his attention and she wriggled slightly to lessen the tension. Gently, he removed her dress and let it slide onto the floor. His eyes passed over the curves of her body, his hands gliding over a fair skin and brushing her hair between the thighs. He responded to his own touch of her. Her hands pulled him to her, she felt the stiffness touching her. He hesitated, but inside she could feel her love for him responding. They rocked and rolled and swam together using the whole expanse of the bed that afternoon living like nothing either of them had ever experienced until the tide of love engulfed them and they fell asleep in each other's arms. Both of them were unsure what lay ahead and whether this relationship, so beautiful for the time being, would be anything other than transient. Rudi passionately wanted her to be with him forever. He'd told her so and she'd laughed.

'You never told me how you got here, remember you said '*Later*',' said Rudi.

Maria propped herself up sliding her hand under her chin and looked into Rudi's eyes.

'You know I was born near here. After my eighteenth birthday, they opened the gates for me and there I was standing outside looking up and down the street, not knowing what to do. It was a very strange feeling. I watched people passing wanting to say something, but I couldn't find any words. Eventually, I started walking towards the centre of town. Looking at everything, drinking in the atmosphere of freedom. I think there was someone up there looking after me as I never felt afraid.'

'It must have been me!'

'Maybe, Rudi, maybe.' Maria touched his bare chest and rubbed the glistening hairs.

'It didn't take long to find a small job that gave me food and lodging. I continued learning and tried to forget the past. I was determined to make something of myself and there you have it. A rural librarian living on her own and going nowhere happily, until you, Rudi Stanik, criminal and Enemy of the State, came waltzing into town!'

They laughed and sank into each other's arms again.

'Maria, how do you want to spend the rest of your life? You are too good to be here languishing the days away. Don't you believe in fate? Me, purely by chance, arriving here. Meeting you.'

'Yes, I do. Most things to me are somehow connected but fate, that is the difficult one. What is the future? You tell me, Rudi?'

Well, I'll tell you what I want. I want to live a free life where I can make a choice, not have it made for me. Living here away from Moscow there seems to be less State interference. Maybe it's an illusion, you tell me, but, nevertheless, I want to get away. I spend nights talking to Jack about the West. I can't wait to sample it.'

'I don't know what it's like in Moscow, but there are some here who still hanker for the return of the Tsar. You would never notice them, but I know who they are. I see them every day purporting to follow the State line but bending a little here and there. If I could make a wish, Rudi Stanik, I would be living with you somewhere warm overlooking the blue ocean in a little house with two children,' she laughed at the prospect. He took her in his arms.

'My wish too, but I need your help and trust. You know all the information you've given me. Some I needed and others were a cover in case someone other than you queried the requests. To protect you.'

'What are you suggesting?'

'I escape and as things get a little easier, politically, as they will, you've read the new edits and

137

the state announcements. Sooner, rather than later, people will be allowed to travel abroad and one of them will be you. I'll see to that. Only a year or so, maybe longer, but it will happen.

Maria looked at him thoughtfully. 'So, I do all I can to help you escape and remain here hoping that one day,' she paused. 'That's a big ask, Rudi'

'I know but remember I don't exist as a citizen. I have no identity. Nothing. How can I stay hidden forever in the forest, growing old and weary? Seeing you furtively every now and again. Sooner or later, I fear that I will be arrested yet again.' He started to cry but quickly recovered his composure. 'I want you to believe in fate, Maria. I want you to take a chance. I want you to use those connections of yours and get Jack and I identity papers for that ship.' He sat back and let his hands fondle her blond hair as she turned away in thought.

Could she, would she, do this for him?

CHAPTER 22

Skovorodino Siberia USSR

As September turned into October, Rudi collected enough clothes from street markets slowly and without suspicion. Jack and Rudi stuck rigidly to the daily exercises. Those parts of the body that complained with pain and stiffness in August succumbed to the vigorous regime and accepted the part that they were to play in the near future.

The lake swims under cover of darkness extended from thirty minutes to what was now over three hours covering several miles each outing and feeling there was more to come. The lake water was turning cold now that November was well established and summer a slowly fading memory. Still the two continued to stretch their bodies to the limits of endurance sometimes physically sick with exhaustion. Could they succeed? If they were being realistic their chances were slim of even getting as far as the port of Vladivostok.

But they were driven by the pain of lost families and the belief in exposing Matthew Johnson as a double agent and those who help him.

**

Rudi had always tried to be honest with Maria. He had fallen desperately in love with her and her with him. The thought of leaving her was beginning to be unbearable. She had been true to her word, risking her position, to provide them with presentable paperwork. He'd spent hours talking to Jack about his feelings for her and worrying about what would happen to her once they'd left and if they did succeed, how he would be able to get her out of Russia.

Jack had always been positive in his outlook for the future. He, like Rudi, could not see the Soviet Union surviving, isolated in its ideology. Something had to give. After all the cruise was an invitation for change, albeit, a small one.

On the last day of November, Rudi had agreed to meet Maria at the library as usual.

'I have a big surprise for you,' she said as soon as he walked in. She was beaming. He had thought that their last time together would be a bitter-sweet affair of love and regret, but her mood had changed that.

'Come, I want you to meet someone important.' She gathered her coat and fur hat and took his hand. So far, he had not had a chance to say anything, save 'Hi' and kiss her gently on the lips and gave her a long hug. She wriggled free and took his hand. 'Come on or we'll be late.'

Maria took Rudi's hand and they walked to the house she shared with the owners. To Rudi's surprise they were greeted by several of her friends and the owners all in traditional folk dress. Everyone clapped as they entered.

'My surprise, said Maria.' The answer is 'Yes'. I will be your wife, and this is the start.' Then she whispered, 'before we have to part for a while.'

Rudi was speechless as she explained that before setting off to church a special ritual had to take place. The gathered few started singing songs that Rudi had never heard before. One of Maria's friends held out his hands and took theirs together and tied them with a scarf, then Maria led Rudi around in a circle three times, smiling and laughing infectiously.

As they slowed their circling, she leaned in and spoke softly in his ear. 'The magic bit, now.' From the table came two small cut loaves. One was handed to Rudi and the other to Maria. They put the two pieces together above their heads as they sat together facing the guests. Rudi felt Maria crumbling her part of the bread and did the same with his as the pieces of bread descended over the two of them. Glasses of vodka were handed around and everyone cheered and drank to new couple and wished them well. She leaned into him, 'Don't worry, no-one of them knows our plan. I'm going to tell them that you are looking for a teaching job, should they ask. The church service will have to wait."

The two of them wandered outside away from the happy few who had resorted to a few raucous folk songs.

'Now you are sort of married, Mr. Stanik, you can go to America and sometime soon send for me.

Promise? They will look after me in the meantime. No-one will talk, they all hate those in Moscow with their ideological nonsense.'

'Nothing would give me greater pleasure, my love.' With those words he kissed her and they wandered further away from the house into the cold, holding hands. Rudi was the happiest man alive.

'Fate,' she shouted. As Rudi disappeared into the night, he shouted back the word 'fate'.

CHAPTER 23

Skovorodino Siberia USSR

The SS Soviet Union was due to sail on the 7 December. Early on the morning of the first, Rudi awoke after a fitful night. All he could think of was how to survive for Maria. He was cold. The outside temperature had fallen well below freezing and the small log stove had struggled to keep them warm. He put the coffee pot on the hotplate and turned to see Jack staring at him with a smile on his face.

Jack sprang from his bed, shivering at the sight of the frosted windows and the cold air searching and catching the inside of his lungs.

'Well, let us begin our adventure, Rudi.'

Shuska and Theosk, outside, had heard the stirrings from within the cabin and started to bark. Rudi left Jack to prepare their breakfast and stepped into the crisp white snow covering to feed the dogs who would transport their belongings over the next few days journey to the railway station at Ushumun.

Rudi was glad to return to the warmth of the stove stamping the snow off his boots and shaking his hands free of his gloves. They both sat down relishing the thought of their last hot meal for the next two days. Eggs hard over as Jack prefers them, bread and coffee. Jack scrapped the last bit of home-made jam onto the bread and ate it, savouring the sweet taste on his tongue. Jack poured another cup of coffee and eased back on his chair. There was still no sign of light outside and there wouldn't be for another few hours. He lit his pipe, fondly stroking the bowl. The new pipe that Rudi had bought was to be much more in keeping with the image they would be trying to portray for the next two weeks.

Rudi collected the two hessian sacks from under Jack's bed and into each one they proceeded to empty the cabin of its contents. The two men carried the sacks into the wood and threw them into the hole that Jack had hewn out of the frozen earth over the last few weeks. Both men filled the hole and covered it with earth and branches. Jack hesitated momentarily as if saying a silent prayer over a fallen comrades' grave. He turned and they both gathered the shovels and stowed them on the sledge patting Shuska and Theosk as they passed, who mournfully turned their heads as if to ask when they could move.

The first part of their journey was through a thickly wooded valley following closely the Selemdzha river which would eventually turn east away from their route to the Ushumun. Despite the light covering of snow their progress was slow as the route was narrow and uneven. After about two hours they left the trees behind them as the valley opened up before them. They were now started to make good progress. Both Jack and Rudi were experts in cross country skiing. Rudi had persuaded

Jack to fashion skis when they first settled down in the cabin and since they had undertaken journeys of many miles in the winter for exercise and fun.

By 5pm they had reached the point where the river turned east through a narrow limestone valley. They had covered about 40 miles according to Rudi's calculation. The valley was well covered with vegetation in the form of large clusters of trees and following Rudi's gaze along the side of the rock outcrop Jack pointed to what they were searching for. Both men took off their skis and led the dogs along a narrow path to where they left the well-worn track and climbed upwards over a treacherous terrain intermittently covered with deep snow. The wind that carried the powdered snow off the surface bit into their faces. Daylight was fading fast and the night sky closing in on them sent longer crimson shadows over the snow. They reached the long, shallow cave and Rudi uncoupled the dogs and let them inside. On the floor there were remnants of a previous fire and Jack went to gather sufficient kindling and dry wood that had been left by others who had toiled through this inhospitable winter landscape. Hot coffee and the comfort of the flaming fire lifted their spirits as they dined on dry bread and salted meat.

After another fitful night, their morning started early. Rudi poked the smouldering embers and rekindled the flame to boil water, causing the dogs to stir. Their warm breath caught the freezing air. With the dogs fed and their stomachs warmed by the hot tea and bread, they tied the dogs to the sledge and looked down from the ridge towards the rising sun throwing fingers of yellow light along their route. There were few clouds in the sky and without the swirling snow they expected to make good progress. The valley looked peaceful and white, the shelving ridges gently undulating beneath its winter blanket.

This part of south eastern Siberia had until the early 1970s only been served by the traditional trans-Siberian railway, but now with a new rail link running to the north of Lake Zeya to Sovetskaya Gavan it was possible for Jack and Rudi to avoid the sixty or so boom towns to the north and with the hope that the train to Vladivostok would prove to be a less risky route, Jack glanced at his watch. The train would be leaving in 24 hours and they were still thirty miles away. Their hope for a good day was beginning to turn sour with a change in the direction of the wind during the early afternoon and with it came heavy cloud cover and falling snow, impeding their vision and slowing their progress. The prospect of boarding the train clean and tidy as they had hoped faded as night started to close in. In the last few hours, the countryside began to change from the valley and the mountains of yesterday to the undulating highlands of an ancient landscape. Finally, with an hour to spare, in the distance lay their destination, the small town of Ushumun just visible through the driving snow. Rudi was the first to enter a deserted side street that appeared to run parallel with the railway track. Neither of them could see any activity. They slowed their progress looking for a suitable place to leave Shuska and Theosk where they knew they would be taken care of and valued.

Presently, they saw a small farmhouse with outbuildings and unhitched the dogs from the sledge and ushered them quietly inside one of the outbuildings with the sledge. They removed their travel clothes and gave the dogs something to eat. It was a sad parting as they hugged them and silently rubbed noses. 'You'll be all right here,' mouthed Rudi as they left. It wasn't long before they joined others on the platform awaiting the train for Vladivostok.

At the same time back in Skovorodino, Maria left the doctor's surgery holding her belly, smiling to herself. In eight months, she would be a mother to Rudi's child. It was too late to tell him, but she'd pray for him each day until they met again.

CHAPTER 24

Vladivostok

Jack had already carefully studied the pictures that Rudi had found. The SS Soviet Union had been built in Germany during the 1930s. On 5 June 1942 it had been hit by a U-boat torpedo and sank off Murmansk without survivors. In 1949 eight Soviet salvage companies had raised her from the seabed and she had been refitted to carry freight and passengers. There were a great many factors that Jack had not liked. The sides of the ship did not slope down from the deck but bulged outwards in a smooth curve. The portholes appeared to have central hinges so that they split the openings and were too narrow for a human body to fit through.

The advertising material described the ship as being stable in rough seas because of the fins below the surface from bow to stern. If a person were to try to jump overboard, it would not be possible from either the port or starboard cabins or lower decks or from the upper decks. Jack concluded that to avoid contact when jumping from the ship one needed considerable speed before attempting the dive. The stern was probably their only hope, but a final decision could only be confirmed when he had seen the ship at close quarters.

They knew that their plans would be hazardous and to avoid the propellers and the surviving wake would test their fitness and they're planning to the nth degree. His experience told him it was possible for a fit man to survive. He knew that their acclimatisation in the cold waters of Lake Zeya would stand them in good stead when they hit the warmer tropical waters. Their voyage would take them across the Sea of Japan and through the Straits of Tsushima-Kaikyo. Here a wreath would be laid in memory of those who lost their lives when the Russian fleet was destroyed in 1905 by the Japanese. They would head out into the Pacific Ocean towards the Equator. The exact route was to be a secret.

As Jack and Rudi boarded the SS Soviet Union they felt tense as if all eyes were focused on them and them alone. If they had been casual observers, they would have realised that with all the chaos of the last-minute activities by the crew and departing friends of others around them no one except those checking their tickets knew they had boarded. There were given instructions as soon as they appeared on deck as to how to find their cabin. The feeling of freedom had yet to penetrate their hearts as they made their way through the first door into the corridor that led along the ship towards the stern. They climbed the staircase towards the next deck as a voice rang out behind them.

'You two, what you doing? Papers, please.'

Rudi turned to look at Jack. His eyes showed the fear of a thief caught in the act of stealing. He felt the blood coursing through his veins throbbing at his temples. Jack sensed Rudi's fear and was stepping down the staircase. He purposefully put down his case and handed the tickets over. The man cast his eyes over the papers and looked at Jack's face. Not a flicker of distress was apparent.

'First class. You are going the wrong way, my friends'. He pointed to the next exit down the corridor.

'This is reserved for the crew. I hope you enjoy your holiday.'

Rudi joined Jack at the foot of the staircase and walked slowly away. They both felt the stare of the man as they found the next gangway. Rudi clutched Jack's coat as they turned towards their cabin.

'I can't take too much more of this.'

'Nonsense. You will fine. You handled the train journey better than I. We'll be on the way soon and you can start to relax.'

There were only a handful of cabins on their deck. Rudi had borrowed money from Maria and had used all their savings towards two first-class tickets as otherwise they would have had to share their cabin with strangers and their absence would have been noticed too soon. They opened the cabin door. It wasn't luxury, but it gave them the solitude to relax and restore their energies.

Rudi broke open the bottle of vodka and poured two healthy glasses and as they looked out from the safety of their cabin over the harbour. The evening was still, and the lights of Vladivostok danced on the black water beneath them. Rudi turned to Jack.

'I propose a toast. To your mother of Parliament, Jack, may we live to see the freedom she upholds.' They raised their glasses and clinked together.

'To you, Rudi, for giving me that chance.'

A crackle from outside the cabin made them pause. It relayed the captain's orders to make ready for departure. Both men stood motionless by the cabin porthole and watched as the mooring ropes slackened and slipped into the water. The vibration of the propellers beneath their feet made the ship tremble as they saw the gap widen between them and the quay and the black water swirl around them. As they were taking another healthy sip of vodka, their reverie was interrupted by a knock on the cabin door. Jack stood and opened the door and came face-to-face with a commissar.

'I have been appointed to organise various matters during this voyage.' He handed Jack two black scarves.

'These are to be worn by you at all times outside the cabin. You are now part of my group.' He smiled as he made his announcement with satisfaction. He then explained the itinerary which was designed to control all passengers for the entire voyage during their free time.

As Jack sank back on his bunk after the commissar had left, Rudi turned to him.' It won't work, there'll be a revolt before the night is out.'

'I hope so because if not we'll never be able to leave prying eyes behind during the voyage.'

That night at dinner all those with the black scarves sat together looking at all those in their red scarves. Arguments were already rife, regrouping was taking place, scarves were being thrown to the floor and the bolder amongst the passengers were sitting where they wanted. The various commissars were watching helplessly as the ship pitched and rolled gently on a southerly heading. This precious holiday for most was clearly not going to be stifled by a few.

It was at breakfast on the first day that the captain gave up the idea of a timetable for entertainment in favour of an announcement of a series of events for those who wished to attend. There were few up and about at this time as the revelry of the previous evening had taken a heavy toll. Jack and Rudi took their first stroll around the deck paying particular attention to the stern, watching the wake created by the twin screws that powered them through the water towards the Straits of Tsushima. It was not obvious to any observer of the two men, but each was able to take in the stabilising fins and the fact that they stopped about two metres before the propellers at a point where the wake was thrown off the hull. As Jack had surmised there were two narrow places where they could simultaneously jump to freedom. Another bonus was that at the end of the main deck where they were standing were two large refuse containers which would discourage passengers from congregating during the voyage. If they were able to stand on the other side of the gunwhale, they would have to jump about fourteen meters into the water, less than Jack had thought, but nevertheless still a difficult task. Rudi turned and leaned against the rail.

'It is possible?'

'Definitely. Our run and jump together with the ship's forward speed at the time of the jump would help to throw us well beyond the propellers but into the turbulence of their wake, bumpy but doable. What we need now is to find a navigation chart. I know we have the constellation chart of both hemispheres, but the small map that we used when planning this little adventure with will not help us with the exact timing of the jump.'

On their way back to the cabin, both men were able to study the route which until an hour ago had been kept a secret. They studied the ships course that had been marked on the chart of the Eastern Pacific that now hung in the dining room showing its intended journey to the Equator and back. The route was annotated with dates across the East China Sea close to Taiwan and then the eastern shores of the Philippines turning eastwards entering the Celebes Sea reaching the Equator between Borneo and Celebes.

After a few days at sea, it was apparent to Jack that the Captain maintained the routine of passing close to land during the day and using the open seas at night wherever possible.

It was on the fourth night that Jack and Rudi made their final plans. During the day Rudi had befriended a young lady with whom he had discovered during the course of conversation had a keen interest in astronomy. It was unlikely that either Jack or Rudi could have asked to visit the bridge without raising some suspicion, but with this young lady in tow the problem seemed far less daunting. Whilst the young girl chatted to the first mate, Rudi edged closer to the navigation chart. He took in all the details that Jack had requested and committed them to memory.

'So, it is to be the island of Siargao,' said Jack lifting his head from Rudi's small map.

'Nineteen miles long, sailing time along the shore about one hour. About 12 miles to the west. Time of arrival about 19.30. Jump time 20.00.'

He felt in charge again after so many years in the wilderness. His clipped synopsis of the plan reminded him of Buster before the missions they had undertaken together.

'That is some of the deepest water in the world, the Mindanao Trench,' remarked Jack, musing nostalgically about the H.M.S.Vernon training school. Rudi was listening and letting Jack remember times gone by. Suddenly he regained the present with the start.

'Sorry, we've more important matters to deal with.'

'No, Jack, I was fascinated. You have never really talked of the past quite so animatedly. You're beginning to live again.'

Jack looked at his watch. Both men were ignoring their hunger. Both had missed breakfast and whilst Rudi went to lunch, he had picked at his food anxiously. Both men drank water heavily throughout the day. It was a painful part of their immediate preparation. Their attention was held by the present, no thoughts of the past now the time was approaching.

It was 19.55 hours as Rudi and Jack walked along the deck.

CHAPTER 25

Celebes Sea

Alert, observing every detail, passing others taking their evening stroll, Jack and Rudi climbed to the upper deck, Rudi scanned everything around him and removed the small binoculars from his inside pocket. On the port side he focused the lenses. He moved methodically in an arc searching for land. The sky was casting over, gone were the high cumulus clouds and blue skies of the afternoon. They had been replaced in a matter of hours by a strong wind that was blowing from the south and bringing with it a heavy swell and overcast sky. He took the glasses from his eyes and handed them to Jack. There was a flash of lightning over to the west in the blackening sky.

'What can you see?' Rudi asked impatiently.

Nothing. Nothing at all,' replied Jack taking the binoculars from his eyes.

The air held the strains of dance music from the boat deck near the stern as they approached. They made their way between strolling couples in and out of the shadows as they clutched self-consciously their towels and flippers, mask and snorkel sandwiched between them. They made their way down the companionway onto the main deck towards the stern of the ship. As they approached, they stopped in their tracks as they heard the laughter of several men in front of them. Jack crept forward unobserved. Three deckhands were sitting on chairs drinking and whiling away the evening.

'We've got to get rid of them. Our chance only lasts another 15 minutes or so.'

Rudi looked anxious and nervous as the stress began to show. Jack's behaviour by contrast was controlled and logical.

'We'll wait here under cover,' he ordered. Both men lifted the flapping ropes that the wind had loosened and pulled the canvas covering the lifeboat over their heads. In the pit of the lifeboat, time hung suspended in anticipation. Jack positioned himself so that he could just observe the feet of the third sailor as he was stretched out on the nearest chair. They waited. Above their heads they sensed the intrusion of the occasional light as the storm came closer and it was with relief that they heard the first heavy drops of rain fall onto the canvas above their heads. Jack raised the canvas cover a little more. The feet that he had focused on had disappeared and with them the three men had taken cover from the rain.

They hauled themselves from the cover of the lifeboat and dropped silently onto the deck. They slowly made their way to the stern. The fear of being discovered now began to dissipate as they shed their clothes. They looked at each other, standing there in socks, trunks and vest with their scarves tightly guarding their masks, flippers and snorkels. Jack took Rudi's hand and pressed half the supply of grease into his palm. They smothered the exposed parts of their skin as best they could.

'Spring up and jump as far as you can upwards as we practised. It will throw you farthest away from the stern. Wait for my signal. See you soon my friend.'

They parted and made their way separately to their agreed positions. The ship plunged in and out of the water as the swell increased. Jack climbed the rail and held himself steady with his feet in front and arms behind him looking down at the swirling water beneath them. He looked over to Rudi as he crouched into a springing position. He held up one hand. Rudi acknowledged. Within a second both men had jumped up and out from the ship. The blackness swallowed them both together as they were lost from sight through the swirling spray. Jack hit the water feet first and disappeared underneath the foaming wake. Years of training allowed him to sink effortlessly downwards knowing that with a lung full of air, he would bob to the surface without any effort.

Despite all Jack's lectures, as soon as is Rudi hit the water, he tried desperately to resurface without waiting, using up vital energy that he would need later on if they were to survive. Despite his best efforts, the binoculars he was carrying had been dislodged by the force of the dive and disappeared beneath the waves.

Jack surfaced first, untied the scarf, letting it float away, and put on his flippers, mask with snorkel attached. There was total darkness all around him. As he floated up on the crest of the swell, he could just make out the lights of the SS Soviet Union fading into the night. A flash of lightning illuminated the sky around him giving him the opportunity to look for Rudi. He remained motionless in the water scanning to his left. By rights they should only be a few meters apart, but Jack could not see him. He pushed his mask onto his forehead and called out to his friend. The sound of his voice was lost in seconds. He shouted again. No response. He waited. Almost imperceptibly he heard a cry. It was impossible to orientate the direction that it had come from, but logic told him to move to his left. The rain that had started a few minutes ago had stopped and the wind, so strong on board the ship, was lost on the surface waters. As he swam slowly onwards, he heard Rudi's voice carry louder through the air. A wave carried Jack high above his surroundings and momentarily he saw Rudi about twenty meters away moving towards him. Both men put out their gloved hands in greeting. It was their real first moment of freedom together.

They turned on their backs and waited. The black clouds overhead, carrying a heavy weight of water in their clutches were being driven slowly away by the strong winds. The night sky to the right was beginning to show vital signs of the storm abating. They both searched for the brightest star so that they could determine in which direction to swim. The feeling of fear that had coursed through Rudi's body had now been conquered and he and Jack were together. Suddenly, above their heads they saw that the blanket of darkness had parted to reveal the twinkling firmament. There it was, Jupiter, as Jack lifted one arm high above him. Slowly both men turned over and with the rope fastened between them, they began to swim westwards. Their progress was short lived as the clouds threw a heavy curtain of blackness across the sky again.

They both felt the need to press on, but they knew that with the huge swell that occasionally tossed them in all directions, it would be useless to do so. They turned over again and waited. It seemed like an eternity, but after an anxious wait, they sighted the stars again. This time they were able to keep swimming as the clouds that shielded the night sky dispersed. They swam for several hours, and now and again rose high on a wave that gave them a panoramic view of their watery wilderness before them. They would not expect to see land until much later so their spirits remained high. They had to make as much progress as they could before dawn broke and their the stars were lost for another day.

As the horizon behind them began to glow with the dawn of a new day, the yellow and orange light danced on the water in front of them. The colours changed from their welcoming warmth to the coolness of the blue as the stars faded and were lost. It was Rudi who first noticed the small cumulus clouds that were building up in the morning sun directly in front of them. They quickened their pace without communication as Jack who was in the rear also noticed the tell-tale signs of the moisture rising from the mountainous land that formed these beautiful cotton balls silhouetted against the azure blue of their background.

Rudi looked at his watch. They'd been in the water now for 12 hours. Several more than they calculated. The heat of the sun unmolested, bore into their exposed skin now encrusted with the salt that had dried. The grease that had been protecting them had been washed off over the hours they had been submerged. Every few hundred meters each man turned over for protection, constantly sprinkling water over their skin. On the crest of another wave Jack and Rudi saw with heightening joy the first outline of the rocks and trees of the island of Siargao. As the morning turned to afternoon and then to early evening, it became alive with fish diving and dancing through the waves. They were accompanied by birds eager to collect their evening meal before darkness set in again. Jack and Rudi had almost exhausted themselves in their attempt to avoid another night in the ocean, but the current running along the outer reaches of the island was carrying them away from land. Jack was now very tired, and his legs dropped downwards giving him little forward movement. The rope between them tightened and Rudi stopped, looking back at his friend. He swam over and held his shoulder.

'Come on, Jack, we're almost home.'

The words were lost in the delirium etched across Jack's scorched face and head. Rudi removed Jack's mask and cupped a handful of water over his face. Jack opened his eyes as the salt stung his forehead and Rudi plucked the salt from his lashes.

'Rudi, you can make it, don't stay for me, I'm not afraid of death. I've seen too much of it for that. Just let me go to sleep.'

Jack struggled to shed himself of the snorkel mask. Rudi fought with his friend to restrain him. It wasn't difficult as Jack was obviously near exhaustion. Rudi replaced both his and Jack's mask and snorkel and turned to Jack on his back and nestled his head on his chest gripping his arms underneath Jack's body. With no arm action but only using his feet Rudi was able to move forward slowly.

Both men drifted forward not noticing the change in the sound around them that had come with a change in wind direction. Somewhere ahead of them in the fading light, came the noise of thunder and yet there was no hint of lightning in the sky above. As if mesmerised by its calling, Rudi moved through the water hauling Jack's inert body with him. As he did so, the waves began to tip over, allowing white ripples of water to be blown from their crests. The intensity became frightening as the noise increased. He was finding it impossible to hang on to Jack's head. He looked around over his shoulder, and as he did so a huge wave engulfed him. He spun over and over underneath the foam his body being pressed downwards by a force. He was unable to resist, but he struggled automatically kicking his feet and flailing his arms trying to break the surface again. Jack had gone momentarily, until he felt the rope tightened slacken and tighten. He resurfaced into still water. He grabbed the rope pulled himself towards its end. Jack floated to the surface. Blood was streaking his face from a gash along his left eye. His mask had been ripped off and hung shattered around his neck. Rudi pulled off his gloves and fumbled to feel Jack's chest. His heart raced as he detected a rhythmical heartbeat. He clasped hold of Jack and started to move to shore. The thunder of the waves over the reef receded. Suddenly he felt his body drop and his unsteady feet touched the soft sand beneath.

He dragged Jack up the incline of the gently shelving beach to the safety of the ridge underneath the towering palms and the green lushness of the heavy undergrowth behind. Rudi slumped down and cradle Jack's head on his stomach.

CHAPTER 26

America Denver Colorado 1987

Matthew Johnson had risen slowly but effectively and was now the CEO of his own highly successful Worldwide Security Corporation, 'WSC' for short, from small beginnings with capital payments from unnamed sources within the espionage industry during the latter part of World War II and the Cold War of the 1950s and 1960s and contracts that did not bear too close a scrutiny. He had now manoeuvred himself and his company away from small time work into a global setting, still using contacts from the past that had themselves become influential and could open lucrative doors for him. He had covered over effectively and sometimes ruthlessly the history surrounding his past so that now he considered himself untouchable.

It was late at night and all his head office staff had gone home.

He swivelled his chair around and looked at the man in front of him. His eyes took in the mean look that time could never dull. The man offered his hand, Johnson ignored the gesture but took in the distinctive lime perfumed aftershave.

'Sit down, please,' said Johnson. The man complied.

'Anatoly, you come highly recommended. Mr Granetti tells me you worked well for Mario Flavioretti, and if anyone can help me, it is you, so I am advised.'

Anatoly's face remained placid without emotion as Johnson handed him a file, having first extracted several photographs.

'I need your help to secure the continued unblemished future for WSC. Failure is not an option.'

Johnson held up one black and white photograph, faded with age, but still making the faces identifiable. It was of two men in naval uniform. One in his fifties, the other younger. He handed them over to Anatoly who studied them and read the words on the back.

Johnson then handed over another photograph, colour this time. She was a pretty woman and dressed in naval uniform. Anatoly read the note and smiled for the first time. The rest of the file contained several copy newspapers reports, memoranda and a blurred photocopy of a foreign newspaper, showing two men; one face had been circled in ink. An enhanced version of the face was attached to the back. Anatoly compared it with the black and white photograph he had studied earlier. He held it to the light and nodded, from Anatoly's years in surveillance, he knew they were one and the same person.

Johnson felt his heart pounding. He'd been right. It was Jack Sanderson. The report from

165

Moscow had alerted him, but they had only just warned him of the sighting and now time had passed without a trace, Sanderson had vanished.

'Well, Mr Johnson, what do you want from me?'

'I want you to find Jack Sanderson. I want you to find out if anyone other than the Russians know about him being alive. These are some names and addresses that will give you a starting point. I want you to report back to me before I decide on the best course of action. I will place in your account enough for your expenses.'

'I have not agreed to your proposal yet.'

'But you will, as I have just entrusted you with the future of WSC and that is something very dear to me which you cannot ignore, if you reflect on it.'

'Are you trying to threaten me? I hope not.'

'No, just so as we understand each other.'

Anatoly nodded. He turned and left the offices of WSC. His job had changed over the years. He was now no longer just an eliminator. He had learned quickly. He was very efficient and thorough in dealing with problems.

Johnson sat back and turned to reflect on the snow-covered mountains on the horizon now glowing in the clear moonlight. He shivered momentarily as he thought back to his sometimes, unseemly past. He rose from the chair. The years had done him well. His face and arms were bronzed enhancing his full head of white hair. He looked fit and well and had kept himself occupied with his young family when WSC allowed.

Life was now kind to him, and he was never going to let the past interfere, never.

CHAPTER 27

Escape from Siargao

The sun rose quickly warming the two bodies that lay as they had fallen the night before. It was Rudi who woke first and dragged Jack so he could lean against the bank of sand and grass that had been woven into shape by the sea and the wind. At least there, the palm trees offered considerable refuge in their shadows from the intense heat that would soon be the midday sun.

'We've survived one night without shelter, but we may be here for a long time. We need to build or find ourselves a temporary home.'

With that Rudi disappeared along the white sand beach that seemed to stretch for miles in both directions. Jack lay alone, his eyes drifting in and out of focus. He felt very tired, lethargic and extremely hungry. He must have fallen into sleep again as when he awoke, the sun had moved quite considerably. He struggled to his feet.

'Hey, look what I've found.' Rudi was holding up a collection of native fruits, their colours making Jack's mouth water in anticipation.

'I've been to the northern tip of the island. I'm absolutely certain that this place is uninhabited, just as we feared.'

They were talking and planning as they crudely devoured their first meal in freedom. By early afternoon they had selected the location for their encampment and were busy foraging for building material. Soon they had their off-ground accommodation and their first pieces of furniture, two makeshift hammocks. Within weeks they had built enough for their needs and were now supplementing the fruit diets with fish and nuts.

'I never thought of our lakeside cabin as a palace but compared to this...,' smiled Jack as he flicked away one of the many curious insects that became their constant companions.

'At least it's warm, just like California.'

'Shall I fashion a surf-board, so you can practice in anticipation?'

Rudi laughed. 'You've got plenty of time, Jack, so start tomorrow!!'

Each day was different, although to an outsider it would have seemed monotonous and tedious. Exploration was a task reserved for the morning before the sun scorched the island. It was during one of these expeditions southward they discovered the island had been visited recently. A tropical storm, that raged most of the night and left them drenched but clean, had uncovered a series of ropes tied to the base of a palm tree that lay, partly obscured, in the sand, stretching into the sea and secured to an outcrop of rocks.

They had travelled this way before but had not noticed anything. Last night's storm had unwittingly given them hope of rescue. Searching further they discovered, hidden under a network of living plants a dry storage area with large tin trunks, several benches and a table. Paraffin lamps with fuel still in them hung down from the ceiling. The newspaper they found stuffed into a recess was brittle and fell to pieces, but the recent date was decipherable.

'What shall we do? Move in, it's better than our place?'

'Think, why would someone try to hide everything, especially the rope anchorage? No, Rudi, we need to be careful, very careful. We know this place is deserted. The only reason to come here has to be its remoteness from spying eyes. Something murky happens here. What is this region known for? Black market contraband, human trafficking, drug manufacture and distribution. Need me to go on?' asked Jack.

'From what we've seen, I think it must be drugs. They can carry a fair amount in a small boat and that rope seems too small for a large one.'

'I agree, Rudi. I think we should leave our discovery as if it were untouched. All we can do now is wait and hope and then tell the truth and hope for some humanity. After all, they, whoever they are, will never have heard of such a story.'

'Probably worth more as a newspaper story than their drug smuggling!'

'Well, we'll see.'

The weeks turned into months and there was no sign of any visitors. Their daily visits to the site were unrewarded and by now both men were beginning to see their freedom was, in reality, a different form of captivity. They had not seen any ships passing and began to doubt whether they would ever be rescued. From the whiteness of years unused to the sun, their skin browned and cracked under the tropical skies, protected only by the shreds of their garments and the fullness of their hair.

The solitude was never a problem and Jack was able to call upon his years of experience in helping Rudi come to terms with their life.

'Never let go of your dreams,' Jack constantly reminded him. 'Never lose hope or your self-respect.'

As the sun was settling behind the topmost ridge of the hills that formed the backbone of their island as it did every night casting long shadows over their encampment near the beach and beyond, Rudi was sure he could see the silhouette of a boat. Jack looked but was uncertain. With the fading light, any hope of tracking it was out of the question. They decided that they would take it in turns through the night to keep watch. Whatever the danger, they did not want to miss this opportunity of rescue.

After their meal and undercover of the dark shadows both men trekked south towards the den they had discovered. They approached silently, their hearts pounding seemingly creating the noise that could mean their own discovery. Nothing was happening. They could see nobody. As Rudi sat down under a large date palm, Jack saw the look of despair on the face of his young friend. He consoled him as they sat looking out to sea.

'You have some shut eye, I'll take the first watch,' said Jack.

The only light was that of the crescent moon in the early days of its cycle. It highlighted the foaming crest of the water that crashed and spilled foaming over the coral reef except for one small gap, wide enough for a boat to traverse. That small area held Jacks sole attention. The small waves rhythmically lapping over the shore in front of him glinting as they occasionally caught in the reflection in the pale yellow light. Jack sat there, hands clasped around his knees, watching the gap and waiting. Now he heard the intermittent noise of an outdoor motor caught in the offshore breeze disappearing and then re-appearing. Jack, alert and focused, shook Rudi gently, putting his hand across his mouth. They lay down, still and watched as the occupants made secure the anchor rope and waded into the shallow water.

Voices echoed through the night. Hurricane lamp lights danced among the undergrowth. Jack could make out three men. One had entered the den and was lighting other lamps. The other two were carrying waterproof bags which they had lifted out of the boat. They followed into the den. Jack held Rudi firmly.

'Not yet,' he whispered.

Within minutes they heard the noise of the second engine. They had a clear view of the occupants from their vantage point on the ridge amongst the palms, there were two men in the second boat. One remained and turned the boat around, shouldering what looked like a powerful automatic rifle. The other struggled out of the boat and lowered his bulk into the water. He held on tightly to the strap of a wallet bag he was carrying. He dragged his overweight body up the beach and into the den.

'Now,' said Jack releasing his grip on Rudi

They both slowly made their way forward. The place appeared to be unguarded. The two of them crouched, Rudi in front, Jack behind, and listened to the detailed conversation unable to understand the language being spoken.

'What do we do now?' whispered Rudi. Jack shook his head and mouthed the word 'wait'. They watched concentrating on what appeared to be an illicit transaction before them. On the table in bundles were thousands of US dollars bills as well as a pair of weighing scales and packets of white powder. On the ground lay open several other metal boxes stacked with packets of white powder.

Their concentration was so overwhelming that when the muzzle of a handgun scraped across Jack's cheek, he froze momentarily then rose slowly pulling Rudi with him. The gunman motioned them forward and followed them inside.

'Well, well. What have we here, Robinson Crusoe and Man Friday?' The large man spoke in English quickly recognising that the two men before him were not from these parts. He laughed. The others, unsure of what to do, started laughing too. 'Come on, you're not to be afraid.' He poked his stick into Jack's belly. 'I'm sure you're not here to rob us, are you?' Don't look like pirates or undercover policemen to me.'

Jack spoke first. He started the narrative at the point of the train accident avoiding any details of the trials or any other events that could put either of them at risk in the near future. He told the unbelieving faces that stared at him that they'd escaped from imprisonment in the gulags and then of the escape from Russia by diving off a cruise liner and swimming here months ago. They had lost track of time, so he didn't know how long they'd been marooned here.

Every now and again the fat man acknowledged the story by nodding or making some other gesture with his podgy fingers. At length, Jack finished and looked into the fat man's eyes. The man stared back, there was the faintest of smiles on his face. He fondled the foul-smelling cigar he had been smoking as Jack and Rudi stood in front of him. It was now being pampered and sucked by his generous lips as he rolled the smoke around his head with his hand.

'You haven't told me your names.'

'I'm Jack Sanderson and this is Rudi Stanik.'

The fat man was silent as he thought. No-one moved.

'Let me tell you mine. I am Mister Bander. Always use the word 'Mister' and then we know who is the boss. Isn't that so men? He looked around and the others nodded deferentially. 'Well, my trip is paid for by these,' he said pointing to the bags. 'Getting them home to Sabah will be easy, but what am I to do with the two of you? You have been very inquisitive, haven't you?'

'Mister Bander, you can sell our story for cash and get the purchaser to help us to escape as part of the deal.'

Mister Bander chuckled and looked around. The others began to smile and then laugh.

'And why would I want to take so much trouble over two castaways that no-one knows about?'

Jack and Rudi had played their hand and it appeared they had lost. Mister Bander thought for a while, keeping the tension between the two of them at fever pitch. He rose from the table. Took the gun from one of his associates. He approached Jack and put a gun under his chin, cocking the trigger as he did so.

Reactively, Rudi shouted, 'No!' and dived towards the fat man. He never reached him as the butt of a rifle struck the back of his neck and he crumpled into the dirt floor. Mister Bander cursed the stupid reaction of youthful loyalty.

'You fool. One of my men could have killed you.'

'But?' whimpered Rudi from the floor, holding his neck with his hand while staggering to his feet.

'I was trying to demonstrate to your friend the seriousness of any breach of confidentiality. I believe he has the message. I hope for your sake that you do too.'

'We will leave as soon as I have completed this transaction.' said Mister Bander. 'Take these two aboard then come back for me.'

The ball of fire rose from the horizon in the east. They had been travelling for about an hour and the fishing vessel dragging the shore boat behind was making good progress along the string of islands that form an arm stretching between the Philippines and Borneo dividing Sulu from the Celebes Sea.

It was an impossible task for anyone to police these waters so the chance of detection at sea was extremely remote.

As the boat rounded the south-western tip of Sibutu Island, it was early afternoon and the man in the wheelhouse turned the boat into the protection of the small cove densely overgrown with mango trees. There they waited for several hours dozing in the tranquillity of the gently rocking boat listening to the cries and chatter of the monkeys as they dived through the undergrowth chasing each other and disturbing the parrots that were resting in the afternoon heat. The darkness of another dying day slowly prompted Mister Bander and his men to make ready for their undercover return to Tawau.

Jack and Rudi spent the first day getting used to civilisation again. It felt good now that they were cleaned and shaved. Mister Bander had agreed that the two of them would remain with him and that he would arrange a meeting with a newspaper reporter.

He seemed more relaxed now that the tension of the handover transaction had passed. He had been trading in these waters for longer than he cared to remember. Trust was a dangerous pastime, even with his own men with one or two exceptions. It was obvious that Mister Bander was enjoying this new experience. Jack was gaining the impression, as each hour passed, that mutual trust was becoming a reality. Rudi and he would not put a foot wrong.

Their first meal of red meat for years came as a welcome and savouring experience. It had been cut by Mister Bander from a joint to celebrate the completion of his successful trip. Around the table where his wife and his two eldest boys. Both took after their father and were already tending towards overweight. The wall of eyes focused on Jack and Rudi, they felt embarrassed as the first tentative piece of pink flesh pass their lips, then another and another. The boys burst out laughing, followed by the whole family and finally by Jack and Rudi. Their faces must have been a picture as they devoured the goat meat. Despite living in the world of a local drug overlord, their stay with Mister Bander was relaxed; they felt no danger under his protection.

Mister Bander arranged through a business associate to call the newspaper offices and put his proposition to them. It was on their fourth day in Tawau that they were advised that a meeting had been set up. Two days later on the other side of the island in a hotel room in Kota Kinabalu, George Kwong set up a tape recorder and microphone and waited for his celebrities. Introductions were made, Mister Bander was present but said nothing. If anyone could read his thoughts, they would not have been surprised that he had admired the courage and determination of these two men. Even in his world, no-one had the daring and endurance to survive what they had been through. He had made it very plain that he had no intention of mentioning Siargao. He didn't want anyone sniffing around. The island had served him well for years and he wanted it to do so for many more to come. George Kwong left Jack and Rudi to tell their story. He had made additional notes as they talked but did not interrupt them. The session lasted into the evening. This hotel room was to be their home for several days while George Kwong with Mister Bander and his contacts made the arrangements for Jack and Rudi to leave Kota Kinabalu.

The choice of America had always been Jack and Rudi's preference and the confirmation that their Panama registered freighter would take them across the Pacific Ocean, through the Panama Canal to Puerto Rico seemed the answer to their hopes and prayers. George Kwong took the fateful picture of them just before they left their hotel room in Kota Kinabalu for the short taxi journey to the waterfront where they were to be smuggled onto the ship. There was no final goodbye. Jack and Rudi had said all that was to be said a few days ago when Mister Bandar handed them an ornate solid silver coin bracelet each, featuring two braided chains with the statues of Buddha in the Borobudur Temple.

'Some say they have magical powers of protection. I have my doubts, but I suppose it is what you believe yourself that matters,' said Mister Bandar, raising his left arm to reveal a similar bracelet, smiling as he did so, then he stepped forward with his arms apart and gave them both a farewell hug and had walked to the hotel exit and left without another word.

Jack and Rudi had no idea how long they were to be imprisoned in this decaying hulk. They knew that they would have to trust the captain. George Kwong had given him only a deposit for the moment, the main payment would be released when he could prove safe delivery. His story had potentially very lucrative avenues in the future but for now the seed corn he'd invested was very little. He blessed Mister Bandar's reputation.

Their route would take them along the western coast of the Philippines to Manila where several days passed as the ship discharged part of its cargo of machine parts in exchange for completed items. It had been agreed for the sake of security that Jack and Rudi would blend with the crew and undertake some of the tasks with them. The learning process started as soon as they were out of sight of Kota Kinabalu and by the time they reach Manila, some three days later, both men looked part of the scene and were beginning to be accepted by the others. There was one exception, a man named Paulo Aires, a man of little humour and even less conversation, but very strongly built. He appeared not to mix with the others, but Jack and Rudi tried to befriend him, especially as they had to share quarters with him. The rest of the crew had warned them, in whispered conversations, that he was not a man to be trusted.

After Manila, the ship headed north and then due east, south of Taiwan, out into the Pacific Ocean. It was during this long slow voyage across the waters stretching from horizon to horizon that Rudi, who was closer in age to Paulo, began to find topics of conversation that brought the man out. Paolo talked about his mother who had brought him up in the slums of Santiago without ever knowing who his father was and then seeing his mother die after a hit-and-run in a dilapidated local hospital when he was 14 years old. He was also interested in Rudi and his life of deprivation in the USSR. The increasing empathy between the two was leading Rudi to talk too much and Jack feared he was unaware that he was giving too many details of their past to Paulo. Jack had kept his eye on the two of them during the hours of working together on deck or in the cabin after supper when dark covered the horizon, Jack could hear them discussing matters in whispers well into the night.

With Rudi's indiscreet disclosures, Paulo considered that he must confide in the ship's Captain. There was very little opportunity to arrange a meeting without anyone knowing. He knew that they would be docking at the American island of

Guam the next day and he would seize his opportunity before then.

It was 7am when the Santios Hispana docked. Rudi and Jack and the rest of the crew had been awake since 4.00 making ready. All the crew had hoped they would be free by early evening. It was hot in the hold as they struggled to keep up with the dockside gang. Sweat rolled off everybody's body as the surrounding air became heavy with dust and flies. By five that afternoon they saw the last crane load disappear through the open hold onto the quayside. Jack sank onto an empty crate and remained immobile as he collected his strength, looking into space, snapping with his hat at the persistent flies that seem to be invincible as they darted to and fro, momentarily alighting onto his exposed skin and leaving an irritating bite. The rest of the crew had left him and were anxious to use all their spare time in town. Captain's instructions to Jack and Rudi were clear, no onshore excursions were permitted. Jack wearily made his way up the metal stairs out of the hold into the warm air with a breeze coming off the dockside. The deck was deserted as he walked to the stern and the crew's quarters. Rudi was almost dressed as he entered the cabin, the day's dirt and grime washed into the waters below.

'Bring something nice back for me,' laughed Rudi as he watched Paulo walk down the gangplank. The chances of Rudi and Jack getting through dock security on this former American Pacific base were remote and at this point were not worth the attempt to escape onto another island.

Jack slowly let the tide of sweat and dirt washed from his tired body. The warm refreshing water from the shower slowly revitalised his weakened muscles as he lingered for a long time, moving each part of himself into its path in turn. It was at least half an hour later that he wrapped a towel around his waist and made his way back to the cabin. Rudi was lying back on his bunk reading.

'Rudi, how much have you told Paulo of our past?'

'Why do you ask?'

'We've been told not to trust him. You heard the others. I just think a man like that has his eye on the main chance and I'd hate to think, having got this far without......'

'Come off it, Jack, you're being a bit paranoid, don't you think.?

'Maybe, but tell me'

'I've told him about prison, escape, life in Soviet Russia but nothing about your Naval past. He thinks you are Russian too. Look, don't worry about it, he'll say nothing. What could possibly be in it for him?'

Jack let the matter rest with the words *what could possibly be in it for him*, spinning through his mind. Fatigue soon took over and he fell into a deep sleep. He was awakened by the noise of the returning crew, with their intoxicated singing and laughing, most had difficulty in finding their bunks. He was unable to regain sleep tossing and turning and then finally rose to walk on the deck. He could see Paulo slowly returning between the shadows of the giant cranes that slept motionless against the night sky. He watched as the man climbed the gangplank and turned towards the stern. On the spur of the moment, he decided to follow. Paolo walked towards the officers' quarters and the light from the Captain's cabin filtered under the door. Paolo knocked quietly. There was no answer, so he knocked again with resolution. The door opened and the Captain appeared in a sweatshirt and white shorts.

'What you want at this time of night, Aires? The rasp of the irritation put Paulo off his stroke for a moment. He hesitated.

'Captain, I'm sorry to come at this late hour. It's about those two new ones on board. I've been talking to the younger one. Rudi, the Russian, he has told me.....'

The captain pulled Aires inside the cabin and closed the door. Jack crept closer and crouched down. He listened intently. Before Paulo had finished, he made his way back to his cabin. He shook the sleeping Rudi violently out of his dreams.

In hushed terms he said 'Paulo's told the captain all about you. We have a problem to solve.'

'What? What's he told him?' Jack related what he had overheard.

'Oh God, Jack, I'm sorry. What can we do?'

'Nothing. You do nothing. Continue as if nothing is wrong. Keep talking to Paulo but watch

183

yourself. We have a long time before we see land again and they can't do anything here. We all need time to think.'

'Who needs time to think?' The words caught them by surprise. Rudi felt adrenaline spurt into his stomach as he froze in the shadow of the cabin's lamp.

CHAPTER 28

South Pacific Ocean

On deck, long shadows of the rising sun-bathed the deck as the ship rolled gently making her way towards the Hawaiian Islands. Jack took a deep breath, expanding his lungs in the salt air and watched across the deck, the smoke from the diesel engines drifting away into infinity. The crew set about their usual daily tasks, mostly maintenance on this part of the voyage so that by midday they could be out of the heat.

He could see Rudi listening to Paulo as he related the escapades of the previous night. All traces of the heaviness and fatigue had vanished as he watched Paulo consume the fat enriched lunch. Jack kept a very close eye on Paulo all that day and the next, even at night, he slept fitfully whilst Paulo rested unconcerned through the darkness.

By nightfall on the third day the ship had covered about half of its three thousand mile journey to Honolulu. The weather had been kind. Jack was sitting on deck pivoting back and forth on his chair watching the churning foam from the stern being carried far out into the distance towards the golden horizon waiting for the setting sun. Paolo was below him leaning on the rail looking out to sea. The second officer approached him and words that Jack was unable to hear passed between them. The officer left and Paulo remained leaning against the rail. Jack left his chair to go and search for Rudi and found him reading in the cabin

'Get out to the stern and stay with Paulo,' he ordered. If there's been a meeting arranged, he'll have to make some excuse to leave and then we'll know. Give me the thumbs up sign. OK?'

Rudi was up and away and found Paulo still leaning against the rail at the stern. They talked, casually observed from above by Jack. He had rediscovered his pipe and with the supply of tobacco being no problem he was happy to roll the smoke around his mouth until it was taken away on the shallow breeze.

Evening clouds were building up in the West and together with the fading light of the sun gave the Ocean a black sinister feel, occasionally reflecting the lights from the ship that now glowed brightly. Paolo shifted his stance and Jack looked towards Rudi as the two moved away from the railings. He noticed the sign and moved to where he had expected Paulo to walk. Unexpectedly, Paulo climbed the stairs towards him. Jack retreated into the shadows of the ill lighted lifeboat recess and took off his boots. His feet felt the chill of the metal underneath. Where was Paulo going?

At a safe distance he went in pursuit. He could hear the heavy footsteps in front of him as they disappeared down two flights into the hold. The air was heavy with the smell of diesel fumes and newly painted steel heated under the day's sun. It was difficult to see and he waited until his eyes had adjusted to the dim interior. He could still hear the footsteps echoing away from him. They stopped some way in the distance, and he heard voices. He crept slowly and carefully forward until he was near enough to make out most of what was being discussed. What he heard came as no surprise.

He was unable to talk to Rudi until the early hours of the morning. Paolo was snoring peacefully as they both left the cabin and disappeared into the deserted bathroom block

'They're going to wait until Puerto Rico. The Captain wants to get his final payment and then put us in some hovel. I could not hear the rest of the conversation, but we're their hostages this time. They know a lot about us now, so the dollars are talking even for two smuggled deck hands. Not something we want to let happen, Rudi.'

Rudi had not really thought of anything except getting away as soon as possible. His idea of jumping ship in Honolulu was the first possibility, but that was too clean and too American for the moment. They needed time to acclimatize. Over the next day both men became preoccupied in their separate thoughts. After supper that evening, they strolled the deck while Paulo nursed a headache in the cabin. Finally, they both agreed to wait and see and to continue the voyage to Puerto Rico.

After Honolulu, the ship ploughed through the ocean for the next seven days, catching the equatorial counter current that slowed its progress to Central America and the Californian coast. It was early on the eighth day that Rudi felt the ship slowing and changing course. They were now approaching the Panama Canal from the South. Rudi and Jack were up on deck as they entered the first section of this fifty one mile waterway. The sheer stone cut sides towered over the Santios Hispana as it edged slowly forward.

'The dream of one man,' said Rudi interrupting the silence. 'That dream nearly came to an end when Ferdinand de Lesseps abandoned work only ten years after it was started in 1879. Malaria took the lives of so many men a hundred years ago. It was the Americans who cleared a zone five miles on either side as part of their agreement to complete and operate the canal, so thanks to the Yanks you won't be bitten today, at least not by a mosquito.'

'You know, Rudi,' said Jack relaxing a bit, 'it's hard to imagine now that the first ship passed through this canal as the political structure of Europe tottered and began to fall after the assassination of Archduke Ferdinand in Sarajevo and the guns of Germany were preparing to sound the beginning of the First World War.'

'The 20ᵗʰ Century has been a torrid time, so far. Political readjustment is always fraught with differing ideology leading to violence and supported by stubbornness. We were just two pawns in the grand scale of things.'

'And now we are free.'

'Are we?'

'That depends on the next few days, Jack.'

During the nine hours that it took them to negotiate the canal with its three groups of locks raising the ship up to Gatun Lake some eighty-five feet higher than the Pacific Ocean and then down again, the fears of Rudi and Jack were temporarily forgotten as they passed fourteen ships following three to the front and four astern on that day.

It was early evening when they left Colon and started to make swift progress across the nine hundred miles of the Caribbean to San Juan, the capital of Puerto Rico. The captain of the Santios Hispana anchored in the waters off the oldest part of the 16th century city. The small island upon which the Spanish explorers first set foot is now connected to the main and modern part of the city by a causeway and bridges. The sight of the jumble of houses and decaying buildings overseen by the two great Spanish forts that dominate the clifftops surrounding the bay, gave Jack and Rudi hope that within the next few days they'd be free and that their decision to avoid Honolulu was the right one, so long as Paolo Aires didn't interfere again.

CHAPTER 29

Puerto Rico Central America

That night as the ship rocked gently at anchor, sleep did not come easily and when it did it was shallow and fitful. Rudi and Jack were both glad when morning arrived; and orders were given to get on deck. The ship waited. As it entered the berth to unload its cargo, the smell of tobacco leaves bundled in heaps hung in the early morning air from the wharf next to them. Opposite across the water, the sugar refinery was discharging its nightshift workers; refrigerated containers of oranges and bananas stood waiting to be taken away across the water to Europe.

The gantry slowly moved towards them and the jib of the crane was lowered into the hold. At this time of morning, it was not unpleasant to work. The air was still chilled by the night and sun had little time to warm the air. They were told that they would be working for two days then with one day off, then another two days for loading.

It was during their lunch break both noticed the Captain leave the ship. He returned during the early afternoon unseen by them. When all hands had finished for the day and were getting ready for a night out, Jack and Rudi were summoned to the Captain's cabin. The agreed photograph was taken with the newspaper date clearly showing as Jack and Rudi stood against the stern rail with their backs to the vista of San Juan bay.

'You will remain on board until I have been paid,' he ordered. 'I am sorry, but this time you will have to be locked in.'

Rudi protested in vain.

'Bring me Paolo,' the Captain barked into the intercom.

Paulo arrived and listened as he was given instructions. He then prodded Rudi in the back and escorted the two men into the bowels of the freighter. In a room without any natural light, Paulo closed the door without a word and with the sound of the double click of the lock, their plans of escape dissolved. The faint noises of the outside world occasionally filtered into the silence of the cabin. The light flickered now and again as the generator cut in and out. Rudi paced back and forth trying to focus himself, irritating Jack whose thoughts were being interrupted.

Several hours passed until they received their first meal brought from Paulo. He returned later with several blankets. They spent an uncomfortable sweaty night and most of the next morning locked away. They saw no one so by the time Paolo called again, they were desperate to relieve themselves. They were escorted one at a time along the gangway with Paolo waving the barrel of his gun haphazardly about. They both knew the layout well and it was clear there was only one way out.

When their evening meal arrived, Rudi complained of feeling ill and persuaded Paolo to accompany him to the lavatory again. Reluctantly he agreed but remained on guard outside in the gangway. Time ticked away as he waited and waited and eventually, he went to investigate. He banged open the first cubicle, and then the second with his boot, holding the gun outstretched in front of him. The third was locked, he bent down and when his call to Rudi went unanswered, he searched under the door. His eyes focused on the boots and trousers and the smears of blood he could clearly see on the floor beside the lavatory pan. He tried the door again. It would not move. He retreated a few paces and charged the door with a shoulder. It flew open with the noise of splintering wood. Before his massive bulk could regain its balance, Rudi smashed the seat into the back of Paolo's head. The black Bakelite shattered into several sharp pieces piercing Paolo's skull. Blood poured from the wounds. His golden hair was staining with rivulets of red. Rudi stared at Paolo; he clearly wasn't dead as he heaved his body up from the floor. There was no time for regrets.

'You shouldn't have tried to double cross me,' shouted Rudi pointing the gun at Paolo. 'One more step and I'll fire.'

Paulo made a fatal error as he tried to raise himself from the floor. The blast echoed down the gangway as Paolo sank to the floor. He convulsed once and was silent.

Rudi searched the big man's pockets, taking the keys, passport, and money. He locked the outer door and ran back to cabin and unlocked the door. They knew that they had little time to make their escape but were thankful that it was going dark as they crept onto the main deck.

Several lorries, under the dock arc-lights, were loading and unloading, their drivers passing the time of day with each other. Jack and Rudi emerged from the shadows and made their way unobserved towards one of the vehicles that had a tarpaulin loosely covering its load waiting, they assumed, for the driver to allow the police and officials to do their final check. Rudi ducked under the trailer chassis followed by Jack. They remained motionless looking around until they were sure they could continue. Rudi loosened the tarpaulin ropes and climbed inside followed by Jack. He was able to re-thread the two rings and put the rope back through the canvas. They felt their way amongst the packed pallets that were covered in plastic. There they waited until finally they felt the vibration of the engine and slowly the vehicle drove toward the exit.

It stopped. They heard the driver get out of his cab and voices passing along the side of the trailer. They were now under the lights of the custom post. Fear tightened their muscles, and their bodies became coiled springs. Torchlight searched the gaps between the pallets and underneath their loads. The inspectors light hesitated and returned. The two men were in animated conversation. The tarpaulin was lifted higher. The customs man climbed on to the edge of the trailer to investigate further. Rudi remained motionless as the light moved towards him. The beam passed over his boot. He'd been seen. His mind was in a confusion of loyalty. He passed Jack Paolo's gun and wriggled away from Jack. His eyes flickered momentarily to his left at Jack.

The beam of light settled on Rudi's face and he raised his hands and jumped down and lunged at the surprised lorry driver and sent him sprawling to the ground. In the panic that followed, the customs official un-holstered his gun but by then Rudi, darting left and right in and out of shadows had covered most of the distance towards the Santios Hispana. Adding to the confusion, the ship's Captain was yelling from the bridge that one of his crew had been murdered. He needed immediate help.

Rudi heard the radio crackling orders for security back-up as men swarmed over the chaotic quayside with no-one knowing quite what they ought to be doing. In the confusion, Jack was able to pick his opportunity and disappear into the night. He looked back at the docks as he rested against a stonewall that had been warmed under the tropical skies which were now ablaze with red as the sun set, intermingled with yellow of the searchlights that glowed in the distance. The stark shapes of the cranes reaching into the sky like rearing preying-mantises. It spun a surrealistic web. A volley of gunshots bounced off the lorry nearest the exit. Jack saw Rudi climbing the fencing and vaulting over the top and dropping to the ground where he was lost from sight.

Now they each were on their own. Jack had passed unseen through the main gates in the moments that followed Rudi's run for freedom and walked across the causeway of the bridges. Nobody had taken any notice of the tramp. He entered the oldest part of the city and settled upon a vacant site surrounded by decaying metal shuttering. He pulled back a small section of it and squeezed through.

Judging by the blackened embers that protruded from the side of the brick wall that confronted him, it was obvious that this building had been destroyed by fire some years ago. Probably an uninsured loss and curtained off by the city authorities. He searched amongst the debris and found an entrance to what looked like a cellar. He lifted several pieces of masonry and boarding and squeezed between two charred beams and lay down on the floor of the cellar. He lay Paolo's gun next to him and settled as comfortably as he could amongst the ruins.

When he awoke, the shafts of light pierced the gloom of his world. He watched as every movement he made cast thousands of minute particles of dust in the whiteness of the light. He felt every movement of his aching body. He rubbed his legs and his feet to free them from the numbness that had gradually overcome them during the night. The stinging pain of the blood bringing them back to life hurt him. He stood up and searched the cellar, his home for the moment. At the bottom of the stairs where he had lain was a corridor. He passed through it ducking to avoid the broken beams and boards. Through a half open door, he saw a washroom and apart from being in need of a good clean was undisturbed by the desolation that had occurred above. He then entered another larger room. It was furnished with a small wooden table lying on its side with two upturned chairs. In the corner opposite him was a small sink with cupboards above. He walked over to it and turned on the solitary tap. A small trickle of water dripped and ran away down the drain. It was a start. He righted a chair and table and sat down. He started to count Paulo's US dollars, there must have been fifteen hundred of them to begin with. At least Rudi had half to help him along. How long Jack's share would last, he had no idea, but it was a fair start.

He decided that to begin with he would only venture out under the cover of darkness until he felt fully comfortable with his accent and demeanour. He knew that the commotion and death of Paulo in the docks last night would mean for a while that the police would be on high alert, looking for Rudi and himself and worst of all they had that recent photograph. He needed to change his appearance; back to Siargao, that Robinson Crusoe look again. He was now grateful that he'd allowed no-one to cut his hair too short. He had no idea this time how long it would take him to get to the United States of

America legitimately. He'd just bide his time and time was one thing at the moment he had plenty of.

CHAPTER 30

Kota Kinabalu Sabah Borneo

Anatoly had been reading intermittently for several hours and had devoured most of the novel by the time the 747 cabin crew made ready for touchdown at Bombay's Sahar International Airport. He looked out of the window as the vast Arabian Sea gave way first to the developing offshore oil industry and then to the port traffic seemingly stationary in the waters outside India's most important commercial and industrial city. He strained his neck to glimpse the triumphal arch built in yellow Bombay basalt by the waterfront to commemorate the landing of King George the fifth in 1911, as the giant plane banked slowly in the early afternoon sun. He folded down the corner of the page of his book and placed it in the pocket in front of him.

He would have to wait patiently for an hour while the exchange of passengers took place. He fondled the small bottle of Scotch he had saved from earlier and added it to the remnants of the ice in his glass and looked around him. He felt relaxed despite the obvious discomfort of long-haul flights.

His next stop was not scheduled in the airlines ticket registration computer. Many travellers never made it to their scheduled flights, and he would be assumed to be one of those at some stage. All his papers were in order and he was confident that no one would be able to trace his movements in retrospect. He relaxed his head against the rest and closed his eyes. Before long the 747 taxied out onto the runway and within minutes they were airborne again stretching towards the evening skies gathering over the reaches over the northern tip of the Indian Ocean. The plane's course took them over the islands of Nicobar and on to the northern reaches of Sumatra and then down the Straits of Malacca to Singapore.

It was late evening and the winter evening rain had just stopped as Anatoly exited Singapore's Changi airport onto the pavement that was steaming a little after a day of temperatures in the mid-30s centigrade. An equatorial climate never suited him, but it was a relief to smell the fresh air mixed with the Oriental perfumes emanating from the luxuriant bushes along the side of the taxi rank. He gave the driver instructions and settled back in his seat. He liked Singapore, this Lion City. It was his fifth time and he felt at ease. To him who regularly faced danger, it was the safest city in the world. The taxi turned off the tree-lined boulevard into the business quarter that spilled from the site of the old Raffles Hotel into Collyers Quay and then along Robinson Road. Finally, it came to rest under the fan shaped protection of the entrance to the Oberoi hotel. He thanked the driver and was escorted to the reception desk.

In his bedroom, he made his way over to the ample balcony and drew back the curtains to admire once again the night lights of the busiest harbour in the world with its natural deep-water anchorage. If he wanted to travel on without delay, he would have to be up early the next day.

It was 8am as he arrived at the offices of Mansfield and Co Ltd situate in Ocean Building, agents for the Straits Steamship Company. He had walked from the hotel avoiding the large puddles accumulated from the overnight rain. It was warm and he was dressed casually in a linen suit with light open toed shoes. He made his way to the ticket counter and bought a single ticket to Kota Kinabalu in Sahab on the northern part of the island of Borneo. The 'Raj Brooke' was due to sail at first light in the morning and would be at sea for four days.

He made his way back to the hotel and in Raffles Place he entered the John Little Building which housed the tourist promotion board. His reception was nothing less than he expected in the city, efficient, smiling and extremely helpful. The reception lady left her desk and returned with another more elderly woman.

'I believe you've enquiring about back copies of our newspaper,' she queried.

'Yes. I'm undertaking some research on the dates between 1986 and 1988.' Anatoly replied.

The lady beckoned him to follow her. They descended into the basement. Lining one wall from top to bottom were all the back copies of the Straits Time annuals. A small table sat in the middle of the room with an angle poise lamp waiting to be used.

'1986,7 and 8 are up there second from the end. You're taller than me.'

'Thank you,' said Anatoly bowing slightly and then reaching up and removing the 1987 volume. It was extremely heavy as he struggled to ensure that no damage occurred as he placed it gently on the table.

'Please call me if you need any help.' With that she was away up the stairs.

His mind was full of expectation as he fingered through the first few pages expecting to see reference to the two men in the photograph in his pocket. It was 4 February in the 1987 edition that caught his eye, eight days after the first report. The photograph was the same. He read with heightening excitement this short article that accompanied the photograph. Only one of the names of the two men given in the article meant anything to him.

'Hadn't they realised their immediate future would only be protected if they remained hidden,' he said to himself.

Matthew Johnson had been right; he would find out much more across the water over the next few days.

The next morning could not arrive soon enough. He thanked the ladies for their help and tucked his notebook into his jacket and left.

Once on board the 'Raj Brooke', he found he was one of three passengers on this cargo vessel that plied its trade throughout the Indonesian and Malaysian islands. The other two were ageing students making their way to speculate on the prospect of finding work in the forest hardwood industry that was ravishing Sabah's countryside whilst making it the richest part of the Malaysian Federation. He spent his days reading in his cabin with private shower and toilet, walking on deck, reading and acclimatising himself to the tropics.

Four days of hard work would bring his fitness to a peak. Nobody on board paid much attention to this American except when the Captain and senior officers and the two other passengers sat down for their regular evening meal together. He talked of his time and youth in Los Angeles, all part of his new identity. No one would question any of the details and his work in the rich harvests of the computer industry. He practised enough to know what he was talking about and his visit to Sabah seemed to all concerned reasonable with the technology of the offshore oil and the interior development of the copper industry. At one point, the Captain had queried his choice of travel.

'Why the Raj Brooke, a short flight would have been better. No?'

'Good question. I need to be seen to be able to cope with the rigours of the climate as I am obliged to spend some time in the interior coping with all that those surroundings can throw at me. It is very dry in California and it will take some time to get used to and this trip is just the beginning.'

'Yes, I see,' said the Captain letting the matter drop.

It was late on Thursday 25 November that the ship entered the harbour of Kota Kinabalu. The sky's crimson reflection danced off the ripples of the wake as it washed against the other ships anchored in the bay. He leaned against the rail watching the crew go about their preparations for docking. There were no unusual formalities as he walked down the gangplank towards the two uniformed immigration officers. He handed them his passport which they fumbled through. He had not bothered with the Visa as there was a reciprocal arrangement with the US allowing him to remain in Malaysia for up to 3 months.

'Business or pleasure?' The older man enquired eyeing Anatoly unblinkingly in the face.

'Primarily business, computers and afterwards a few days exploring your country,' came the reply

Both men nodded and he was on his way to the only taxi that was sitting patiently awaiting the ship's arrival.

'I need a good bed and a good meal, what hotel do you suggest?' Anatoly was leaning into the taxi as he asked the question.

'Get in, I will take you to the best place I know.'

The driver didn't offer to open the door but remained fixed in his seat as the Anatoly struggled into the back seat with his suitcase. The town had grown up from the almost total destruction of the Second World War and was formerly known as Jesseltown in the days of British colonial rule. Little character showed itself as the taxi made its way through the wide boulevards. Even at this time of night it was busy, and the town was well lit from the fluorescent orange lamps that lined virtually every street. Most of the shops were still open and the warm air drifted into the taxi as it slowly negotiated the narrow confines of the side road that led to the Excelsior Hotel. He paid the driver in US dollars at a favourable rate to him and entered the hotel.

He checked into his room, had a quick shower and went downstairs to the restaurant. He ordered beef and chicken satay with a side order of nasi goreng and half bottle of the local sweet wine. The waiter was a little surprised when he asked specifically for the accompanying chilli and peanut butter sauce to be heavy on the chillies. To finish, he ordered fresh mangosteen and enjoyed the cooling effect of the pulpy white flesh inside the tough purple rind that tasted a little of strawberries. Anatoly was satisfied and rewarded the waiter handsomely.

Sleep came well that night. He'd never been sailor and the motion of the ship ploughing through the water, rolling and pitching interfering with his sense of balance had subsided. At first light he was up and dressed. Armed with a street map and a copy of yesterday's newspaper, he sought out their main office in town. The reception was manned by a smartly dressed but roughly hewn man who guided him to a second floor office. He was met by a man dressed in an open neck shirt and fading tan trousers that hadn't seen the press for several years. He introduced himself as George Kwong, assistant reporter and part-time helper to the archivist. He explained that his job was to file and cross reference as much information that each newspaper contained. He complained that without a computerised system it was a long and laborious job, but soon technology would be introduced. He had been promised.

'I'm interested in looking at your newspaper for 27 January 1987.'

He followed George Kwong along the corridor to a small room.

'Wait here, I'll be back in a few minutes.'

He returned carrying the January 1987 copy daily papers.

'I'll pass by in about 15 minutes or so, see if you're all right.'

Anatoly opened the heavy binder and located the date he was looking for. His eyes widened again as he looked into the face of the older man that appeared on the front page in front of him, the same Jack Sanderson. This time he took out his notebook and started to jot down the further information he needed. At the end of the article, he saw the name George Kwong. Interesting he thought.

CHAPTER 31

Kota Kinabalu Same day

That afternoon, Anatoly walked into town from the hotel, street after street searching and eventually finding what he was looking for. The cost was immaterial, the secrecy was absolute for buyer and seller. The penalties for exposure were too great.

George Kong entered the bar of the downtown drinkers' nightspot, 'The Durian Belanda', named after the tropical fruit with the pungent odour used in Malayan ice cream and custard flavouring. He looked around and saw Anatoly sitting in an ill-lighted booth at the far end of the bar. He was sipping a cold beer from a bottle and reading his notebook.

He rose to greet George and ordered another beer. Anatoly cross examined George, coaxing out details that did not appear in his article. Details which he was ordered by his editor not to print, for the moment, to protect Jack and Rudi during their voyage across the ocean. George was a bright young man and took his reporting, whenever he was allowed, very seriously, checking, and cross checking all the facts before he wrote anything.

Several matters had prompted him in this case to indulge his investigative mind. He had some idea why the original story had been subsequently heavily censored suspecting that Mister Bandar's hand rested somewhere on the contents. He too had been involved. Smuggling illegal immigrants was a serious offence. The episode was quietly forgotten at this office of the Straits Times. Naively, he told Anatoly things he should not have. So, what, he was being paid well. What harm can be done, he thought. The two men were now long gone, lost in a big world out there. Several more beers were consumed as the men chatted. George seemed to be taking the alcohol too well for Anatoly's liking. Already he had had several measures of vodka from the bottle in his pocket when George had occasionally left their booth to replenish snacks from the bar. Eventually Anatoly said he had to go and both men made their way out of the Durian Belanda into the humid air outside. George staggered slightly and leaned against Anatoly.

'Come on. Let's get you home,' said Anatoly.

George put his arm around Anatoly's shoulders; the distinctive lime scent of Anatoly temporarily heightened George's senses as the two of them stumbled along the street towards the harbour. Anatoly had planned his route well. He always did his homework. There were few people about as he took a shortcut between a row of concrete warehouses.

George was vaguely aware of his surroundings and muttered something about the wrong way, but Anatoly took no notice and tightened his grip around George's waist. George's body was getting heavy now as the alcoholic induced sleep invaded the man's head. Not far now thought Anatoly. He carefully looked in both directions. Not a soul in sight. He lay George down in the shadow cast by the second warehouse and rolled up his left shirt sleeve. He removed a length of cord from his pocket and tied it around George's bicep. There was little resistance as George seemed to have fallen asleep. Anatoly extracted his afternoon purchase and plunged the needle into the waiting vein. He slowly injected the contents of the syringe into George's arm. He left the money in George's pocket and the needle wrapped between the fingers of his right hand. The rubber gloves would find another resting place further away. Just another accident.

CHAPTER 32

Sandakan and Tawau Borneo

Anatoly returned to his hotel and paid his bill in cash. In his room, he unpacked his suitcase and carefully repacked the contents in the backpack that he had bought earlier that day. From the depths of his shaving bag, he extracted a small bottle of hair dye and stood in front of the mirror carefully re-colouring the roots that were just showing through. After a wash and shave he retired to bed for an early start the next morning.

The sun was barely visible over the horizon when he walked out of the hotel unnoticed by the night porter. Further down the street he summoned a taxi and was taken to the bus depot. Even at this time the place was bustling with travellers, mostly workers waiting to be taken to outlying districts, dressed as they were for a day's labour under the sun.

He bought a one-way ticket to Sandakan, the commercial capital of this province and the headquarters of the timber industry. He had no intention of remaining there, but in this land of mountains, there was little choice but to skirt the coastal plains. He boarded the bus, somewhat more luxurious than he expected but still, by Western standards, pretty grimy. He wanted to relax but refrained from choosing the more comfortable seat at the front and decided to sit near the back where he could remain relatively unnoticed. He unfolded the early morning English newspaper and scanned the pages. Nothing worried him at this stage. He needed time and space to think and relax and the next few hours on this long journey would give him that.

He settled into his seat and started to read the unfinished novel from the flight to Singapore. Every now and again he would stop and gaze through the dusty window at his surroundings as they changed from the greenness of the coastal plain to the tree clad slopes of the mountainous interior as the bus dragged its weary way up the hills that wound past the slopes of Mount Kinabalu. The clouds that daily obscured the summit were already in place allowing his imagination a chance to wonder upwards to its summit. Human life seems so transient and insignificant by comparison with the force of this massive granite giant which pushed its way through the softer rock that surrounded it as the earth split open millions of years ago to allow its gradual movement upwards until its efforts ceased, and the pinnacle stood waiting to be eroded away by the elements.

His thoughts returned as he gazed at the new occupants who had entered the bus. Shabbily dressed, one of their number made eye contact as he passed his seat and made his acquaintance with the friends occupying the rear seat of the bus. After a few moments he felt a tap on his right shoulder. His heart raced but his face remained impassive. The passenger stood up and was now breathing heavily into his face. They eyed each other momentarily. What did he want? Anatoly's heightening panic evaporated immediately as the passenger pointed to the discarded newspaper that lay next to him.

After a brief stop to allow everyone to stretch their legs and refresh themselves in the shadows of a roadside service station which offered scant relief from the sun they were on their way. It was early evening as the bus made its way steadily down the hillside offering a panoramic view of Sandakan Bay. The last rays of the burning sun had left the hillside and the fresh moist air of the receding trees wafted through the open windows of the bus mingling with the smell of exhausted passengers.

In the town's main square, he collected the rucksack from the top of the bus and shook the dust and grime of the journey from it before hoisting it on his back. He was unused to this sort of travel but the unexpected evidence from the meeting with George Kwong had changed his itinerary.

He made his way up into town searching for a place to rest his weary head. The street he now entered was illuminated by assorted neon signs offering accommodation. He walked along Pine Beach eyeing all he could see as he passed. Having reached the end, he turned and made his choice and entered the Sulu Sea Hotel. A bald man sat behind the reception counter and without a word pushed a registration form towards Anatoly. He took the pen and filled in the form and handed it and the cash for the night's stay to the uninterested receptionist.

He was escorted to the first floor and the door to number 13 was opened. Anatoly closed the door and lay on the bed for several moments collecting his thoughts. After changing his shirt and removing the dirt of the day, he descended to the street and walked along the seafront. After a refreshing beer and several instructions from the bartender, he walked back along the front towards the tourist office. He suspected that it was probably shut but was surprised to find a light illuminating the immediate pavement outside. The sign on the door indicated it was outside office hours, but an attentive knock brought a young man to open it.

'I am sorry to intrude at this hour,' said Anatoly.

'I am touring your beautiful country and want to visit the Hot Spring Park at Tawau. I have spent several days visiting Mount Kinabalu and your National Park,' he lied knowing that anyone in the travel business loved an enthusiastic tourist and usually helped. This was to be no exception.

'That is not going to be easy for you; our roads are not good between here and Tawau. It will take you several hours of hard travel.'

He took out a map from under the desk and laid it out on the top. He fingered the route as it passed Lintang, the fishing port of Ladah Datu and then to Semporna and finally Tawau.

'There is a small bus once a day which goes direct so you will not have to change,' he said with emphasis.

'You have to book in advance and tomorrow is already full.'

'I haven't a lot of time left to me before I have to return home to work. Are you sure it's full? I will make it worth your while.' Anatoly pulled a small bundle of US dollars from his top pocket. The young man's eye watched as he peeled off several bills.

'Look,' he said picking up the telephone and dialling a number quickly. 'I can see if there have been any cancellations.' The young man jabbered away in the way in Malay and after a few moments replaced the receiver.

'Tomorrow morning, then. You must be there by 6am, make yourself known to the driver.' He handed Anatoly a ticket having scrawled a hurried note on the back. Anatoly handed over the dollars he'd counted out and thanked the young man and left.

The next morning at 5.50am Anatoly was settled into the front seat of the smaller Mercedes bus by the driver, the others boarded around him. Outside on the pavement an argument had started between the driver and two other Europeans who were waving and pointing at their tickets. The driver was shaking his head and replying constantly in Malay which was obviously incomprehensible to them. At length, they appeared to give up and wandered disconsolately away. The driver returned to the bus and announced in both Malay and English that they were now leaving. He counted the numbers, one spare seat, then started the engine. It was a journey Anatoly tolerated but wished the hours away, meticulously planning his next move.

His hotel in Tawau was modest but comfortable. He slept until long after dawn. He had chosen a room with a balcony looking out to sea to the south over the rooftops of the commercial district. Dressed in shorts and an open neck shirt, he sipped his coffee under the awning shading the table and surveyed his surroundings.

**

Far away in Kota Kinabalu, on the other side of the island, George Kwong's body lay in front of the pathologist as he searched painstakingly every inch of the cold skin. In front of him was the head of police and his assistant, Ahmed Suharto. They waited for his initial conclusions. Suharto had already established George's movements for two days ago. Had the man he was drinking with anything to do with this? He waited to hear the cause of death of this young man. He couldn't persuade the newspaper's owner to hold on too much longer before running the story of the death of one of their own, but he wanted as much time as possible.

The Excelsior Hotel had given Suharto as much as they could after they traced the taxi driver, but no one had seen Anatoly leave, so at that point the trail went cold.

**

In Tawau, Anatoly wandered back inside away from the burning sun. It was Sunday and he would probably not make much progress today. However, he needed to try and decided to wander out of the hotel again.

George Kwong had trodden this path before him, so he knew exactly what and who he was looking for. His white face attracted attention as he made his way along the waterfront towards Kampong Tawau, a village on water. Even today wealthy members of the community still liked to live as their forebears in these water villages. It was a strange notion to Anatoly, but he accepted the different cultural needs of others. His eyes searched among the tangle of timber struts and the washing drying on a myriad of lines strung aside the walkways. The occasional splash of water and children's shrieks of laughter interrupted his search. He had learned from George Kwong that this town was the headquarters of smuggling between the Philippines to the north across the Celebes Sea and Malaysia. That had been the source of the vial that killed George Kwong two days ago. Anatoly had come here unarmed despite the air of menace. He was not here to settle any debt but just for help and he hoped and expected it was not going to be seen as a threat to the boss man he was looking to speak to.

He felt the presence of someone behind him, the occasional scuff of a sandal tread. He didn't look

215

round, just slowed his pace a little and quickened again. He was definitely being followed. He turned towards the gangplank securing a small white and blue outboard dinghy. His follower was upon him in a second, pressing a point into his side and shuffling him forward. An arm from behind grabbed his neck. Anatoly did not object, a sign of welcome. Both Anatoly and his assailant descended into the gloom of the interior of this timber house; the smoke from an internal cooker hung in the air. He was searched and ordered to sit down. A large man, with perspiration dripping from his forehead in sympathy with the increasing daytime temperature, appeared in front of him. He poured himself a drink from his personal bar and turned to Anatoly.

'Will you join me?' He asked.

'Thank you, Mister Bandar,' said Anatoly.

'You seem to know who I am, yet to whom do I owe this pleasure,' he asked sarcastically.

Anatoly gave his name and explained the nature of his visit. Mister Bandar sat, making no comment as he heard the story so far. He had not appreciated the significance of the transport he had arranged for Jack and Rudi. He had taken them as part of a mercy mission with a little payment for his trouble; they had seen the humane side of Mister Bandar. His voyage to the uninhabited island was to do business and he had found them by chance. He had appreciated their story of repression, imprisonment and escape. He too had seen the inside of a prison in his youth and vowed that he'd never succumb to it again.

Mister Bandar was wary of this man. He could read the ruthless eyes, the lack of compassion that had left Anatoly concentrating on self and self alone. Anatoly was a professional. He wouldn't come here unarmed, otherwise.

When Anatoly had stopped telling his story, Mister Bandar rose and wiped his brow with a handkerchief. Anatoly knew then what George Kwong had told him had been verified by Mister Bander's silent nodding.

'What you ask of me is very little but without it, you have nothing. If I tell you what happened after they arrived here, what guarantees do I have that you will keep your word of secrecy?'

Anatoly thought for a moment.

'I can offer you nothing other than dollars, lots of them and, of course, I need you to arrange a passage to Manila for which I will pay, that way you will be able to ensure that I have departed in silence,' said Anatoly.

Anatoly knew he was about to take a great risk with his freedom but considered he could read Mister Bandar opposite him. He continued after a few moments of reflection.

'There is also another and more significant reason why I will never return here and when I tell you, I am in your hands. He related the story of George Kwong. Mister Bandar remained impassive as he listened. There was no love lost between him and the press despite his dealings with George Kwong.

'I will consider your request but until I have verified this, you must wait. Where are you staying?'

Anatoly told him and rose to leave.

'I will send someone to see you. Wait in your hotel this evening after 9pm,' he ordered.

There were no handshakes as Anatoly left and walked away from the waterfront town. He spent the rest of the day preparing, making sure he did not become another of Mister Bandar's missing persons.

The telephone call to police headquarters in Kota Kinabalu was registered at 2:15pm that Sunday afternoon. Ahmed Suharto listened as the unidentified caller gave him a description of George Kwong's killer. The caller then confirmed the situation to Mister Bander.

Anatoly had spent a fruitful but hectic afternoon and it was early evening before he returned to his hotel. He had spent a great deal of money, but it was worth every cent. He spread his clothes on the bed and spent some time straightening out the creases before re-packing them in his rucksack. He had told the hotel proprietor that he would be leaving the day after and had reserved the room for another night. This information was relayed to Mister Bander. He attached the knife to the inside of his right arm. He threw the arm in an arc to test its efficiency. Satisfied, he strapped the 4mm Browning handgun to his inside left shin and let his trousers slide over it. He rose and examined himself in the mirror. At

8.30pm, unobserved he lowered his rucksack from its first floor balcony with a length of rope he had acquired that afternoon. As it settled in the shrubbery below, he released the rope and slid it to the ground alongside. The lamps from the street opposite cast convenient concealing shadows.

Looking as if he was out for an evening stroll, he left the hotel. Hidden in the shadows opposite the entrance was an ill-dressed man watching, he recognised Anatoly from the description. His backup had not yet arrived, so he had no choice but to follow despite feeling the tiredness of the journey that afternoon. He felt the gun in his pocket nervously. Ahmed Suharto saw Anatoly retrieve the rucksack from the bushes and detach it from the rope. At a secure distance, he started after Anatoly.

Anatoly walked at a steady pace towards the bus station. He had been aware of his follower from the start. One man was no match. He bided his time. There was little point in backtracking and trying to throw the man off his scent. He walked to the taxi rank outside the station. There were three taxis with their drivers idly leaning against the first car's bonnet smoking and passing the time of day. He approached and they all stood, the first driver beckoning him into the car. He offered to stow the rucksack in the boot, but Anatoly declined, placing it on the seat beside him. As the car started away, he turned slightly and smiled to himself. A second taxi followed at discreet distance. Ahmed's radio crackled as he gave instructions to those he expected to assist back at the station.

A car accident in front of them delayed their progress. Anatoly relaxed back into the rear seat just leaving himself enough room to watch the events. Despite it being Sunday, there were plenty of cars on the route along the coast road. The taxi driver pulled into the roadside café in a small village five miles from Tawau. The driver remained for a few moments counting his fare. Anatoly had been generous. The hotel cafe was full of locals enjoying their Sunday night freedom before work the next day. He felt a little out of place as he sat near the bar, but nobody took any notice of him. He had arrived here earlier than was necessary, but as he had not anticipated being followed, perhaps it was just as well he had the extra time. His gaze wandered over to the window as the second taxi stopped on the other side of the road. The passenger got out and ducked behind a line of parked cars.

When Anatoly had finished his drink, he picked up his rucksack and walked out into the night. The light breeze off the sea filled his nostrils with salt air. He recognised the landmarks he was advised of earlier that afternoon and strolled down the road opposite towards the water's edge. His ears picked up the sound of his follower. Anatoly eyes flicked back and forth until he found a place to drop his rucksack momentarily and sidestepped into the dark recess of a boarded shop door entrance and pressed himself against its cold surface. He breathed shallowly. It was over in a second. His knife severed the carotid artery and bronchial tube with a sweeping curve unhindered by any defence as his surprise was total. The body stood motionless for an instant against the window of the shop before the darkness of death crept upon Ahmed Suharto as his legs buckled at the knees and slid to the ground. His eyes stared out, blurred at first then unseeing. Suharto breathed his last tentative choking breath taking in the aroma of lime as he felt the warm blood, his own blood seeping into his lungs and down over his chest and with it went his life.

Anatoly needed to know who he was. He searched the body. Whatever had decided Mister Bander to inform on him would have to wait. Revenge was not his top priority, but he would not forget. He never did. This policeman was not likely to have acted alone and Anatoly's present whereabouts were likely to be known. He wiped the blood from his knife and with a change of clothes from his rucksack, he was within minutes boarding the waiting motorboat

CHAPTER 33

WSC Headquarters Denver USA

It was Sunday afternoon and the WSC offices were deserted as Anatoly stood in front of Matthew Johnson and handed him his Report. Anatoly looked as he had the last time they met. Very different from how he'd be described in Singapore, Tawau and Sandakan, thanks to having spent some time again with his Manhattan "barber".

'Do sit down. Coffee?' Johnson was much more friendly this time.

'Black one sugar. Thanks.'

When the fresh brew arrived, Anatoly sipped his coffee as Johnson continued to read the report. He admired the elegance of Johnson's study and cast his eye over the rows of leather-bound books exuding wealth from the shelves and the vertical row of Imari plates hanging either side of the entrance door. Two generous smoke blue glass globe lamps stood either side of the bay window mirroring the velvet curtains that hung. He put down his cup and strolled over to the bookcases casting his eye over the classical American and English authors, Steinbeck, London, Twain, Alcott, Salinger, Fitzgerald, Dickens, Orwell, Shakespeare, Bronte. The list went one.

'I've read them all, but my favourite has always been Hemingway.'

He folded his arms across himself striking a psychologically aggressive pose.

'O.K. So you reckon he is holed up in Costa Rica somewhere.'

'I'm certain. The Santos Hispana was destined to unload her last shipment there and it would be a good starting point to get to the US and a sympathetic embassy that would listen free from corruption and publicity.'

'Yes, I agree. Your report about San Juan contains the details of the incident at the harbour. I want you to investigate first-hand, just to be sure that it is Sanderson.' As an afterthought Johnson said, 'No trouble mind.'

Johnson then unlocked a drawer of his desk and handed Anatoly an envelope which he took and flicked through the bills inside.

It was mid-afternoon as the American Airlines DC10 banked to port and rose into the clear blue sky. This time Anatoly didn't need anything on Sanderson or Stanik, he knew these men and had got the images clearly in his head.

CHAPTER 34

Puerto Rico

Anatoly had his feet up on the queen size bed sipping a cool draft of lager. He had been on the go for several days since the meeting with Johnson in Denver and it wasn't long before his mind began to drift, and sleep enveloped him. When he awoke the sun had set and the glow of the streetlights and neon signs danced on the bedroom wall though the open window.

He looked at his watch, 8 pm. Soon he had washed and dressed and left the hotel behind. Slinging his cream linen jacket over his shoulder he embraced the air and the exercise. It wasn't long before he stopped, lit his cigar and watch the smoke gently spiral away from him in the gentle breeze. He looked as if he somehow fitted in this place. The gentle tan from his Manhattan barber gave him that Central American 'I'm one of you' look.

He walked towards the main entrance to the wharf. Two guards stood talking.

'Hi. James Ricardo, Central America correspondent, Washington Post.'

Anatoly flashed a plastic card in front of them.

'Smoke?'

He proffered two cigars that were eagerly snapped from his hand.

'What can we do for you?' asked the small stockier guard as he stuffed the cigar in his top pocket for later.

'I gather there was some trouble a while back and thought it might make a story. Either of you on duty that night?'

'Maybe, maybe not?' said the taller of the two showing his misshapen yellowed teeth through a sarcastic smile.

'Look, I'll pay if you have something interesting for me. You will have to trust me on this.'

The taller man looked at his watch.

'I'm outta here in half an hour. You got wheels?'

'I'll take a walk and be back then with a taxi. O.K.?'

They sat in a bar near Anatoly's hotel. The tall man introduced himself as Pedro Andreas. As Anatoly sipped his beer, Pedro told him all he had witnessed that night. Most of which Anatoly already knew.

'It was utter confusion at the time. I was inspecting a routine cargo that had arrived. This man darted out of the trailer and ran back towards the cranes and ships away from this exit. I only realised afterwards that this was a strange thing to do. Most would have run in the opposite direction towards the town.

'I ran after him. He was too quick for me. Pretty fit I'd say. My mate called for reinforcements, we immobilised the lorry and closed the gates. It's a big place to search and it was only when the dogs arrived that we stood a chance of capturing him.'

He lit another cigarette and gulped another mouthful of beer.

'We thought the dogs had him cornered but the Captain of the freighter...'

'The Santios Hispana'

'Yea, that's it. Well, he arrived shouting that one of his crew had been battered to death. The dogs were told to follow him on board. What we saw was awful. There in the toilet is this big dude, blood everywhere. We all waited with the Captain until the police arrived. We just forgot about one stray illegal immigrant. Must have escaped over the perimeter fence into the night.

'Did you talk to the Captain? Was the big dude part of the crew?'

'He was really shocked even for an old sea dog who must have seen most things in his time. Yes, the dead man had been part of the crew for years.'

'What about the rest of the crew?'

'They were all out on the town. Only got back in the early hours. I told them what had happened as they straggled back.'

Pedro stopped mid-sentence, trying to remember something locked away in his mind. He savoured another mouthful of beer and slammed it down on the table.

'I remember. One of the crew when questioned in our interview room said he'd warned them he was no good. I had no idea who '*them*' was only that they were the two new guys who joined them in Kota Kina...something or other, in Indonesia. Making their way to the U S,' he added.

'Kinabalu?'

'Yea, that's it.'

This was enough. Anatoly knew he was in the right place.

CHAPTER 35

October 1990 London

Lieutenant Commander Susan Sanderson R N had planned her week. It was now Friday, and she had decided to apply for some well-earned leave. The drive from her Cornish retreat to London had been swift and uneventful. Back at her flat she checked her mail and changed into her dark grey suit with silk blouse and tied her scarf in a generous knot around her neck. She looked in the mirror. Her tired eyes looked back at her as if saying 'OK, we know what to do and how to do it, so stop worrying'. She pushed her anxiety aside and brushed her short brown hair close to her head. 'A handsome woman', she'd been told. She smiled.

'That's it then', she said bending down to pick up Soxy, her faithful Burmese brown cat, who was glad to be out of the car again and home. The cat nestled her head into Susan's neck and purred loudly.

'Now you be a good girl and I will be back at two.'

She picked Soxy's claws carefully from her jacket and placed her on the radiator shelf. She did not notice her journey through London's underground from Clapham in the south to Whitehall in the center, her mind was elsewhere sifting through the tangle of information that coursed through her brain. Out on the road, she lifted her collar and umbrella against the cold wet grey morning and jostled with the many as she hurried from Charing Cross along Whitehall. She stood under the classical portico in the small courtyard and shook the rain from her umbrella, folded it and entered the building. She acknowledged Bill's greeting as he stood smartly to attention hardly glancing at her identity tag that now hung from her lapel. She climbed the steps to the cavernous interior of one of Victorian England's legacies to the nation, the Admiralty, and made her way to her secretary's office on the first floor.

'Good morning, Alice,'

'Good morning to you, Commander Sanderson.'

Alice was never at home addressing her as 'Susan' despite continually being asked to do so when they were alone.

Susan entered her office and booted up her computer. She trawled through her current files to find one that would be suitable to disguise the eventual site she wanted and could be linked without suspicion by those trawling in security. She knew it would be impossible to conceal completely, but Alice had unwittingly coached her well. The screen flashed file after file at mesmerising speed passing her eyes. She found what she wanted and pressed 'enter'.

Alice arrived with her black coffee with two sugars.

'Don't know how you can drink it like that and stay so slim. Look at me and I diet constantly,' she said, rubbing her generous tummy gently and smiling ruefully.

'Don't go, Alice.'

Susan watched the screen flickering as she sipped the coffee. The dates rolled passed from 1950 onwards.

'Alice, can you run me off an authority for the Bolton papers and get Admiral Wood's authorisation.' This was her cover to gain access to the archives.

Susan was trying hard to be herself since the previous night. Her world had been turned upside down by the news that just maybe her father had not died when she was a teenager in 1956.

All week she had been trying to put together a string of unconnected events created by the off-chance encounter with a file marked 'Operation Wild Cat'. A copy of that file was now safely stored in her safe. Today, Susan carried a small camera in her briefcase. The risk she was about to take today could leave her career in ruins and a long prison sentence to deal with under the Official Secrets Act. There was no question of jeopardising state security as far as she was aware. It was a breach of trust so fundamental within these walls whatever the circumstances. Her burning desire to find the truth was, however, overwhelming and armed with

Admiral Wood's authority and her camera she descended the stairs full of hope.

A few miles away in Cheyne Walk, Robert Jenner listened intently to his informer. He then made a call to America.

CHAPTER 36

Later the same day. Cawsand South West England

In her bright red MGB sports car had twin gurgling Weber carburettors and with Soxy curled up on the front seat, she had made the journey surprisingly quickly for a Friday night as she stretched her legs for the few minutes it took the chain ferry to travel from the city of Plymouth across the river to Torpoint. Salt air felt good in her lungs as the sun began to fade and the silhouettes of the dockyard cranes and ships that lay at anchor became a blur in the darkening sky.

After four miles through undulating farmland, the twinkling lights of Cawsand were below her as she descended into the tiny community that in the past had been the haunt of smugglers, the home of fishermen and even Lord Nelson and Lady Hamilton. The smoke from the fires that brightened the small cottages lazily drifted upwards until it was whisked away by the breeze coming off the waters of Plymouth Sound. Now it was the retreat for those who wanted peace and tranquillity amongst the remaining faithful Cornish folk who lived permanently at peace with the world.

She put the key into the lock of her front door with the sound of the waves braking over the rocks below. As she entered, Jason Roberts, the local storekeeper, stopped by with her box of pre-ordered groceries.

'Evening, Ms Sanderson. How was your week in the smoke?'

His ruddy face shone in the glow of the lights of the Ship Inn. His cockney accent was now overlaid with twenty years of Cornish drawl. He had retired from his wholesale carpet business in London's East End to semi-retirement and was now well over seventy, still lively and, most of all, never too busy to help.

'Fine and glad to be back, Jason. How's yours been?'

Slow, now that autumn is upon us. I'll put these on the doorstep and be off. Bye, my lovely. See you soon.'

Susan now raced up the stairs. She hoped she had not been too curt with him not offering a dram. She dumped her belongings onto the settee and let Soxy out of her cage. The bay window curtains were open, and she looked out at the small boats that lay at anchor with their green and red lights dancing rhythmically on the swell.

Normally she would sit with a gin and tonic unwinding from the journey, but tonight was different. She disappeared into her dark room with the unexposed film. Hours later she emerged with a handful of photographs and sat on the floor setting them out in sequence. Soxy tiptoed across them nuzzling her head into Susan's face.

'O.K. I forgot to feed you. Come on.' Soxy ran ahead into the kitchen and waited with her usual cry of delight as the food was forked into her bowl.

Susan returned, poured herself a drink and put on the electric fire. It was going to be a long night. The first photograph was dated 17 April 1956. On the next was a report from Lieutenant John Folleigh. Its contents were later confirmed in a similar report by Petty Officer Daniel Ryan.

'It was 07.10 hours and they were standing outside HMS Vernon, the Royal Naval Diving School in Portsmouth, observing the Russian cruiser and her two destroyers anchored across the water. Over to their left, they had seen Commander Crabb and Lieutenant Sanderson quietly enter the water from a position obscured from the Russian ships. Next, they turned their attention to the Russian cruiser and almost simultaneously they saw two Russian divers jump into the water and take up positions around the stern of the ship. Their report noted that it would have been impossible for lookouts posted on the Ordzhonikdze or the other two ships to have seen Crabb or Sanderson enter the water.'

It was either an incredible coincidence or the result of communicated intelligence. Susan did not like coincidences.

CHAPTER 37

London. October 1990.

Susan's request for leave was granted and the confirmation sat on her desk that Monday morning. She needed more information that was locked somewhere in the thousands of reports that passed through intelligence files daily. It was her job to track some of these, so her trawl through past intelligence reports was entirely acceptable. Linking information, trying to find a pattern. She was looking for something but what? Date after date flashed on the screen. Reports of sightings, press cutting national and international, breakdown in security, deaths, changes in personnel and so on. Some she read with fascination, other not.

Alice walked in with coffee.

'Something bothering you, Commander?' she asked seeing Susan who was rubbing her eyes and staring out of the window. Susan explained very simply what and which dates she wanted to search without offering any explanation as to why and in any case, Alice would not have asked.

Alice, loyal and dedicated, could sometimes offer a different approach to life and computer logic in particular. She walked around the desk and peered at the screen. Susan backed away to give Alice more room.

'Never assume these things know what they are doing and why, talk to them simply,' she muttered as she fed various answers to the ever-changing screen and stood up, flexing her wrists and fingers.

'There, try again.' A smile of mute satisfaction crossing her face momentarily.

Ten minutes later, Susan burst into Alice's office and gave her a beaming 'thumbs up', finding it difficult to hide her excitement. She knew she had hit on a possibility as she printed the brief details of a report. Access to the full report was denied.

A few miles away, Robert Jenner gazed out across the Thames. He knew then as he put down the phone that he had been right to be worried about Susan Sanderson when he'd telephoned America.

'Why such a vague report of a train crash in Siberia should appear in the first place and then be covered with a blanket of secrecy,' she mused. The dates were a long time ago and yet no follow up information.

By the time she decided enough was enough and packed up for the day, Alice had already wished her a good night and left. Susan had the rest of the week to tidy up her files so long as her search paths were covered as much as she could. The printed material was safely stored in her briefcase. The rest of the week passed as normal, so that on late Friday afternoon, she bade Alice 'goodbye' and left for her well-earned leave.

As she turned into Whitehall, it began to drizzle. She unfurled her umbrella and began to walk briskly to the Underground station. Behind her, unobserved, Anatoly, hidden under a black umbrella started to follow; he had flown to England at a few hours' notice from Johnson and was still feeling the effects of the flight from New York.

Jenner's description had been excellent, and he was glad she had decided to leave earlier than expected as he was cold, and his trousers began to soak up the rain. The walk would warm him as he followed the shapely legs and the immaculate straight seam of her black stockings as his eyes followed the seam upwards. There was little chance of him being spotted amongst the throng of office workers also making their way home. Susan entered Charing Cross station. He waited several meters away from her on the platform and followed her into the same carriage settling well away from her but observing closely.

He knew at Clapham South, his job would be more difficult. Luck was on his side, as the rain intensified, and Susan had to hold onto to umbrella with both hands against the blustery rain that whipped across Clapham Common with little chance of looking behind her.

She did not see the figure that crossed to the far side of the road as she turned the key in the lock and let herself into her apartment halfway down

Thurleigh Road. A few minutes later the hall light extinguished itself and the front path was now in darkness again.

Anatoly saw her close the curtains to the front room as he crossed the road and walked up the path. He noted that there were two other flats in the building but no sign of life in either as they were both dark. He crept down the side path and silently vaulted over the side gate as it bent and swayed but withstood his weight. The first window, even though ajar was too small for a man of his size to squeeze through. The rear garden was overlooked but no-one was going to see him on a night like this.

'Come on, Soxy. I know you don't like this weather, but neither do I; out you go.' Susan opened the French doors and reluctantly, Soxy went out for her night prowl.

Anatoly darted into the recesses of the bay; Soxy arched her back against the intruder and hissed loudly. He crouched down and patiently beckoned the cat. 'Thank god it wasn't a dog,' he said to himself. Soxy came to him and as he stroked her, she shot out her left paw and dug it deeply into his right cheek. He cursed loudly and saw the blood on his left hand. Soxy ran to the door crying to be let in.

As soon as Susan opened the door, the cat ran in and disappeared behind the settee. Barely had she time to take in the cat's frightened behaviour when a boot jammed itself inside the door. Anatoly hurled himself into the flat, knocking Susan off balance and backwards into the room. The blade of his knife flashed in the light of the table lamp as he gripped it expertly in his hand.

He grabbed Susan as she recovered her senses and swung her around, holding the blade of the knife against the skin of her neck. She struggled violently until she felt the warm trickle of blood ouze down her neck. Anatoly stuffed a rag into her mouth to stifle her screams. The scent of lime caught her nostrils as he forced her to the floor and tied her hands behind her back; secured her wrists and ankles. Finally, he pulled a length of material from his pocket and blindfolded her. He went to the door and looked out. No further lights had come on and satisfied that no-one had heard the struggle, he closed the curtains.

He looked into the nearest mirror and examined his face. Two long raised cuts with a thin line of encrusted blood colouring them. Damn, he cursed that animal. He knelt close to Susan as she took in the aroma of his scent again. For the first time he spoke. There was a slight accent in the depth of his American. Where from she couldn't immediately tell.

'I've a message for you, Commander Sanderson. Stop your research now. Next time my orders might not be so lenient!'

Anatoly rose and left through the front door.

Susan remained unmoving on the floor for some minutes. She started to cry and Soxy re-emerged and stroked Susan's face with her head. Susan crawled into the kitchen and pulled herself backwards against the cupboards into an upright position and prized open the cutlery drawer. Several minutes later she was free from her restraints. She steadied herself as she reached for the telephone. She made three calls, one to Sydney, Australia, one to the Qantas desk at Heathrow London airport and the last to her mother.

The most important journey had been to the family home at Buckland Court in Devon. She had not spent as much time talking to her mother as she should have done about her father's disappearance when she was young but now was the time for that conversation, albeit briefly. Soxy was keen to explore her temporary home again to reunite herself with its smells and excitedly left them to talk.

Susan had many questions and wanted just a few answers. Her mother started talking for the first time in years. Susan should have felt safe for the first time in many hours, but the more her mother talked, the more disquiet crept into her.

The following evening, Susan was sitting in the fifth row of the Qantas 747 as it waited for final traffic control clearance for take-off. Covering her tracks had meant a few hectic and lousy days.

She closed her eyes, reflectively fingering the scar on her neck. She smiled at the thought of Soxy running about at Buckland Court playing with mice and voles being constantly scolded by her mother for the trouble she was causing.

Her mother had never remarried after the strange and untimely death of her husband; Susan's father. Now only her brother knew her whereabouts, for the moment at least.

CHAPTER 38

New York America

Anatoly returned to his loft apartment overlooking the East River in Manhattan. In the privacy of his own world, he removed his glasses and bent over the bathroom sink and carefully removed the dark brown contact lenses and washed his hair thoroughly, under the cascading warm water; brown dye slowly coursed into the drain. Nobody, not even Mr Johnson CEO of WSC, would be able to recognise him. He took pride in his anonymity.

An hour earlier, he had visited his usual photocopying booth and taken the whole file that Johnson had compiled and arranged it as best he could into the dimensions of a book he'd aptly called 'the Dark Side of Sunday', the day of the discovery of Crabb's dismembered body in his diving suit.

Dressed in his track suit, he poured himself a whiskey and opened the floor safe and took out one of the many passports that had served him well over the past few years. He looked at the photograph that stared back at him and picked up the telephone and dialled.

Half an hour later he was travelling north on the subway sitting in the corner with a complete vista of the carriage. He felt at home in this dingy world below ground. The air was warmer but on this particular route away from downtown the atmosphere was always a little menacing, even in the mid-afternoon. He watched those who he recognised as living on life's edge. He had been there once and never wanted to return. He could identify people who might pose a violent threat on any street, in any town, anywhere. They presented little opposition to him. He fingered unseen, under his left arm, his companion of many years, asleep, safe, waiting to be unleashed at a microsecond's notice. Today, he hoped no fool would see him as a target and regret their decision. No one did. Get in your retaliation first was a motto that had kept him alive so far. The train slowed and he rose and exited onto the platform.

He entered the shop two minutes later and locked the door pulling down the blind over the 'back soon' notice.

'So, what is it today?'

'I am looking forward to warmer days', said Anatoly pulling out a copy of the picture from the passport together with the passport. The man took the passport upstairs to his brother together with instructions from Anatoly and returned.

No further conversation took place as the proprietor loosened Anatoly's collar and folded the gown into it and allowed his skilled hands to mould, and colour the hair into the photograph pinned to the mirror in front of them.

One hour later, he glanced at the passport with its newly endorsed entry visa and then compared himself against the passport photograph. Satisfied, he handed over ten one hundred dollar bills and left.

He had reckoned to be away for about ten days, so the root colourer in the new unopened toothpaste tube he had been given should be enough.

By nine pm the next day, he was sitting in the departure lounge at Kennedy airport reading the updated version of the 'Dark Side of Sunday' waiting for the announcement of the flight to Sydney. He had bought tickets straight through but arranged for a stopover in London for 24 hours at Johnson's last-minute request.

Previously, he had made a call to London and having given the correct ID password had spoken to Johnson's man there, Robert Jenner, and arranged to be met at Heathrow. Jenner had been instrumental in helping Johnson set up 'GSC' and in return Johnson had given him a generous consultancy salary and shareholding. During the flight he read and reread the 'Dark Side of Sunday' until he was so familiar with the characters that he could see the troubling new ones in his mind's eye and probably where they fitted into the story. He hoped there were no surprises, he did not like them nor did he like returning to Sydney so soon after the elimination of one man for the Granetti's for not complying with debt obligations. Surveillance and reporting on the Sanderson woman was not going to be so easy, but that would have to wait until he had dealt with the nuisance Sydney Times reporter who had stuck her nose too far into the Granetti family's business. Johnson had told him that the family wanted permanent closure on this one. Now he had two paymasters, albeit, both through Johnson.

Outside the concourse, he had been told to wait by the number 6 coach stop and would be picked up in an uninspiring grey Rover. Jenner's description not his. The car blended in with the overcast miserable damp air that hung over London. Anatoly opened the door and got in the back seat. The driver turned, shocked at the apparent arrogance of Anatoly.

'Get out. This is not a taxi, I am waiting for someone.'

'Robert Jenner's house as fast as you can; he's expecting me' shouted Anatoly. He gave his ID as Jenner had advised.

Without another word, the driver exited the airport with his passenger towards Cheyne Walk in London's luxury Borough of Chelsea.

The front door was opened by a man in his sixties, dark hair with a slight greying around the temples and a upright elegant stance. Heavy black-rimmed glasses hid the age lines around his eyes. Robert Jenner was dressed elegantly in a dark charcoal suit with light grey waistcoat. When he spoke, his voice was private school, Marlborough

College, followed by Cambridge University where he read Law and Russian gaining a double first.

'I would say 'good day' but it seems a little inappropriate, don't you think? Do come in.'

They settled in front of a large crackling fire and Jenner poured two generous whiskies.

'Matthew told me to give you some more background for your investigation.'

'Had Johnson been honest with Jenner and told Jenner the whole story and what his instructions were', thought Anatoly. He would let Jenner do all the talking.

'Well, as you will undoubtedly know, when I left Cambridge, I joined the Civil Service and spent some time assisting in the Admiralty in the post 1945 war reconciliation attempts between the West and the strengthening threat from Eastern Europe and the expansionism of Soviet Russia. I had high level security clearance but not the highest. This gave me enough access to some top-secret information.'

Anatoly nodded as if Johnson had thought all this information was necessary and let Jenner continue. The more he knew the better he could look after himself.

'I survived the internal enquiries that followed the exposure of Burgess and MacLean as Soviet spies although some still believed that there were others involved. Only later did Kim Philby and Anthony Blunt come to light. It was a terrible time for the secret service. Blown apart literally.

'Anyhow, since Matthew contacted me several weeks ago and described what he had found out, I have spent most of my time ferreting around. Very carefully, mind you.'

Jenner poured another glass of whisky each, poked the fire back into life. Anatoly now knew that Johnson had been open and frank with Jenner.

'I can now add some interesting information to that which you already know.' He sat back and slowly proceeded to fill in some of the gaps in the 'Dark Side of Sunday' so that Anatoly was able to scribble notes to some of the pages. What he had learned would certainly blow GSC out of the water together with Matthew Johnson and Robert Jenner and no doubt some of the older politicians would fall as collateral damage. He concluded that his contract with the CEO of WSC needed renegotiating, but that could wait until his return.

CHAPTER 39

Sydney Australia

It was going to be a scorcher. Even when Nick awoke, the air-conditioning in his small, elegant apartment in the Rocks District of Sydney was struggling to cope with the rising temperature. Pulling back the curtains of the sitting room, he again marvelled, as he did every morning, at the view across the bay to Manley, from the sheer strength of the Bridge to the seashells of the Opera House at both ends of his spectrum. It had taken him a long time to settle on this location in the old converted Bond Store. Well away from that Victorian 'prison' which he called school back in the UK where he had spent his formative years coming to terms with authority. His partners lived in the suburbs and spent a great deal of their lives travelling to and fro. Such a waste. Still the apartment was not the place for children. He could walk a few minutes south and enter the 'holy shrine' of Green Boswith and Litefoot, Attorneys at Law.

He showered, dressed and grabbed his wallet. The previous night he had arranged for a taxi to pick him up at the end of the cobbled street next to the Argyle Arts Centre. All the boutique shops and studios were still asleep as he strode purposefully to the corner. Only the coffee shops were beginning to awaken with the sound of tables and chairs being dragged across the ground to their positions to satisfy the hunger of the early office workers and stray vacationers still suffering from jetlag interrupted sleep.

Always five minutes early just as he liked to be.

The taxi turned south onto the Bradfield Highway heading for Botany Bay and Mascot. He opened the window, and the warm breeze brushed his face. It would not be long before he arrived at Kingsford Johnson Airport.

**

Tilly, an investigative reporter at the Sydney Times and Nick's girlfriend, did not notice the journey at all, she was so engrossed in her conversation with Dr Simon Copplestone that she was surprised when he drove into the central police station.

Months earlier, Tilly had a car accident caused by a slightly drunk driver. There was very little damage to either vehicle, but it was clear that Tilly was shaken by the experience and wanted to call the police and ambulance. The other driver was not keen.

'I am a registered doctor, please let me deal with this.'

She had done, and no report was made to the Medical Council. One day Tilly might need to call in the favour and yesterday that day had come.

'If you are happy to wait here, I will only be fifteen minutes or so,' he said as stretched over to the rear seat to retrieve his brief case and then opened the car door.

'I'm happy to wait,' nodded Tilly.

She hadn't mentioned that she had already tried unsuccessfully to question the police without success and that she thought her presence would cause some friction.

She settled into her seat and put her feet on the dashboard closing her eyes. It had been a long day already and it was only late-morning. She drifted in and out of sleep.

'You startled me,' she said pulling herself upright and trying to straighten her dress.

'I can see that. Sorry. It wasn't that complicated, actually. I would rather not talk inside the car; shall we find somewhere less obvious than here.'

They headed out of downtown to a quieter suburb and stopped outside a small café. As he went to collect the drinks, Tilly set up her recorder on the table in the quietest and farthest corner from the door. Copplestone handed Tilly her white wine spritzer and set down his coffee.

'No names, I am an informed source. OK'

Dr Copplestone prompted by the whir of the cassette recorder started talking.

'Looking at the limb, I found out that it had been severed at the shoulder by a clean-cut incision. With a shark attack you would expect more evidence of, how shall I say, violent ripping of the skin and tissue. No, it was definitely not a shark attack. The condition of the blood, tendons and muscle tissue suggested to me that amputation had taken place sometime post-mortem.'

Tilly had already found out that the recorded shark attack blazed across the news channels last night was now part of a more sinister investigation by the police.

'So, we are definitely talking murder, not suicide or accidental death,' Tilly summed up as she fingered the stem of her wine glass.

'Was anyone else present?'

'Yes, Inspector Richards. He pointed out the tattoos and said that it should not be too difficult to ID the corpse. He had already seen the missing persons file and had two possible John Does. No names were mentioned. He merely wanted me to confirm what the police pathologist had already told them. That was it'

Copplestone drained his coffee and stood up. 'Good luck. We are equal now. Agreed?'

Tilly nodded.

Neither of them had noticed Anatoly in track suit and dark T-Shirt who followed then at a discreet distance.

CHAPTER 40

Sydney same day

Tilly stopped and looked both ways before stepping off the pavement. Anatoly thought for a moment that she may have seen him but reassured himself that it was not possible. There were too many people around and whilst that was good cover, it was going to make his job that much more difficult. Tilly passed several shops stopping to gaze into some of them. It wasn't far now just a couple of blocks. He quickened his pace to get closer. She paused again at the road crossing watching the traffic pass. She was the only one waiting.

'Hit by a passing car. Jaywalking. Didn't stand a chance'

He moved closer, quickening to a run.

'Tilly, what are you doing?'

The voice of Jeff came from a passing car that had slowed down and pulled to the side of the road.

Anatoly continued his run side-stepping Tilly and disappearing across the road into the shadows. Perspiration was streaming down his face, cursing himself for taking this job. He could have refused but as they pointed out tactfully and forcefully, it was his unfinished business. He had never turned down the Granettis or any other introductions they had made in the past. He had to remind himself that now he was not about to let them down now. It was their reminder to others that interest on loans must be paid on time. The bloke obviously had not understood business and Anatoly had fatally reminded him, but the disposal had somehow gone wrong and now this reporter was in it, way over her pretty little head. Silly girl. The situation needed correcting very quickly.

He looked back. Tilly was in deep conversation. She got into car and he watched as it turned the corner and disappeared into the Sydney Times underground car park.

Upstairs in the newsroom, Jeff guided Tilly to sit in the seat next to him. He punched several keys enthusiastically to retrieve the 'Missing Persons' file. He looked at her, smiling, as the computer searched its memory.

'I found out something important by chance and so I needed the names earlier than I had expected. Sorry,' said Tilly apologically as she knew Jeff was always pre-occupied with some story or other.

He nodded and tapped in the print commands and collected two copies from the printer.

'Wow, so many *'missing'*. I had no idea, and this is just the past three years.'

Tilly studied the dates and dismissed most on the list. She mumbled to herself, 'what had Copplestone said? 'Two possible candidates both on file with distinctive tattoos.'

She searched the list scanning the descriptions which had been given to the newspaper from the Police's Missing Persons Bureau.

'Got one', said Tilly. 'Number 15, Guy Rosen, aged 32, six foot two, blond hair, lived in Paramatta. Tattoos on both arms but no description.' She put a cross in the margin and continued her search.

'The other, James O'Ryan. Number 23,' pointed Jeff.

Tilly turned the page quickly.

'He's the one, I know it! Well done, Jeff.' She tore off the relevant part and put the rest in Jeff's shredder and stood up.

'Oh, my God, look at the time. I'm meant to be at a dinner part in twenty minutes. Got to dash. Thanks, Jeff. Tell Ed I will ring him tomorrow.'

'Tilly, where have you got to be? I'll give you a lift. You should not be walking around at this time of day alone. Too many weirdos.'

'Across the bay in Manley. You can give me a lift to Circular Quay, if you like.'

Within minutes, Jeff pulled up outside the main entrance and Tilly walked towards the booking kiosk, pausing to turn and waving her thanks.

Anatoly who had been watching Tilly, saw her and Jeff enter the Sydney Times building and also noted their departure in the direction of the harbour and hailed a taxi. It was worth a chance. As he paid the driver, he looked around but could not see the woman he was tailing. He entered the Quay building and casually walked its length. There were no barriers. This was a commuter point of entry into the city from outlying residential districts over the bay and handled thousands of commuters every day. Speed was the essence of the design.

There were passengers quite a few waiting for the hydrofoil. In the distance he saw it ploughing its narrow furrow across the water. His eyes darted back and forth scanning the shadows looking for the woman in vain. Just as the considering leaving having made the wrong assumption, he noticed her exiting the ladies' room. He retreated out of sight. 'Pretty' he thought. He loved the legs and the way her recently brushed hair lay around her neck. She was talking to herself and looking constantly at her watch as if she were late for something.

She looked up and moved towards the entry gangway as the hydrofoil began to slow its approach. It was getting quite dark now even though it was a clear night. She hugged herself to keep out the creeping night cold. Within minutes the Quay was alive with noise as those disembarking and others rushing on board to secure the best and warmest seats.

He kept his distance, hoping that as a smoker, she would remain outside. Just another body floating in the harbour, an unobserved disappearance, he thought to himself.

But Tilly made her way inside to sit with the majority of passengers. He would have to wait for another opportunity. He was always patient; you had to be in his line of work.

Tilly opened her bag and began to listen to her recorded interview with Dr Copplestone. She thought again of the possible events that had led to this man's death and its discovery as a murder. Tomorrow she would trace the wife who had reported him missing. She had her address. Now she told herself to relax and to look forward to an evening of conviviality amongst friends. She then dictated the contents of the missing person printout into the machine before tearing the paper into small pieces and dropping them into several different garbage bins as she walked around the cabin, readying herself to grab the nearest taxi.

As the hydrofoil slowed, she went on deck looking back at the illuminated Opera House and Sydney Bridge and the shimmering skyline of downtown Sydney. It was a beautiful vista. She closed her bag and placed the recorder in the top pocket of her blouse out of habit. Not very chic but always available for use very quickly. As she approached the waiting line of taxis, Anatoly pushed in line just behind her. She told the driver the address.

Anatoly flashed a badge and told the next driver to follow.

'Just stay behind and don't lose it', he said authoritively. The driver obeyed instinctively. You couldn't tell undercover police these days.

After a few minutes, the taxi in front pulled into a parking bay on the side of the road lined with plane trees and intermittently lighted by streetlamps that strained to illuminate the footpath. Tilly started to walk across the road and follow the footpath. Anatoly's taxi passed by and he looked over his shoulder to see where she was heading. She turned into a side path as Anatoly struggled out of the taxi heading towards the path. He left a generous few dollar notes on the passenger seat.

Before Tilly knew what was happening, he grabbed her from behind covering her mouth with his gloved hand and twisted her around unbalancing her. One muffled shot into her chest and Tilly slumped into his arms breathing in his unusual scent. He let her fall gently to the ground, snatched her handbag and disappeared. He removed his small moustache and dark wig which would find their way down river with the tide later.

'Subject dispatched as ordered,' said Anatoly as he spoke to a local Sydney member of the Granetti family's contact from the airport. Last night, he had answered a call from Jenner to tell him that Susan Sanderson had left London on the Qantas flight arriving the next day. As he wondered towards the Arrivals hall, a tannoy announcement for Susan Sanderson from the arrival of Flight 267 from London, caught his attention. He surveyed the crowd waiting. Susan Sanderson wouldn't be expecting him and, in any case, she'd never recognise him now. He looked at all the faces and saw Tilly's partner, Nick Sanderson walking quickly towards the woman he recognized.

CHAPTER 41

Sydney - the same day

Singapore was behind her now, the last lap had begun. The film was starting and there was little activity around her, as Susan closed her eyes, quite exhausted from recalling the horrific assault, and the question 'why?'

What evidence had she uncovered that was so important to hide. If she had known of Robert Jenner and his web of informants, she would not be on this plane. She would have taken the advice dished out in her flat at Thurleigh Road. The scenarios throughout most of the journey had not made sense to her. She needed a rest but still found herself wandering through the jungle of possibilities.

It was early, too early for Susan as the bubble of excitement started in the cabin at the words 'fasten your seatbelts'. A new day was dawning, the plane began to bounce and flap as it banked over the blue ocean to make its final approach to Kingsford Sith International.

She eyed the expectant faces that lined the concourse as she pushed her luggage before her. Susan and Nick saw each other at the same moment and for the first time in their lives they recognised the lost past. Unquelled emotion spread through their bodies as they wrapped their arms around each other. Tears of uncontrolled joy poured down Susan's face. They were momentarily lost in a time warp as others passed by. Anatoly watched, no emotion on his face.

'I love you sis, it has been far too long.' They embraced again.

He pulled away from her and noticed the bruising and scar on her neck.

'What happened?'

'I have no idea, only what I told you on the phone. Where is Tilly?'

'Afraid there's been an accident.'

'When? Is she all right?'

'Yesterday. Yes, she's fine. The hospital expect her to be out in a few days. I didn't want to worry you even more.'

They walked towards the taxi rank. The heat hit Susan momentarily taking her breath away so different from grey old London.

'Are you OK? Since your call, I haven't had time to think. Look at your neck. That bastard could have killed you.'

'If he wanted to, he could. He was told not to, but just to frighten me. Nick, it's been a very long day. Later. OK?'

'We will get you settled and see Tilly.'

'That's great by me.' Susan had relaxed for the first time in several days.

The journey downtown was relatively quick. Susan settled herself into the spare room of Nick's flat.

Nick told her that he had persuaded his partners to let him have some leave in view of her imminent arrival and Tilly's accident.

Anatoly followed their path to Nick's apartment in the Rocks and waited. It wasn't long before they appeared again and walked to the nearby taxi stand.

Would Johnson sanction this unscheduled surveillance? Now was not the time to ask; he'd make sure his report left no room for doubt. He needed a favour, one that would be called in later; he had no doubt about that, but as he had worked for the man several times in his limited field of expertise, he felt sure he'd oblige. He made a call whilst on route from the airport to Mario Flavioretti and took a room in the Rocks hotel across the road from Nick's apartment. Flavioretti's man arrived within minutes. Anatoly, now dressed in a Sydney Telecom jacket and carrying a black plastic case with similar markings, waited for someone to appear at Nick's apartment block entrance door. He smiled at the old lady exiting as he held the door open for her. It did not take long for Flavioetti's man to let himself and Anatoly into Nick's apartment. The security locks were ancient and easy to breach. Within minutes, he had installed two communication microphones and left undetected; all he had to do now was wait in his hotel across the road and listen.

Susan and Nick were shown into the Intensive Care Ward; Doctor Drake Miles ushered them aside.

'She's much better, regained consciousness an hour ago, but is still very fragile. Not too much excitement, just a few minutes.'

At the Sydney Times offices, Ed Warren and Jeff were waiting for news of Tilly. The phone rang. Ed snatched it from its cradle and listened intently to Nick on the other end.

'Any news yet,' asked Jeff as Ed slung the receiver back down, grabbing his jacket.

'Yeah, come on, she's regained consciousness.'

The Times had paid for a private room to be used for Tilly's recuperation once out of danger. The clinical colours and fresh antiseptic smells were alien to the world of organised chaos at the Times. Ed did not feel at home, he hated hospitals.

'She is still very poorly so don't tire her too much. She needs all the rest she can get.' With that said, the nurse left closing the door behind her.

Tilly looked very pleased to see them despite an array of tubes and lines attached to her and monitors clicking and flashing her vital signs.

'Til, good to see you.' They both gave her a peck on the cheek.

'Hi, guys. Excuse the sight.' They took two chairs and dragged them closer to the bed.

'Going to tell me why you didn't take my advice,' chided Jeff.

'Actually, I did. It wasn't until I was a few steps from my dinner date that someone grabbed me from

261

behind and shot me in the chest and ran off with my bag. The police were here earlier and told me they assume it was just some opportunist. There have apparently been several such similar attacks, but this is the first with a gun. I did not tell them anything other than about the attack. One of the officers left his contact details on my locker over there.'

Jeff walked over and copied the name into his notebook.

'Do you think it had anything to do with the list?' asked Ed.

'How could it, I have only been on the case for a day or so, with no leads or conclusions.'

'Look, you rest and enjoy the break you never had! Anything you need? We'll see what we can find out. Can't have a top reporter the subject of an attempted murder, can we?'

It was obvious to Ed and Jeff that she was already too tired to continue.

Back in the office, Ed Warren telephoned the police station. He scribbled furiously on the pad beside him as he listened intently to the information being given by police headquarters. The conversation came to an end. Ed flipped the pad back to the first page.

'It appears that they haven't recovered the bullet from the scene. The doctors told them that Tilly's tape recorder in her blouse pocket had disintegrated on impact with the bullet and some of the fragments were embedded in her chest. The recorder undoubtedly saved her life. They also told me that the tape inside the recorder was shredded and they could not retrieve any information from it.'

Jeff sighed.

'Shame about the tape. Tilly and I, before she left for Manley, had 'discovered' the probable owner of the arm from the Missing Persons File and that she had taken part of the computer printout to continue her investigations. Was there any mention of papers found on her?'

'Nothing else was found in her clothing,' said Ed.

'Do you remember the guy Tilly was talking about?'

Jeff rose and walked to his desk and returned with a copy of the printout. He remembered that he and Tilly agreed on two possibilities and that Tilly's instinct had told her that the second Missing Person was their man.

'James O'Ryan, known as Jimmy. Ed, can you see if there is anything about this guy on our database?'

Moments later Ed shouted 'Yep!'

'James 'Jimmy' O'Ryan. Aged forty. Owner of the Pleasure Drome off Bondi. Small time crook in his early days. Nothing on his record for the last fifteen years. Has other interests in clubs in Paddington. Owns the Piazza Parlour down in the Wharf. There's an unsubstantiated note here that he may have links with Mario Flavioretti.'

'Mario Flavioretti, I've heard that name before. Fill me in, Ed.'

Ed leant back in his chair and clasped his hands behind his head.

'OK, know all, let's have it,' said Jeff

'Allegedly part of the New York Granetti Family. Nobody here knows much about his activities except that all appears to be legit and worth an awful lot of dollars.

'I know, Jeff, that this is not your kind of work, but while Tilly's recuperating, can you make a few enquiries? I'd like to run another piece after Tilly's attack story has run its course. Get O'Ryan's address and anyone who can ID him and as much info as you can about him and his activities. Go carefully, you never know with these people.'

'You mean I can end up with a chest wound as well!'

'That would make another good story for the Times.'

That afternoon, Jeff found himself admiring the coastline around Bondi watching the surf crash against the rocks at the southern end. He pulled into the long graceful driveway of O'Ryan's house and stopped under the shade of several pines that had bowed away from the prevailing wind over the years. He mounted the steps and pressed the bell admiring the craftsmanship of the portico albeit a little overbearing for his taste. After a few moments, the door was opened by a woman who had clearly endured a few sleepless nights and was red around the eyes as if she had been crying.

'I am sorry to intrude. I assume that you are Mrs James O'Ryan?'

'Who shall I say is here?' She said pointedly.

'Jeff Green of the Sydney Times. Might I have a few words?' he asked, smiling endearingly.

'I am Mrs O'Ryan. You'd better come in.'

She led him through the cavernous entrance hall into a room that was clearly a study.

'I suppose I've been expecting someone from the Press sooner or later. Do sit down.'

Jeff waited for Mrs O'Ryan to take her seat and then chose one opposite her. He took out his notebook.

'I understand that you have recently been asked to attend the Homicide Department of the Sydney police. I'm sorry to be direct but can I ask you if you identified your husband?'

She held her head in her hands and Jeff knew the answer.

'They eventually managed a partial print from a fingertip and matched it to their database. He'd been in trouble with the police when he was younger, but you probably already knew that.'

Jeff nodded.

'He said to me on the day I last saw him that he was going fishing.'

'That would be 8 April,' Jeff interrupted. 'Did he go alone?'

'I don't know who Jimmy was going with this time, he went fishing quite a lot these days. He never told me if he was having company. He was quite a secretive man about his business dealings, but I didn't mind. I suppose it was to protect me.'

Jeff turned to his notebook.

'I just want to find out if this was an accident or not, as we have reason to think that.........' He stopped, wondering if he was going too fast and she would cease being co-operative. 'I can assure you that the information will be treated with total confidentially and we will do nothing to undermine your security without your written permission. We have lawyers to deal with these situations. I know you said that Jimmy was secretive, but did he talk to you recently about any business deals?'

Mrs O'Ryan thought for a moment as if deciding whether to trust Jeff and the Sydney Times, finally she walked to the desk and picked up some papers.

'Since he went missing, our accountant and I have searched through all the papers here and in his safe but found nothing.' She paused. 'However, I have thought about something he had told me several days before he disappeared. Apparently, the Bank was being very generous in supporting a new venture. Here.' She passed the sheaf of papers to Jeff.

'See if you make anything of them?'

Jeff scanned them.

'Nothing really in here, is there?' He was just about to hand them back when something caught his eye. Scribbled lightly on the corner of the back of one of the letters was the words 'ring Mario'.

'Mrs O'Ryan, have you ever heard of a Mario Flavioretti?'

'Not that I can recall, No. Never. Why?'

'Oh, it's a name that came up in the office before I came here. That's all, nothing really.'

CHAPTER 42

Sydney Later the same day

Jeff settled into the sofa while Ed Warren leaned his elbows on his desk.

'Well, what happened with Mrs O'Ryan. Get your foot through the door?'

'Yes, but nothing gained from Mrs O'Ryan herself as she clearly had no knowledge of Jimmy's business activities and really did not want to know. Ex-criminal and all that. But all is not in vain as Jimmy clearly had some dealings with Mario Flavioretti. I found "ring Mario" scrawled on the back of one the letters she showed me.'

'Wow, Jeff. Well done!' shouted Ed as he sprang back in his seat, spirits lifted.

'So, what have we got to trade with the police? I think we may know more about Jimmy O'Ryan deceased than they do. Let's set up a meeting with Sergeant Field.'

In the quiet confines of the Bulletin Place, a forty-seater shoe box on the first floor sparsely decorated that doubled as a café within a stone throw of the Sydney Bridge which Jeff knew at this time of day would still have space for them. Jeff and Ed waited for Field who entered a few minutes later with Inspector Farmer. Unusually, Jeff insisted on cocktails all round and went to order four Ring-a-Roseys. The two policemen look apprehensively at the mixture of gin, grapefruit and rosemary, sipping it tentatively until they smiled and downed the lot in one go and ordered another round, after all, it was out of hours and an unscheduled rendezvous. When Ed had finished telling them what they had uncovered, Farmer started to speak.

'You seem extremely well informed and I won't ask the sources.'

'What is the quid pro quo, Inspector?' asked Ed.

'The forensic boys have managed to put together their best guess. We think that O'Ryan had been silenced for some reason, hauled into a metal trunk or something like that and cast loose out at sea. On the arm there were traces of paint and metallic scrapings. The arm had been amputated and they think the whole body was dismembered before it was squeezed into the metal container. We just don't know until we find the remaining parts of the body. Whatever happened next, the container opened, and Jimmy's arm ended up in our morgue. However, I'm more interested in your mention of Mario Favioretti. We have nothing but suspicions currently. He is well connected and very well protected. What makes you think he's involved?'

Jeff took over at this point.

'From my conversation with Jimmy's wife and other information that our colleague Tilly collected, we suspect that Jimmy's rapid rise in business acquisition and property over the last few years would have required investment over and above what his Bankers provided. Ed found a photograph in our celebrity archives showing the two of them at a function last year. Their faces conveyed a closeness. At least that was our impression.'

'Can I borrow the photo? Maybe the Coroner at the Inquest would be interested in calling him as a known associate and see what happens. Boys, can you sit on this story for a while, please?' asked the Inspector.

'Yes, on one condition, if I may,' said Ed Warren.

'You agree to meet with us regularly to exchange information. It will benefit both sides. You know, in Tilly, we have one of the best incisive reporters in town who could be an asset for you as well as us.'

'We'll do our best, guys, but we have constraints.'

'As we do,' said Ed.

A faint smile crossed Inspector Farmer's face. 'Indeed, you do.'

CHAPTER 43

Sydney General Hospital

Susan and Nick arrived and parked their car in the pickup zone. Tilly was waiting for them, sitting in a wheelchair with a hospital porter on hand. Susan still embraced Tilly cautiously not knowing what would hurt, but this time whispered 'we're two of a kind' holding her face gently in her hands as Tilly noticed the scar and bruising for the first time. Nick stood watching, waiting to take hold of his first love in his arms and get her safely away from the hospital.

'Home at last!' said Tilly lowering herself cautiously onto the settee. She smiled when she noticed the 'Welcome Home' banner draped across the sideboard. 'Thanks'.

Tilly, although still easily tired, could not wait to question them both.

'Come on you two, I'm OK now. Let's start putting things together. Get this jigsaw started.'

Across the road, the light on the recorder flickered and the tape started to turn. Anatoly started to listen intently. He was shocked to discover that the Reporter had somehow survived his gun attack. He had seen nothing in the papers. How could that be? He'd have to reconsider his position carefully, but for the moment, he wanted to hear what they all had to say.

Nick gave a summary of Susan's investigation for Tilly's benefit again. She had written most of it down but now her notes were covered in red pen and question marks.

'First of all, I think about the shooting all the time. I will never forget the scent of lime.'

'What did you say, Tilly? Something about lime. Did you mean smell?'

'Yea, the scent.' Tilly described exactly what Susan had remembered about her attacker.

'You're freaking me out, Tilly. I am really scared now.'

'Can we assume it's the same guy by his perfume?' said Nick.

'Not necessarily, I agree. However, I don't like coincidences even though they are thousands of miles apart,' added Susan. Tilly nodded in agreement. 'Anyway, this guy appears to be a real pro and arrogant enough to think he's untouchable by the smell of him.'

'He may be a real pro, Susan, but he didn't scare you enough to stop you coming here and telling us what happened, and he didn't succeed in killing me. Sooner or later, he'll realise he has two loose ends to deal with. The trouble is we don't know if there's any connection between the attacks, so that's where we start. Susan, he warned you to stop digging. Me, I must have stepped on his or someone else's toes somehow recently.'

'Are we safe here, Tilly?' asked Nick.

'Since the shooting, The Times has offered to look out for us all. They have employed a surveillance team round the clock until this 'thing' is over.'

'So where do we start.?'

As Susan went to retrieve her papers from her case, Nick watched her as she went towards the spare room, his mind drifted back as he thought about the lost years. He had kept in touch with Susan at Christmas, Easter and birthdays, but they were not then emotionally close. Going to separate boarding schools from eleven onwards had stunted those potential ties between siblings. They led different lives and lived in different countries for years until now. It was obvious to Nick that Tilly had taken Susan's place. He had, for the most part of the last few minutes, watched them from afar not really listening to their words. They were surprisingly similar, both in looks and physically. He looked at Susan. The sun from behind her encased her head in a yellow glow. Threads of her fine hair moved gently in the current of air from the ceiling fan. She had joined the Navy after qualifying at Dartmouth in Devon and had volunteered to undertake underwater surveillance training and covert intelligence gathering techniques. He remembered that she loved swimming from her school days taking great delight beating the boys in inter-school swimming competitions, the medals and cups that adorned her dressing table at home. This special

273

training at Dartmouth had led her to joining a little advertised department within Naval Intelligence section of the Navy and to secure and analyse sensitive matters of State where her ultimate masters were politicians.

Nick was drawn back to the present when he heard Susan telling Tilly about the background to the Crabb affair. Susan turned to Nick.

'Did Mother ever talk to you about what happened to Dad?'

'Not really. I remember being told that he had died. I only ever really knew him from conversations at Buckland Court. I just accepted life as normal without him. It was only later that I realised life wasn't that normal', he sighed sorrowfully.

Tilly caught his air of depression she had seen occasionally before when he tried to talk of his youth. Trying to overcome the situation she re-engaged Susan to tell more.

'Operation Wild Cat. It was an unauthorised M16 operation that went badly wrong when Buster Crabb went missing. The mission was sanctioned from the top by the Director of Naval Intelligence, Rear Admiral John Inglis. What I discovered was that contrary to the statements of the day, the mission was not undertaken by Crabb alone, after all he was an oldish man by Navy standards for operational work. He was accompanied by a younger man. No trace of this man exists but as you know the remains of Crabb were eventually found by some fishermen.'

Nick put his hand on Susan's arm.

'Were all the papers you saw, original?' asked Tilly.

'Yes, I broke a few rules to get this far and I know I have put my career on the line and frighteningly, somebody else knows it.'

'O.K.' said Nick, walking to the window and closing the curtains and taking the papers from Susan and putting them in some sort of date order on the floor.

'According to the Coroner's Report from the Inquest, Detective Superintendent Lamport, Head of Portsmouth Criminal Investigation Department, said that he went to the Sallyport Hotel and discovered that four pages from the hotel register had been removed. This covered the first three weeks until 21 April 1956. You said Mum had last seen Dad a week earlier, leaving on the previous Saturday very early in the morning. Look at this note.' He handed it to Tilly.

She read out the scrawled writing, 'The Hotel manager, Richman and staff have been briefed by my men on the Official Secrets Act'.

'No-one from the Hotel is listed as attending the Inquest,' continued Nick. 'In fact, the only other people attending were those from the Admiralty including their own doctor who carried out the post mortem examination of the body.'

'Susan, have you been able to trace anyone who was alive and mentioned in the Operation file?' asked Nick.

'Just before I left, I found out that the Richmans sold up the Sallyport Hotel and are now no longer with us. I traced their daughter to Liverpool. She told me over the phone that her parents were ordered not to talk about the incident, but just before her Dad died, he told her all he knew. Cleared his conscience, so to speak. He told her that he remembered that the one with an American accent, Johnson, gave his address as King Charles Street London.'

'So?' asked Tilly.

'The Foreign Office is in King Charles Street. Coincidence or not?'

'This guy, Johnson, seems an interesting character. Was this a joint venture between the Americans and the British? What happened to Johnson afterwards? Did Richman see if he was the one who removed the pages from the Register and if so what did he do with the car and the other belongings of Crabb and……?'

'Dad,' ventured Susan. There it was for the first time, 'Dad'.

'Yes, seems pretty obvious to me that it was your Dad,' said Tilly.

'From April 1956, Johnson vanishes. The car was never seen again nor anything else.'

'Is the patient feeling a little tired? said Nick as Tilly yawned. 'Do you want to stop?'

'Not at all,' she said stretching, 'What do you know about this Operation,' Tilly looked at her notes. 'Wild Cat, Susan?'

'Well, it was given the go-ahead by the Admiralty because Rear Admiral John Inglis thought that the underwater inspection would reveal important technical information. The Admiralty request was received by MI6's Merchant Navy section. It was they who accepted the mission. It helped me because the request was actually put in writing. Backside protection for someone no doubt, but here comes the cover-up. The Foreign Office was never advised and never asked to give approval. MI6 realised the game was up when the Admiralty reported receiving a message from the senior Soviet naval officer, Rear Admiral Kotov, saying that a diver had been seen close to the cruiser. This message was received initially by the Commander in Chief, Portsmouth. He denied all personal knowledge of the diver but routinely advised the Admiralty.'

'This, I assume is where MI6 went on their damage limitation exercise. The political consequences to the Government could have been catastrophic.'

'Well, I must say you have uncovered some dangerous material even now,' said Tilly, searching through her notes. She turned to them. 'This is where I think MI5's timely help saved some considerable embarrassment. They sent Lamport to the Sallyport Hotel. He could keep the whole affair secret by assuming that Crabb was no longer in their control and by announcing his loss at sea.'

'What about the second man, your father, Susan, Nick?'

Brother and sister looked at each other, Nick put his hand out and Susan clasped it tightly. Tilly realised that she had been talking just like journalists do, aloof from the human emotions that now surfaced in Susan's face. The trauma of her lost father's life being unearthed slowly before her.

'I'm sorry. This must be terrible for you.'

Susan blinked a tear from her eye. She knew now that soon she would know her father's fate. She turned to them looking directly at Nick as he disappeared into the kitchen.

'Apart from this Johnson fellow and some of those at the Admiralty, MI5 and MI6, the men at the Naval Base and Richman. No one else knew that Dad was the second diver.'

'That's still a hell of a lot of people.'

'And one hell of a cover up,' said Tilly.

'Come on, let's eat something,' said Nick, placing a tray of cold meats, salad and a bottle of Chardonnay on the table. 'I've been keeping this for a special occasion. One of the better ones from the Barossa Valley.' He uncorked the bottle with a pop and poured three glasses full, then realizing Tilly was under medication, drank most of hers, before handing her the leftovers.

Across the cobbled street in his hotel room, Anatoly had been listening to the recording of the conversations with heightened intensity. Matters were getting out of hand very quickly for him, Flavioretti and Johnson.

'Tilly, I don't think what happened to you is in any way related to our Dad. Do you? If this lime smelling guy is a pro, he'd have many contracts from different clients.'

'I don't know yet, but you're probably right. Nevertheless, the same man threatened your sister and also tried to kill me. That is a very big connection and I for one am not going to rest until we find him, here or anywhere else.'

'Once he learns you are alive and that Susan is not taking his threats seriously, I am sorry to say he'll find us one way or another. I just hope your protection team from The Times are up to it.'

'Nick, they will be as long as we are careful, OK. What do you two want to do about your Dad?'

'I suggest that we hear the rest of the circumstances of his disappearance,' said Nick. 'Susan?'

'Right, the only one of note was Patricia Rose, Crabb's ladyfriend. She now lives in a flat in Elm Grove North London. She is a very old lady now and suffers from the beginnings of dementia. Like all those with short term memory loss, she kept asking me who I was and what I wanted, but once I guided her away from the present and into the past, she couldn't stop.

'It was really quite amazing. She told me that she had been close to 'Buster', as she constantly referred to him, since his marriage had broken down. She had been devastated by his disappearance and had relived their last few hours together over and over again. She had been uneasy when he told her he'd have to go to Portsmouth. They had to cancel an evening out. Buster had been pre-occupied and was not his usual ebullient self. They had gone to the pub at lunchtime, but he had not touched his usual gin and tonic or barely drunk any wine with his meal. There was never any mention of why he was off to Portsmouth. He never ever told her whether he was working alone or not.'

'I showed her a picture of Dad. She recognised him immediately. She had met him on several occasions. Buster and Dad were like father and son, she said. I asked her whether she thought it was possible they were working together on this occasion. She nodded. 'I never saw either of them again. If he had known anything about what happened, even if he wasn't with Buster, he would have come to see me. I am sure of that.'

Susan consulted her notes again.

'Immediately after Buster's disappearance she went to her brother's villa in Biot in France. MI5 immediately traced her and interviewed her after the discovery of his body. They did not want her to become involved. She was not asked to attend the inquest, nor did she attend his funeral.

'Sometime afterwards she told me she received some mysterious telephone calls. She gained the impression that someone knew more than the Admiralty was prepared to reveal. Each call was very indistinct, and the line was very bad, but she said the accent was distinctly very English and whoever the person was told her that one day the truth would come out, but that now the time was not ripe. Each time the calls were interrupted by a foreign voice and stopped coming sometime in 1960s.'

'So, what about mother, have you raised the subject with her?' asked Nick.

'No, I was waiting to see you. She has accepted life without Dad for years now. Opening up these possibilities that were in the past could have far-reaching consequences for her, mentally and emotionally. She's not in the best of health and I'm not sure what this would do to her.'

'But she must have been told something that didn't add up', interrupted Tilly.

'You've not met Mother. She is a very single-minded woman. She had accepted Dad's death and what she had been told by the Admiralty and with two children to just get on with life. Things were very different in the 1950s,' said Susan with a hint of sadness in her voice.

'It is easy for us to forget that those post World War Two years were uneasy. Churchill' warnings about Stalin's Iron Curtain stretching from the Baltic Sea to the Mediterranean were casting a menacing shadow over Western Europe. Fear was Stalin's method of power retention and his imperialistic outlook sent shockwaves throughout the secret services of Britain and America. Perhaps, if we'd endured that war, the bombings, loss of life, the threat of invasion, the post war revelations of genocide, we would understand Mother's acceptance much more easily.'

'One thing is certain, at some point soon, Nick and Susan, you are going to have to tell her.'

'Nick, you never talked about your father's disappearance from your life,' said Tilly.

'It is strange really. Don't forget I was young. Teenagers are not like they are now. I was shown pictures of Dad and that was it. I don't remember if we had a picture of him on the shelves or anything. He'd died and that was it for me. Death was not a subject that was openly spoken about. Most children were ignorant about any details. I certainly missed not having a father at school, but sometimes it gave me an edge. I was different, someone who'd had a different experience.'

'Susan, what about you?'

'Much the same really. It was only when I told Mum that I decided to follow Dad's footsteps into the Navy that she became morbid for a few days afterwards. We discussed father's career or at least what she had been allowed to know. There was the Official Secrets Act hovering over his career and Mum knew little of what happened outside the house. But she did tell me that he'd left very early on the morning she's last seen him. Later a man from the Admiralty knocked on the door and explained that Dad had been involved in some secret scientific experiments at sea and there had been an accident. They had been unable to recover his body despite an extensive search.' Susan took a deep breath and looked at Nick who had his head in his hands. It was Tilly who broke the silence.

'So, to sum up. Let us accept that Crabb and your Dad went on the mission together. Let us also suppose that Crabb died by accident or was murdered by the Russians. Is it likely that only one body would have been recovered? No, I think it is likely that your Dad was captured by the Russians for future propaganda or bargaining purposes and transported back to Russia on board that cruiser.'

'This is all supposition, but it is beginning to have a ring of truth about it,' said Susan, 'and someone wants to stop us finding out more. The question is who and why?'

Anatoly had heard all he needed now and within the hour he was holding a single ticket to New York.

CHAPTER 44

New York America

Tilly was recovering sufficiently well to attend the first hearing into the death of James 'Jimmy' O'Ryan. Thirty nine witnesses were called by the City Coroner. After three days, the proceedings were halted by a Supreme Court Writ deciding that an inquest could only be held if there was a body and that one limb was not enough albeit clearly identifiable. The Coroner adjourned the case without time limit.

Ed Warren and Tilly ran their story in the Times which provoked a huge increase in circulation and the police continued their investigations but eventually wound down their involvement.

In New York, the Sydney Times was read with satisfaction by Anatoly, sitting in the Alm's restaurant on 49th East Street Manhattan, finishing his first strong coffee of the day. There was only speculation that O'Ryan was missing. What was no surprise was the name of one of the authors of the report. The case was going nowhere so, to hell with her. Let Johnson decide what to do next on the other matter of Sanderson. He paid for the coffee and bagel and left. Once outside he stuffed the newspaper into his coat pocket. It had not been a bad start to the day after all.

Later, his call to Sydney was returned by Flavioretti. He warned Anatoly that this woman, Tilly, was a tenacious terrier when chasing a story and now working on whatever it was, with her prospective sister-in-law, Susan Sanderson, he'd better watch out. Anatoly didn't pass comment but gave his thanks. Johnson was not going to like this at all if he ever found out. Anatoly was not going to tell him and did not expect the Granettis would either as they knew nothing apart from bugging the apartment for him. He considered himself safe for the time being as he booked a seat on the evening flight to Denver.

At WSC Headquarters, Matthew Johnson read Anatoly's report of his eavesdropping on Susan Sanderson in Australia. He had no idea how resourceful the three of them could be. He telephoned Jenner in London and told him what had been discovered and what he now planned and that he would be sending the best photograph of Sanderson he had been able to enhance. Two days later Johnson telephoned Anatoly.

'I'll take over from here,' said Johnson 'I'm transferring your fee and a generous bonus.

Anatoly put down the phone. 'Damn that man, after all the trouble he'd been through for Johnson, he wanted to come face to face with Sanderson himself and what better place would there have been than Puerto Rico,' he said to himself. He knew there would be another opportunity to meet him, but as Johnson had paid him off and thanked him for his efforts, he was out of the picture and had decided to stay well hidden, but there was no way he was going let the matter drop.

Johnson rose the next day and was driven to the airport with Sanderson's new passport in his briefcase, couriered over by Jenner. It wasn't going to be easy looking for Jack Sanderson in San Juan, Puerto Rico with a population of half a million people. It was not his town and he needed help.

'Morning.'

Johnson looked up and stood offering his hand in welcome.

'Sit down. You're a welcome sight. Coffee?'

Johnson recognised his contact. He had worked at head office some years ago, until Johnson had posted him to WSC's Central American base in neighbouring Panama. Resourceful and loyal. Johnson needed him to help in the search.

'I want this man found and not harmed, understand?'

He handed over two photographs that Anatoly had given him together with height and approximate body measurements.

'This is my hotel number. I will await your call when you find where he's living.'

Several days of sun, swimming, good food and general relaxation passed pleasantly for Matthew Johnson.

It was early on the fifth day, the call from reception had woken him after a restless hot night. After showering and a small continental breakfast, Johnson carefully picked his way through the streets avoiding the pools of water that remained from last night's thunderstorm. He eventually sat down overlooking the causeway to the old part of the city. He was ten minutes early, always early out of habit, so he could scan his surroundings for anything out of place. He had not been in the front line for many years and was beginning to enjoy the feeling again.

He took a deep breath and savoured the fresh breeze coming off the water, then saw his contact walking rapidly over the bridge towards him alone.

'Any luck?'

'One of our part time eyes lives in the old city, he cannot be sure but, just after the murder in the docks, this man comes into the store buying candles, lots of them, cutlery and a mirror. Never seen him before, not a local accent, maybe English. He thinks it is maybe the guy in the photograph you gave me. Apparently, he used to come in regularly at first when it was dark but then stopped until last night. We are to meet his son at lunch time.'

'That's great work.' A smile of relief passed momentarily over Johnson's face.

'We'll walk if you like. It's not too humid today.'

It took longer than Johnson had anticipated. This place was making his knees ache and his joints really didn't like the damp air. After twenty minutes, they stopped outside a rundown shop with the pavement littered with pots, pans, nails, clothes and bric-a-brac for sale with several people nosing through it. Johnson was immediately ushered through the shop into a back room where a solitary yellowed bulb made heavy weather of lighting the area with its faded wallpaper, rows of shelving, mostly stocked with dust covered boxes and a flypaper hanging heavily with the deaths of hundreds to one side of the lamp.

Shaking involuntarily the storekeeper told the story again then turned to Johnson's contact.

'He came again last evening, and my son followed him. My son's making a delivery and will be back...'

A young boy appeared, the splitting image of his father years ago, and ushered them to follow him.

Not far away, the boy stopped. He pointed to a gap in the corrugated iron fencing. Johnson pulled at it and peered inside. All he saw was a derelict building site and piles of concrete and rubbish.

'He went in there?'

The boy nodded insistently.

'You two wait over there as if you are discussing something important and keep a look out. I am going in,' ordered Johnson.

Johnson lifted the curled edge of the metal again and disappeared inside. Slowly he crept around the site, looking for tell-tale signs of recent activity, lifting boards and under one such board he saw the first step down into a cellar. It was too clean to his trained eye despite the debris that had been scattered to disguise its use. He carefully descended the steps and found a very serviceable bedsitting room. His curiosity took him further into the room. He noticed, on the table, amongst a pile of papers, language books and Paulo Aires' passport. He silently looked through them, failing to notice a holdall nestling underneath the camp-bed in the corner. He did not want to linger too long and undo all their hard work in tracing Sanderson, so he retraced his steps to the outside.

'Nobody there but it's definitely him. I doubt if he will return during daylight,' said Johnson, then he had second thoughts. 'I think I'm going to wait for him.'

'Boss, shouldn't we wait, just in case?'

'No, I'll be OK. See you in the hotel tomorrow evening. Shall we say 7pm?'

Lying on the camp-bed in the cellar with only the fading afternoon light for company, Johnson wished he was younger. This was now too much for him especially as the humidity had risen with the intensity of the sun. He placed his gun on his chest and closed his eyes and soon drifted into dreams and sleep.

He was awakened by the movement of the entrance door and slid out of the hammock, holding the gun in his right hand, just to be on the safe side, and stood behind the half-opened door. The footsteps grew louder and a hand fumbled and pushed open the door. Johnson held his breath and pointed the gun at the figure as it bent and lit one of the candles which danced then settled casting a yellow glow over the room. There was a hesitation, as Sanderson sniffed the air, something was amiss. He turned abruptly and saw the eerie figure of Johnson and the menancing barrel of the gun pointed at him.

'If you're sensible, you'll just sit down with your hands on the table where I can see them.'

Sanderson did as he was told. Johnson walked around the table and sat in front of him taking out the new passport and comparing the likeness. He put the passport down on the table.

'Pick it put.'

Sanderson pick up the passport and opened it.

'Keep it, Jack Sanderson.'

Sanderson caught his breath at the sound of his name. The strength of the last few years eluded him. He sank back into his chair, his hands nestling his bowed head. Flashing before him, as if caught in a revolving door, came a confusion of bright lights and images from his past. He rubbed his eyes and let his hand stroke the stubble on his chin. He was exhausted.

Johnson looked on. For the first time, he felt some compassion for Jack Sanderson.

'Come with me, we have a lot to talk about and arrangements to make,' said Johnson motioning the gun towards the exit. Jack picked up his tattered holdall and put in his razor, toothbrush and the few things from the table and climbed the steps. It was a short drive back to Johnson's hotel.

Matthew Johnson left Jack to read 'The Dark Side of Sunday'. When he'd finished a realization struck him. He hadn't immediately recognised Matthew Johnson earlier but now he'd introduced himself fully, the betrayal came flooding back. He'd had lots of time alone in the cellar to write and think. Johnson hadn't noticed the sleeve inside the holdall where Jack had hidden his own written recollections and accusations and those of Rudi. Now was the time to seal them in the room's stationery hotel envelope and ask reception to post them, putting the cost on the room bill. He doubted Johnson would check and as they left, he was proved right.

CHAPTER 45

Devon England

Susan and Nick had travelled back to England to talk to their mother and explain what they'd discovered. Tilly had come with them as it was her research that had put the story together. They had thought long and hard about whether to tell Mrs Sanderson all they knew, but in the end decided it was the right thing to do.

Around the relaxing flames of the log fire crackling in the hearth, Tilly set out the whole story to Mrs Sanderson. Soxy was overwhelmed to see Susan again and couldn't stop purring and wrapping herself all over her, never keeping still for a moment.

'So, Matthew Johnson is alive and what's more is extremely rich and powerful. He started the company in 1957. In my view, this was probably with the payment he received for his double dealings over the Crabb affair, but also previously helping the Soviets in WW2. He is estimated to be worth 500 million dollars. Not something he is prepared to jeopardise.

'But there is more, it is only rumour, but it does go to show he may have been playing for both sides. We believe that two Mafia families, the Flavioretti in Australia and the Granetti's in New York were always looking for the main chance. 'We think they approached Johnson sometime when the USSR was beginning to break up under Gorbachov's glasnost. Flavioretti is thought to have used Johnson's contacts and former associates going back to the Second World War and together they set up business for their mutual benefit with organised crime syndicates in the former Soviet Union.'

'Look, Mum,' said Susan, 'we don't want to confuse the issue too much, but there's a real possibility that Dad's still alive somewhere. The threat I received seems to point in that direction and that what he knows could probably embarrass a lot of people in high places but thankfully nothing that would implicate crime syndicates.'

Mrs Sanderson had sat listening to an overwhelming myriad of facts, rumours, accusations and suppositions from her two grown up children and Tilly. She looked sad and pensive, unable to comprehend the enormity of the situation. The three looked at each other now regretting perhaps their decision to tell all, as Mrs Sanderson rose slowly and asked Nick to help her upstairs to her bedroom.

Susan turned to Tilly, 'It's been too much.'

'She's a strong lady. After a good night's sleep, she'll be fine.'

'You think she'll sleep with all that lot flying around her head? I couldn't."

Nick reappeared.

'Is she all right?' asked Susan. 'Should I go and see her?'

'She's asleep already.'

CHAPTER 46

London

Commander Rory Briggs, Head of the SCS or Serious Crime Squad, had flown out to Sydney a few months ago and met with his counterpart, Grahame McCellan of the Australian Federal Police (AFP), the country's principal federal law enforcement agency for the Australian Government. The AFP focussed on preventing, investigating and disrupting transnational, serious and complex organised crime in major airports and delivering law enforcement training for Asia-Pacific partner agencies.

It was Grahame McCellan who made the call personally.

'Rory, we've made some remarkable progress since we last spoke. The man with no real name yet, various aliases and disguises, is believed to be responsible for a lot of dirty business in our Asia-Pacific partners' jurisdiction by all accounts. Death of a newspaperman and policeman in Sabah, the attempted murder of a newspaper woman here in Sydney and the disappearance of a man with a connection to the Flavioretti family. Our men on the ground had a meeting with the newspaper woman's colleagues who had some interesting things to tell them about organised crime here and this particular guy. In and out of the country too quick to catch, save for the fact that he travels back to the same airport every time, Kennedy in New York.

'NYPD couldn't help?'

'No one on their radar fits any of the various descriptions we have of him. We've no prints, nothing, save that he smells like lime juice when he's working.'

'Lime juice!! Interesting, assuming we get close enough!'

'Good hunting, Rory. We need this bastard, alive if possible. Just keep a look out for those aliases on the list I've sent you.'

**

Just before the call for passengers to board the United Airlines flight from John Kennedy Airport New York, Anatoly received a call from one of Flavioretti's men confirming that Sanderson's children and Tilly had left Australia a few days ago and were heading for Britain. This was troubling news, indeed but he kept the information to himself.

Anatoly rang his contact in London, he would be arriving tomorrow. Unknown to Anatoly, his seat number and passport details had already been received in London hours earlier. One of the aliases from Grahame McCellan list had triggered the system. The call confirming that Anatoly had passed through immigration was made. He was observed making a call as soon as he set foot in the arrivals hall and then disappeared into the throng of passengers in line outside for taxis. The silver BMW drew alongside the kerb and Anatoly got into the back seat.

Detective Sergeant Ryan of the SCS watched and followed with his empty suitcase and climbed into the front of Detective Williams' unmarked Ford Mondeo 3 litre police car and followed. They were both out of uniform and looked for all purposes like any other travellers heading for central London.

'We're sitting outside the Marlborough Hotel. The car's in the basement carpark, a Silver BMW. Three series. Registration. Romeo, Yankie, Four, Seven, Two, Bravo. Over,' said Ryan to Commander Briggs.

'Sorry, lads stay put, but follow if it moves. I'll get someone to take over to give you a break.'

'Put the seat down, Boss. I'll take the first shift,' said Williams.

Inside the Marlborough, Anatoly was advised that Matthew Johnson and Jack Sanderson were booked on the early morning flight out of Kennedy arriving at noon London local time.

Anatoly's man recognized the two arrivals in Terminal 5 from flight BA0114 and followed them to car pickup point and reported the details.

'We're off, heading out on the M4,' radioed Ryan at the wheel.

'Keep me posted.'

CHAPTER 47

Bristol England

Robert Jenner's contact at Heathrow had also confirmed that Johnson and Sanderson had landed and had passed successfully through immigration. His part of the bargain, with the provision of the car and details of the addresses in Devon and Cornwall, was now complete. All he had to do was advise them when he knew where the Sanderson's children were staying. He sat back and sipped a strong coffee with just the right amount of brandy. Never too early.

He was startled out of his reverie by the telephone. He picked it up and listened, tightening his grip on the handset.

'Why were the SCS involved?' Jenner asked himself, his contact didn't know. He began to realise the possibility that the plans Johnson and he had put together to save themselves could fall apart at the last minute. Johnson must be told.

All the family were still in the house in Devon according to Jenner's man who was keeping an eye on Buckland Court.

It was time for Jenner to start pulling a few political strings. His first call was to Susan Sanderson's boss at the Admiralty advising them that she had been accessing files normally out of reach to her grade and gave him details of the contents. The next was to Simon Hinkley, Undersecretary of State at the Home Office and the last was to his friend from his Oxford days who was now the Attorney General, Sir Gilbert Rashley.

Johnson had explained to Jenner how he'd arranged things so that no-one in high places would topple least of all himself and Jenner but being followed by men from the Serious Crime Squad was not what he'd bargained for. He hoped Jenner's intervention was going to work.

By late afternoon, having endured an hour and twenty minutes of driving in rain and constant spray from other vehicles, Johnson and Sanderson were glad to turn off the motorway into the City of Bristol for an overnight stop.

It had been easy for Anatoly to follow Johnson and Sanderson from Heathrow along the M4 and into Bristol, light green cars were such a rarity. He watched as they unloaded their cases and checked into the Bristowe Hotel overlooking the city's river Avon. Anatoly was observed making a telephone call.

Good, he thought; *No change, they're still at Buckland Court.* He walked past a couple drinking in the corner but as they appeared to be all over each other, he had not taken too much notice. Anatoly just needed some space. So far, he had noticed nothing to put him on edge.

'Our man's taking an early night in the hotel around the corner.'

Commander Briggs relaxed at the other end of the line and thanked his two Bristol colleagues who would remain in place until morning and report to Ryan and Williams who were staying in a Bed and Breakfast in Filton on the outskirts of Bristol with easy access onto the motorway interchange waiting for the next move, well out of the way so there was no chance of them or their car being recognized.

In his hotel bedroom, Jack Sanderson's mind wandered back over the years, leaping in and out of a jumble of memories unaware that he was drifting into a fitful sleep. He awoke with a start, the sweat all over his body had been chilled by the cool bedroom air and he shivered. The recurring dream had been with him now for years. He was falling into an abyss with water racing past him, air trapped in his lungs unable to breathe, he was desperately trying to right himself, but the sides were too close, and he was unable to somersault to save himself. Then the door clanked open and a faceless man in uniform told him to confess. It was a confusion of his failed mission and Lubyanka prison all over again.

Morning came as quiet relief as he lay cocooned in a tangle of sheets. He was still alive. He looked across at Matthew Johnson. He did not have the strength to strangle the man, at least not here at this moment.

CHAPTER 48

Buckland Court Devon England

Nick was first up and had made a large pot of tea sitting under a rose knitted cosy his mother always favoured and was now tending to the toaster.

It had been an unpleasant night for Anatoly's man alone in the middle of the pine trees giving him a view of the two gates that led to Buckland Court, sitting in the back of his old Landrover with a Thermos of coffee and a bag of sugar lumps for company. As he watched through the binoculars, he could smell the toast in his nose and taste the tea on his tongue, but he had to stay put and wait for instructions.

'I'm leaving Bristol now and will be with you in about two hours,' said Anatoly. 'Keep me posted.' Anatoly didn't wait for a reply.

In the house, the smell of breakfast had lured Susan and Tilly downstairs.

'Anyone seen mother yet?'

Nick poured tea and went upstairs. He knocked on his mother's door and was beckoned in. She was propped up against a stack of pillows and the bed was covered with photographs, mostly black and white. Nick put down the tea and sat next to his mother and put his arms around her shoulders. She nestled into to him.

'If Jack's alive, where is he, Nick?' Nick looked at her, she seemed to have aged overnight and looked so vulnerable.

'I don't know but we'll find out, mother,' said Nick. 'What time does Mrs Simmonds come?'

'Usually about 11 am and makes me lunch and does the rounds. Why?'

'I'd like her to stay with you for the next few days. Susan, Tilly and I have to go to Cawsand. There are some questions that Susan wants answers to from the Naval Station. We'll be back as soon as we can, couple of days,' said Nick as he gathered up the photographs and smiled reassuringly at his mother, kissing her on the brow. After last night he was not too keen to say anything too much.

It was just after 11 am that they said goodbye to Mother and Mrs Simmonds and drove out of Buckland Court.

From the comfort of a breakfast break in the Cafe just down the only road from Buckland Court, Jenner's observer was surprised to see the car pass with two passengers and the woman driving. He rang Jenner who passed on the message to Johnson.

From the uncomfortable inside of the Landrover, Anatoly's man realized he couldn't follow, so within a few minutes, he was knocking on the front door of Buckland Court. It was opened by a large lady he had seen earlier arriving at the house.

'I am expected,' he lied.

'Wait here, I will see if Mrs Sanderson is available.'

She closed the door in his face. A moment later it was opened again.

'Yes, young man. What can I do for you?'

'I arranged to meet the young ladies here this morning.'

'Oh. I am afraid you have just missed them. They'll be back in a few days. Are you from the Naval Station?' He nodded.

'Wait, I'll give you their telephone number, save you going down there.'

How was he going to advise Anatoly that three had left by car for somewhere called Cawsand in Cornwall about an hour's drive away without him following?

'Good work. It's OK. Now I know where they are going, you can stand down. I'll transfer your fee as soon as.' Relief spread over him. He had been dreading meeting the man again. He had recognised the smell of lime on Anatoly as he dealt with the suitcases at Heathrow. It had sent shivers through him when he remembered another occasion when their paths had crossed. He despised and was utterly afraid of him, ruthless and unpredictable. A very frightening combination. He hoped he'd never have to work for him again as he drove away from Buckland Court just as Anatoly pressed the accelerator to the floor of the silver BMW and down the M5 motorway slip road.

D S Ryan picked up the phone in the car. He and Williams had been sitting there for about an hour waiting.

'The BMW is on the move towards the M5. We'll follow for a while, then over to you,' said one of the couple from the Bristowe Hotel.

'We're at the Almondsbury interchange.'

Williams flicked the siren switch as they accelerated to over a hundred in the outside lane, eating up the miles south past Portishead and onto Clevedon. As they approached the Weston-super-Mare junction, the phone buzzed.

'It's about a mile ahead. We'll leave it to you from here.'

Williams turned off the siren as the Mondeo slowed into the middle lane.

'Thanks, guys, just seen it.'

Moments later, Williams in the passenger seat received another call and put it on speaker.

'The warrant for arrest of Anatoly has been issued and Commander Briggs is on his way to Plymouth by plane as we speak. He told the local force that we are on their patch and need a car change. Suggest the Torpoint ferry would be a good place. He told me to remind you to watch and keep well out of the way until reinforcements arrive.' The despatcher ended the call.

'How does he know where we'd headed?' asked Williams.

'He has eyes and ears everywhere on this one, by the sound of it. Probably an intercept, who knows.

Just follow orders, Williams, and we'll see if he's right.'

CHAPTER 49

Cawsand Cornwall England

After Susan's short stop at the local Naval Station, she, Nick and Tilly reached the crest of the hill, they could see the mist and rain squall blowing up from the waters of Plymouth Sound blurring the roof tops of the cottages nestling snuggly in the twin ancient fishing villages of Cawsand and Kingsand below them. The trees had bared their branches of leaves several months ago and braced themselves for another winter of winds that made them resemble well slicked back hair clinging to the shoreline.

They parked the car in the main village carpark and walked towards Susan's cottage, calling in at the corner shop for supplies. Susan made the introduction to Jason Roberts after he had given her the usual bearhug of welcome. They battled their way up the High Street against the driving rain, past the Ship Inn. Now the wind was gusting along the narrow street and with it the stinging salt water clung to them. Despite it all, Tilly was enthralled.

'Wow, nothing like this in Oz. It's so cute.'

Inside Susan's house, the cloak of cosiness wrapped around them. Susan left the curtains open so that Tilly could enjoy the natural experience of this ancient community's life living with the sea. The monotonous drum of the rain on the rattling window frame made them feel safe inside on a night like this. Occasionally, a larger than usual wave struck the rock below obliterating the view completely and sending spray against the window making Tilly step back involuntarily only to return to watch the myriad of bubbles caught in the trough of its recession.

The ring of the telephone broke the silence and brought them back to the 20th Century.

'What?...... Who was he?..... Didn't you ask?' Susan could not disguise her concern or anger.

'When was this?..........Can you describe him?.........No, No, don't worry, Mum, it's probably nothing.'

Nick and Tilly looked expectantly at Susan.

'Someone called at the house just after we left. He said he had arranged to see Tilly and I. She tried to describe him, but it was no-one I recognised. Foolishly, Mum gave him this number and said that we were in Cawsand for a few days. *What a naïve idiot you've been, Mum!!*

An air of foreboding descended on the three.

CHAPTER 50

Cawsand Cornwall England

The drive through Plymouth and across the river into Cornwall had been uneventful. Anatoly had not noticed anything unusual until something on the chain ferry at Torpoint caught his eye. He got out of the BMW to stretch his legs.

His eyes searched passengers assembled in the tight confines of the salon on the right-hand side of the ferry. He saw four men huddled together. Something about them caused him to duck lower. He watched. Car keys were being exchanged. The slowing of the clanking of the chains that pulled the ferry across the estuary signalled the return of those with cars to the deck. He rubbed his hands together to rid them of the cold and was the first driver to get back to his car. Something wasn't quite right.

There had been no time to consider the situation whilst he drove the five miles of the twisting and turning road to Cawsand. There was definitely someone following but then at the top of the hill, he saw in the mirror that the white car had turned right whilst Anatoly continued down the hill to Kingsand. Then it struck him as he parked the BMW facing the sea wall with Plymouth Sound beyond; the driver and his companion in the white car were the same two that had got out as soon as they'd parked their Ford Mondeo to his left at the rear. Anatoly cursed himself for concentrating too much on keeping the green car within watching distance. He was now certain there had been a car change and they were following him. Why? Where were they now? His map showed the two villages were linked together, both were a dead-end with the water beyond. They were somewhere in Cawsand, trying to throw him off their scent, crafty move. He had made the same move but it seemed to him they were unlikely to appreciate that. He was comforted by the dreadful weather. *'Great cover'*, he thought to himself. His mission was nearly over and the two men in that little white car were not going to be a hindrance.

Ryan and Williams had waited until their Mondeo was the last on board the ferry to Torpoint. They stood a good chance of not being observed changing cars with the local police having taken a pre-arranged walk into the misted window salon that was full of foot passengers.

'It's the Ford Mondeo just the left of the silver BMW and one car behind,' said Williams

'Ours is the little white Astra,' said the younger policeman trying to disguise his local Devon accent from these London boys.

'This accursed weather,' said Roger as the Astra turned off the main road in pursuit of the headlights of the BMW, heading into the countryside, the road bending and narrowing as it cut through the vacant fields following the crumbling grey dry-stone walls that skirted it on both sides. The rain drove hard off the headland into the windscreen; the wipers fought to clear any view of the road ahead. They stopped on the crest of the hill overlooking the two villages below.

'According to this map, these roads converge in the middle of the two villages.'

'You sure the BMW turned left and went straight down? OK, we'll go right, just in case we were seen swapping cars. Better safe than sorry, eh?'

As their car stopped in the carpark in Cawsand, Williams opened the glove compartment with the key as directed and placed the two standard issue revolvers in his lap together with two rounds of ammunition. He looked at them admiringly. Not often in the line of duty did he receive weapons from the local police.

Ryan pulled on the handbrake and doused the lights.

'Just in case it gets heavy,' said Williams as he handed Ryan the firearm.

'I think Briggs believes that there is more to be unravelled if we leave the arrest for as long as possible. He can take all the glory as he did in the Goldcrest case.'

'Sometimes risking too much collateral damage, if you ask me, Boss. Never mind that for the moment. Look here. I'm going to walk along the road that follows the houses along the front,' said Ryan as he pointed to the map.

'We were told to stay put as back-up was on its way.

'I know but after that drive, I need some waking up and more importantly we need to be sure we followed the right headlights. Won't be long. Tell Briggs I've gone for a pee if he rings.' Ryan tugged at the collar of his trench coat and set off down the hill towards the sound of the sea.

The village appeared ghostly with the rain and mist swirling around the globes of the streetlights as he approached the village centre. The door of the Ship Inn pub was firmly shut against the elements. Through the misted windows, as he passed, he could see the landlord leaning against the bar, newspaper in hand. He started to head up a gentle incline passing a patchwork of small cottages to his left and right then descending into Kingsand with the Boatel Inn on his right and followed the street that opened out with a low seawall to his right and water beyond. The small shingle beach was being pounded by wave after wave as he avoided the spray cascading over the sea wall. There, about fifty metres away, stood the silver BMW. Ryan watched the steam rise from the still warm bonnet.

He ducked out of sight and retraced his steps along the narrow street back to Cawsand. Through a break in the housing to his left he occasionally glimpsed the raging sea beyond. He shivered slightly as the salt rain stung his face and he bent forward against the wind.

'Hi, the BMW is there but no-one's inside,' said Ryan, startling Williams who had not seen him approach. Gone were the jeans and smart shoes to be replaced by a thick roll neck pullover, flak jacket, grey anorak and heavy boots.

'Glad you're back. Briggs wants you to phone, pronto.' In the car in the carpark, Ryan picked up the phone. He listened intently for a long time then the call ended. He looked around; Williams' eyes followed his Boss. They saw for the first time the light green car that was parked to his left near the street into the village square. The windows were fogged over but now the internal lights were on, he could make out two figures inside who appeared to be talking animatedly.

'Fucking hell. Why don't these f…ing idiots talk to each other,' spat Ryan as he turned back to face Williams. 'That's the car Briggs just mentioned.'

'What's going on?'

'Our man in the BMW has apparently been following that green car over there with the light on inside, all the way from Heathrow. Why the hell didn't we notice?'

'Why should we? Our orders were to track the BMW. Nothing else, Boss.'

'Yea, well, anyway now we know the guy we're following is a real professional and apparently he's ruthlessly good at his job, Williams, hence the issue of the firearms.'

Williams went quiet, trying to assimilate, the situation and then finally said, 'So, we just sit here getting cold and do nothing save keeping our eyes on the car behind, worrying about a professional hit man lurking in the village next door, and wait for Briggs to arrive with an arrest warrant?'

'Shush. Let me think.'

'That was a long conversation with Briggs. He must have said something else, otherwise you'd be a bit more laid-back. There's something you haven't told me, Boss.'

Ryan turned to Williams.

'You're right. I was to keep it to myself on a *need to know* basis, but to hell with that, you need to know the dangers we face.'

CHAPTER 51

Cawsand - later that evening

Briggs told me that his political bosses, in particular the Foreign Office and the Admiralty are worried, very worried.'

'What!' exclaimed Williams.

'You were too young, Williams, to remember the Cold War when everyone in the West feared that Communism was on the march and our democratic institutions were under threat.'

'Boss, so were you. You're not that old?'

'No, but I was old enough to understand what worried my parents when they talked about it. Anyway, it appears that one of those two in that green car behind, Sanderson, has spent years in Siberia as a British spy having been caught in the act of espionage by the Russians in the 1950s. The other, Johnson, runs a multi-millionaire Security Empire used by governments all over. He's trying to keep the lid on a very embarrassing situation for his government, the Americans, and someone in British Intelligence at the time. And we, Briggs and the others in their ivory towers, suspect that Johnson wants to save his own arse at the same time. Apparently, there is no love lost between the two of them, as ours, the Sanderson guy, thinks Johnson was a double agent back then with links to our side and the Soviets and doubled crossed him sending him into the hands of the Soviets and killing his mate at the time.'

'Bloody hell. What about our man in Kingsand. What's he doing here?'

'My guess is he's here to cause trouble. Orders or no orders from Briggs, it's up to you and I to make sure those two old men don't come to any harm,' said Ryan.

'So, what do you have in mind, Boss?'

'Christ knows, Williams, carry on observing but close up. That's a laugh. A sadistic enforcer, a spy and a double-crossing millionaire. We can't be in two places at once and I don't fancy it's a good idea to split up. Great, come on. Let us observe,' said Ryan sarcastically, tucking the gun into his shoulder holster.'

'Do you why they came to this place?' asked Williams.

'How the hell would I know that. Wait. Close the door for a moment. I'll get Briggs on the phone, ask him to give me full details.'

Williams heard him repeat, 'Yes, next to the old chapel overlooking the sea, Cawsand side.'

Just as they were about to get out of the car again to investigate further, Ryan noticed the interior light of the green car had been switched off and then both doors opened, and the two elderly occupants got out and walked towards the sea front down the narrow street leading away from the carpark. Ryan and Williams followed.

'We know where they're going so let's get out of this rain and observe,' said Ryan having walked past the Sanderson cottage, watching the two men hesitate outside huddled together in conversation. Ryan and Williams continued towards the Boatel Inn near where Ryan had seen the parked BMW.

After a cold but long invigorating walk up the hill out of Kingsand and around to Cawsand, Anatoly arrived back at the BMW. He had found both white Astra and the empty green car in the carpark in Cawsand. He took the gun from the glove box and sat waiting. He had no idea which house he was looking for, but his patience would be rewarded soon.

Anatoly opened the rear trade entrance to the Boatel Inn and peered into the bar. There were the two men. *They just don't belong here.'* He thought to himself. One on the phone, the other watching out of the window.' He would soon find out whether their skills were a match for his.

Williams, who was scanning the street outside, saw Anatoly stroll past and up the narrow confines of the High Street towards Cawsand. Ryan and he followed, as they neared the Sanderson cottage, Ryan put a hand gently on William's shoulder, halting him and pulling him into the shadows away from the street, they waited. The rain dripped down their faces as they both blinked away the saltiness from their stinging eyes.

'You stay here and watch my back if he comes this way, I am going in closer,' said Ryan.

Anatoly disappeared out of sight opposite a narrow walkway running between two cottages, barely wide enough a man and his bicycle.

'I'll be back,' whispered Ryan.

Ryan passed the dim lights of the chemist shop on the left; each step he took he was being observed by Anatoly as he stood with his right hand deep in his pocket flicking off the safety catch of his gun, hoping he would not have to use it. Ryan reached inside his coat and unholstered his gun pointing it into the darkness as a sixth sense gripped him as looked at the walkway that he'd noticed earlier.

Ryan thought he had managed to remain out of sight along the twisting street as it rose and dipped amongst the cottages thanks to the mist and rain that howled around him. Anatoly watched as Ryan hesitated then entered into the darkness of the narrow confines between the two cottages. Anatoly crossed the road. Ryan noticed a shadow pass the entrance, too late to turn around, he ran as fast as he could. The end was blocked by an iron gate. He grappled with it and it swung open, he darted to his left and crouched against the corrugated iron side of a shed in the garden as he heard the light footsteps of Anatoly coming to a stop. The gate hinge creaked. Ryan strained to focus in the darkness as he listened to the rain drops bouncing off the shed roof. He couldn't hear anything else until it was too late.

Ryan had no time to react as the pop of Anatoly's silenced gun was lost in the night. Ryan's right knee crumpled, he dropped his gun and slumped to the ground. Anatoly looked around; no lights came on in the surrounding buildings. It was a bad shot; he'd assumed the man would be crouching, not standing upright so he'd aimed low, chest height. He couldn't risk another, so he prised Ryan's jaw apart and stuffed his handkerchief in and he pulled him upright and dragged him to the iron gate, removed his own scarf and tied him to it and left him. He would come back later to finish the job; first there was his mate to deal with. Anatoly made his way back along the High Street.

Three miles away two unmarked police cars travelled at speed towards Cawsand and Kingsand. The first car's lights danced along the hedgerows and low stone walls either side of the road. It was too late when a deer leaped over the hedge and landed in front of the first car. The driver braked and hit the animal head on and swung around as the windscreen shattered and the second car plunged into the side rear door, knocking it into the stone wall as it veered back onto the road and into the hedge opposite. Momentarily, there was total silence save for the rain falling on the twisted metal. D S Ryan's back up promised by Briggs was never going to arrive.

Williams was now worried at the amount of time Ryan had been away. *Watch my back*, had been his last words. Now was the time to follow orders. He looked up and down the street and moved out of the shadows in the direction that Ryan had taken. He stamped the cold out of his feet and swung his arms through the air and started to walk past the Chemist's shop. Where was Ryan?

Anatoly saw him. Williams made his way down the street searching every hidden corner. Just as he stopped to withdraw the small flashlight to focus down the narrow lane that held his boss, he was hit by a tremendous thud in the back pushing the air out of his lungs and stumbled helplessly forwards. Anatoly grabbed him and pulled him towards the cliff edge between two cottages further up the street. Williams had no time to recover his balance as Anatoly pushed him forwards over the slippery moss that clung to the rocks under his feet. Williams felt a strong hand grab his neck, almost encircling it. Below him the waves crashed mercilessly against the cliff thirty feet below. Cascades of foam and brine drenched their bodies. Anatoly tightened his grip and pushed the barrel of his gun into Williams' temple, pushing him closer to the edge.

'Which house?'

'Next to the Chapel.'

Anatoly's vicelike grip tightened again. Williams' began to choke and momentarily looked down at his supposed fate and turned pleading mercy.

'Who are you two and what do you want with me?' Anatoly spat, untrammelled fury in his eyes.

'Serious Crime......' stammered Williams as the wind took his reply away but it was too late, his footing gave way and as Anatoly stepped forward to grab him, his own hands slithered in the rain, gradually losing their grip. Williams' scream disappeared into the night as he dropped slowly at first and then bounced off the rocks below and was lost into the dark jaws of the storm and the swirling waters below.

D.S.Ryan managed to spit out the handkerchief from his mouth and wriggle his hands free. He tied the handkerchief around the bullet hole to staunch to blood and then wrapped scarf around his shattered knee. He pulled himself upright despite the pain just in time to see the Anatoly pass the end of the alley. He took off his shoes despite the cold and stumbled after him. Anatoly stopped at Susan Sanderson's cottage slowly turning the front door-knob.

**

Minutes earlier, Susan answered the front door but, in the gloom of the hallway, had not recognized her two visitors. Before she had a chance to say anything, as they'd agreed, Johnson grabbed her, pushing her forward up the stairs in front of him with his right hand in his coat pocket, jabbing into her ribs. Sanderson following slowly behind. The taller of the older men remaining in the shadows by the door whilst the shorter of the two, Johnson, pushing Susan in front of him, strode towards the fireplace and turned to face them.

'Sit down, all of you,' said Johnson, releasing Susan then removing his gloved hand from his right pocket. 'See, you're not in any danger provided you do as you are told and listen,' his American accent purred with complete authority. Susan, Tilly and Nick did as they were told.

'My name is Matthew Johnson.' He paused as he saw surprise but not shock on their faces. He beckoned to the man by the door.

'This is Jack Sanderson.'

Susan looked at Nick with disbelief on her face. Neither had recognised their father, standing in the shadows. He walked unsteadily over to them, his vision blurred by tears of joy and beckoned his little children into his arms.

It was Johnson's voice that interrupted them.

'Look, I haven't much time. You know the full story as I understand you've all be very busy.' He turned to Jack.

'I want the file of papers you so graciously posted from San Juan, Jack, my old friend. Didn't you trust me?'

Jack turned, still being tightly held by Susan and laughed. 'Whatever gave you that idea?'

'I have completed my side of the bargain by delivering you here.'

Jack searched his coat and produced a small piece of paper from inside the lining and handed it to Johnson.

'On this you'll find a number and an address. That will get you your file.'

'And your other promise? Johnson looked at Jack then at the three. 'OK, I think I can trust you on that one, Jack.'

He knew Sanderson would have no trouble convincing his children and Tilly to end their investigation into peripheral matters. Johnson would have eyes and ears everywhere looking after himself, his empire and those in the Establishment here and abroad who helped him achieve it.

Johnson turned to leave. He heard the downstairs door being opened and the rush of feet pounding up the stairs. Within seconds Anatoly, wielding his handgun, appeared in the sitting room.

'What the hell are you doing, Anatoly?'

'Shut up and move over there where I can see you. Anatoly pushed him towards Tilly, Sanderson and his children. In the seconds of herding Johnson towards Susan and Tilly, they'd recognised the aroma of lime and both recalled in horrible technicolour the night of their individual attacks. Their minds were in turmoil just as Anatoly took his arrogant delight in his victims' recognition.

'Johnson, this is none of your business now. Leave.'

Matthew Johnson turned and started to leave.

'Oh, by the way, thanks for the help in getting me here. You made it too easy. Lost your touch, it seems,' shouted Anatoly as he swivelled the gun towards Jack.

'Commander Sanderson, who do you see before you? Come on.'

'Don't you recognise my father in me, perhaps? My mother always said I looked a lot like him.'

Jack looked hard at Anatoly, but nothing registered.

'Moye nastovascheve imya, Anatoly Petrov.'

Jack looked at him closely, remembering his father, Colonel Petrov, talking about his little son, Anatoly.

'After you disappeared in Siberia, my father's colleagues began to accuse him of anti-Soviet activities. They talked of seeing him talking to you, a British spy, alone on several occasions. Some said he had helped in your escape. He was arrested and shot without trial because of you, leaving my mother and I alone to pick up the pieces.'

Jack pushed his children aside and walked unsteadily towards him, hands in front of him in supplication but also ready to grasp the gun.

'That's not true. I had nothing but admiration for your father. He was a true patriot.' By now Jack was within inches of the muzzle of gun being waved at him. 'Yes, we were on opposite sides, we both knew it. He was a good man, we talked of many things, literature, history, life in both our countries. He was making the best hand he could for you, his son and his wife. Both of you.'

'No. You betrayed him,' he yelled.

Jack held out his hand to take the gun just as Tilly burst forward grappling like a wounded animal with Anatoly. A gun shot rang out as everyone scattered. Jack fell to the floor, blood pouring from the wound.

EPILOGUE

His bedside was surrounded by family as Jack woke up in Plymouth's Naval Hospital. Slowly, he looked around as the blurred picture took shape.

'How are you, my love?' Jack took his wife's hand and pulled her slowly towards him in a gentle embrace; relief and joy of that moment remained for days thereafter.

Only later was Jack told of the vicious nature of Anatoly's life and his death at the hands of D.S.Ryan who had waited on the stairs listening until the first gunshot.

No-one ever talked about Matthew Johnson again. He retired as CEO of WSC and left Denver to live out his days in Bermuda.

Robert Jenner was relieved of his knighthood quietly and most of his friends and colleagues abandoned him. He died within a year a broken man.

The first day Jack returned to the family home at Buckland Court, the phone rang.

'It's for you, Commander Sanderson,' said Mrs Hawkins, who now spent most of her time looking after the Sandersons.

'Some American calling from California, said his name was Rudi, I think. Devil of a noise in the background, some kids running around shouting Maria, Maria.'

Thirty minutes later, Jack Sanderson put down the telephone. His life was now complete as he looked at the diary. Coming here in three weeks. He couldn't wait to tell his wife when she returned from the village.

THE END

GEOFF LEATHER
A DEADLY
PRICE TO PAY
MURDER, DRUGS AND POTENT REVENGE

Hidden away in a Tea Plantation in Sri Lanka the scientists make a sensational discovery in their search for revenge. News of their work on coca plant leaks out and puts their lives and those closest in danger. They need protection and help from abroad.

Surviving an attempt on their lives they arrive in Britain and a covert operation is put together with a former SAS officer, the American Drugs Enforcement Agency and the Columbian police.

Two deaths and one murder are personal. Three grieving families and only one suspect. Can two research scientists, one British Police Superintendent and a Columbian Drug Squad officer take on a powerful Cartel boss and win?

Geoff Leather
PRISONER
441
Genetics. Lies. Secrets and Murder

Dr Solomon Isaacs, a brilliant geneticist with a photographic memory, is released from Belmarsh High Security Prison in London after serving a 35year sentence for a breach of the Official Secrets Act.

Whilst working at the Government's Secret Research Establishment at Porton

Down, he is appalled at the disregard of the Nuremburg Convention on Human Rights.

He copies papers relating to the death of a serviceman during an experiment and thereby follows an exposé of secrets and lies, assassinations and murder.

VISIT MY WEBSITE for more information
www.geoffleather.com

The genesis of this novel was my reading the headlines of various newspapers in 1956. That memory stayed with me from that very early age. Then about twenty years ago I read a book outlining the various conspiracy theories surrounding the death of Lieutenant-Commander Lionel Kenneth Phillip Crabb, OBE, GM. I have taken some of the evidence that is in the public domain and introduced Jack Sanderson [fictional] as Crabb's accomplish on the mission that took place in Portsmouth harbour.

The Cold War during the post WW2 era was a real threat to world peace and so when I visited Moscow a few years ago, it was enlightening to see and visit Lubyanka and the Gulag Museum. This gave me the idea to introduce Rudi Stanik [fictional] and aspects of life during the era of Stalin. Reading "Stalingrad" [1999] by Antony Beevor added aspects of life for young innocent recruits into the Red Army. The Petrovs are fictional characters

501 Labour Camp was real. The Transpolar Mainline construction was a genuine engineering project. There have been fires along the Trans-Siberian railway but not the one I have used in the book so far as I know. Maria [fictional] could have lived through the terrible system of Kolkhoz or collectivism in which millions of Soviet citizens perished through starvation and imprisonment. Any changes of dates have been introduced to suit my timeline. A detailed history of this appalling time is given in Anne Applebaum's book "Red Famine"[2017].

The event that took place on the SS Soviet Union [fictional name] did happen. I embellished the scant report of the event and substituted Jack and Rudi for the real escapees.

The autobiographical books by Greville Wynne, working for MI5 and MI6, in "The Man from Moscow" and "The Man from Odessa" [1981] inspired some lateral thinking on my part in the events process of my novel.

The remaining story and the characters are figments of my imagination and are totally fictional. The places are real

ACKOWLEDGEMENTS

Thanks to David for guiding me through the pitfalls of computing with his vast knowledge of the science and explaining to me in simple terms how to connect loose ends and to May for her additional incisive input.

Thanks to Warren Design for juggling my ideas and thoughts into great covers.

To Chris and Cliff Freeman, Jan Richards and Amanda Towler who struggled through some early efforts with the first draft of this book and gave encouraging words.

To my children, Rachel, Sophie and David, who were never bored with my constant questioning.

To those at Jericho Writers for their invaluable advice.

But most of all to my wife, Judy, who read the drafts, suggested better ways of expression and wording and kept up my spirits when they were flagging.

Readers Download Offer

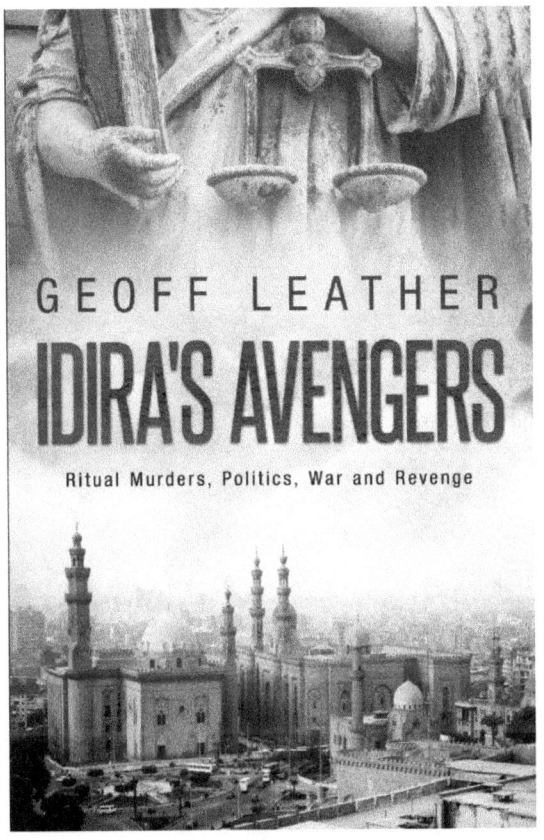

Get your free no-obligation download today.

Visit my website

www.geoffleather.com